Tying *the* Leaves

A Novel

June Toher

Copyright © 2019 by June Toher

Library of Congress Control Number: 2019912287
Names: Toher, June, author
Title: Tying the leaves: a novel / June Toher
Description: Virginia: Toher's Tales, 2019
Identifiers: ISBN 978-1-7334054-0-9 (paperback) |
ISBN 978-1-7334054-1-6 (e-book)
Subjects: LCSH: Global warming. |
BISAC: YA FICTION / Science & Nature / Environment. |
YA FICTION / Social Issues / Self Esteem & Self Reliance. |
YA FICTION / Magical Realism. |

Book design by ebooklaunch.com

For the
Children of Earth

PROLOGUE

Most people don't know what it feels like to suffocate. Not right now anyway. My little sister did almost every week for most of her five short years. When it hit, it hit her hard: her small lungs struggled to suck in enough air and every breath tormented her. We all hoped she'd grow out of it. We never thought something so bad would come of it. Or something so good.

Things might have turned out completely different if we'd never traveled there ... where nobody thought we could go. We wished we hadn't at first. It turned out to be a pretty scary place. Maybe that's why it was the only way. We had to see the truth with our own eyes.

You think you have no power, especially if you're a kid. But we discovered that's only if you believe it.

PART ONE

CHAPTER 1

J amie gazed up at one of those rare phenomena before twilight when a fading sun and a faint moon share the sky like siblings passing on opposite journeys. Inside his house the last glimmer of the day inched its way down the wall. Distant shadows crept in behind as the slow birth of night began.

Then he sensed it before it even happened. He was like that these days: a walking human antenna. He jumped up from his bedroom desk to the open window and scanned the backyard. The grand oak tree towered near the edge of the lawn. A few stray sunbeams danced on its leaves and a slight breeze ruffled its branches. All he could hear was the whistling of cardinals. Maybe his gut was wrong. But before he turned away, a child's wheezing interrupted the cardinals' song. Louder and louder the sound grew, and the birds took flight.

Jamie ran downstairs in time to see his mom tear out of the house. He followed. From one of the oak's low-hanging limbs, his little sister lowered herself onto an old crate at the base of the tree. She leaned forward and clutched her hand to her chest, panting. Her blond curls tumbled around her eyes as she gasped for air and struggled to descend to the ground. Their mom scooped up his sister's trembling body just before her face started to turn blue.

~

Katie was tucked under a blanket on the sofa in their family's den. Eyes closed, she sucked on an inhaler. Jamie stalled in the doorway. No matter how many times he saw his little sister like this, he always quivered a little inside. Ever since that day they never talked about anymore. He'd thought turning twelve would make him old enough to block out the memories. But he was wrong.

He cleared his mind as much as he could, then shuffled over to his sister and eased himself onto the arm of the sofa. Her natural color had returned, but Jamie knew the pressure in her chest had heaved out a lot of her energy.

"Katie, you okay?" Jamie said. He was sure by now Katie knew the routine. Stay still. Breathe slowly. Try not to think about the burning inside. Think peaceful thoughts like rainbows and butterflies and daisies and—

Her droopy eyelids sprung open. She pulled the inhaler out of her mouth and smiled wearily.

"Katie?"

"Couldn't breathe again," she said. "Mommy wants me to rest."

Whenever she had that raspy voice Jamie thought she sounded like a munchkin. She was a munchkin-sized little girl, too. The smallest of her five-year-old kindergarten schoolmates but with the largest green eyes. Right now they weren't their normal emerald shade but a pale, tired green like a faded leaf on a late fall flower.

He wondered how long her asthma attack had been this time. It seemed like the fourth one this week.

He wished he could whisk off her little munchkin self to a place where she'd never suffer. All he could do was try to put on a happy face, but of course she'd probably see through it. Katie was a living mood ring with a sixth sense for people's true feelings. They each had their own way of sensing things, although maybe that wasn't always a good thing.

"Guess where Mommy went?" she said, her voice hoarse but cheery. "To chase Billy out of our tree!" She erupted into a series of giggles then coughs. "Billy and me, we were having such a fun time up on our favorite branch, and the birds were singing to us. They sounded so nice we clapped for them, and they flew all around, and then they landed and sang some more!"

She coughed again but her eyes weren't as faded. "You ought to come up with us sometime, Jamie, and the birds will sing for you too, and we'll show you the spot where we found an empty bird's nest, and a little hole in the bark where we hide special things, but only if you don't tell anybody, which we know you won't." The way she beamed at him, her dimples deepened.

This was how she always got to him.

"Thanks for inviting me up in the tree with you, but didn't Mommy tell you and Billy not to go up there?"

"Well, it's really hard to remember now," she said, her eyelids lowered a bit. "Hey, want to take Billy and me to the mall play center tomorrow? It's Super Saturday."

"Sorry, munchkin. Can't tomorrow. Our class is going on a field trip to the planetarium, where they show the planets on the big ceiling."

"Oh, I wanna go too." Katie sucked again on her inhaler. "If I'm gonna be an astronaut I need to know about the planets."

Jamie glanced up when Billy, the bundle of energy, bounded into the room with their mom. He was glad Billy had healthy lungs. But he wondered if that's why his brother was so much taller than Katie even though they were fraternal twins.

Billy plopped down next to their sister. "Got the wheezies again, huh? When I'm a doctor I'll be able to fix you right up."

"I'll be fine."

"Wheezebomb!" Billy tickled her a little and she laughed and coughed.

"Billy, please don't excite your sister," their mom said.

Jamie studied their mom's face. She seemed so much older these past two years, but she still looked kind of like a short teenager. Curly blond ponytail. Skinny arms and legs. Sarah Sawyer the Skinnybelink. He wished her silly friend would stop calling her that. At least his friends didn't make fun of his own bony body.

Their mom still hugged them just as tightly as before, maybe even more. And she was still pretty strong for being so small. His small mom and his small sister. So much alike in some ways. But Katie was always smiling. And his mom hardly ever smiled at all anymore.

She hadn't always been so serious. Her laugh used to fill the air like a hundred bubbles. She used to say she was one of the lucky ones. And when she'd have them pray about their blessings, she'd give thanks for her happy life. Not anymore. It was like she was always carrying around a boulder. Ever since that terrible day that changed everything.

His mom peered at Katie and seemed to fight a frown. Jamie knew she tried hard to protect their sister. Made sure Katie always had her inhaler. Checked pollution levels before she could go outside. Didn't let her near cigarette smoke.

She cupped Katie's chin. "Honey, I want you to stay indoors for a while so you don't aggravate your asthma."

"But Mommy, I'm okay."

"And I don't want either of you climbing that tree. You're both too little … Now I'm going to finish cleaning up the dinner dishes, and you're to stay put, Katie, please."

"But Mommy, Billy and I want to see the sun go to sleep," Katie said.

Their mom pointed to the den's large picture window. "You can see the sunset from right in here." She headed to the kitchen.

Jamie raised the blinds all the way up the window to a view of their backyard, the sky splattered with several shades of orange behind the falling sun and rising moon. Billy traced the swirls with his index finger. "See, God's finger painting again."

"And the sun and moon are up there at the same time!" Katie said.

Jamie recalled what his dad had told him. "The moon's always there, munchkin, we just can't always see it."

The sunlight shifted and turned some of the white clouds pink. "Hey, now the clouds look like cotton candy," Katie said.

"Yeah, buckets full." Billy encircled a large, invisible bucket with his arms and puffed up his cheeks. Katie giggled and poked both his cheeks as if popping a balloon.

Jamie laughed.

She brushed a ringlet out of her eye. "I bet Daddy likes hanging out with God."

Jamie stopped laughing. "Do you remember Daddy?"

"Not really," Katie said. "Do you, Billy?"

Billy shrugged his shoulders. "No, just a little maybe."

Jamie wanted to tell them everything good he remembered about their dad. But he couldn't yet.

He shifted his attention to their oak tree, at how its leafy branches seemed to wave at them in the wind.

Suddenly, Jamie spotted a sparkly mist in their yard, blinking on and off a few feet above the ground not far from the big oak. He pointed. "Do you see that?"

Katie looked in the direction his finger pointed. "See what?"

"What?" Billy said.

Jamie squinted. "It's gone now. Wonder what it was?"

CHAPTER 2

It was only a thirty-minute drive in the Central Catholic buses from Jamie's hometown in Alexandria, Virginia, to the Smithsonian National Air and Space Museum in Washington, DC.

The last time Jamie visited the museum he'd come with his dad. He tried not to think about that too much now. But he was glad he got to return with his classmates.

His friends had never been here before, so he was eager to show them around. Raj would be blown away because they didn't have anything like this in India. Keisha would love the exhibit on African-American aviation and space pioneers. And Tony, well, Tony would probably enjoy anything that took guts to make it happen.

Yeah, it was all pretty awesome. The largest collection of historic aircraft and spacecraft in the world, from the Wright brothers' plane to the first Apollo Lunar Module. He'd like to share with his friends everything he knew about the place, but he didn't want to sound like a show-off.

After Jamie led his friends inside, his classmates scattered among the exhibits. He hoped to bring Katie and Billy here soon. They didn't get to come when his dad brought him here because they were too little then, so it was up to him.

A lot of things were up to him now. For Katie, Billy, his mom. If only he was sure they could depend on him. He wasn't real sure of much anymore.

Keisha tugged on his elbow. "Jamie, let's all four of us get seats together when it's time for the planetarium show. The sign says they're doing a double feature on the changing Earth and the wonders of space."

That was all he needed to hear because at least there were two things he *was* sure of: his interests in Earth and in space.

~

Jamie's favorite part of the museum was the Albert Einstein Planetarium. As soon as the lights went down, he tilted his head back under the gigantic IMAX domed ceiling and let the magic of satellite imagery transport him high above Earth.

It was as if he were hovering in the upper atmosphere while he watched changes sweep below. Melting glaciers, disappearing islands, dried-up rivers, eroding shorelines, wiped-out tropical forests. Monster hurricanes swirled above the planet's coastal areas and earthquakes cracked open the ground in several parts of the world.

Then he journeyed beyond Earth and experienced the way the astronauts saw it as it slowly shrank to a pinpoint in a field of stars. He traveled to some of the biggest planets and beyond. Red and yellow streaks of light rained through one sector of the galaxy. A supermassive black hole ate a passing star, and a narrow beam of particles seemed to shoot out at the speed of light.

One after another galactic wonder streamed above his head. He joined with the others in a string of collective oohs and aahs. The last scenes brought him back to a view of Earth from outer space. When the film reached its finale, he heard a wave of whispers while the planet slowly faded from view and the lights came on.

The theater started to empty but Jamie stayed seated, his face turned upward toward the blank ceiling, trying to hold onto the image of Earth. A magnificent, big, blue-and-green marble with white swirls above. To him it was the most beautiful planet in the galaxy.

Planted in the aisle seat, Jamie realized that Tony, Raj, and Keisha were waiting for him to let them out. But goose bumps still tingled along his arms, and in his mind he still floated in space. It was such a nice escape from his real life that he wanted to keep floating there.

Tony shoved Jamie's shoulder. "Earth to Jamie. Move it."

~

Jamie followed his friends to the museum store where swarms of other kids inspected books, stellarscopes, star finders, space tablets, toys, and solar-system posters. It was a special treat to have a field trip so early in the 2019 school year, and Jamie wanted to make the most of it.

He found the perfect item and headed to the checkout cradling a stuffed cloth doll. It had a globe of Earth for a body, with floppy arms and legs and a head framed by yellow yarn hair. Its face sported huge green plastic eyes, a white button nose, and a wide pink yarn grin.

"So, dude, now you're playin' with dolls?" Tony said. Jamie knew that was just the way Tony talked because they'd been best friends since kindergarten. A clump of Tony's thick, straight, brown hair fell over the side of his forehead and shaded his eyes.

"For Katie's birthday," Jamie said. "She's got a thing for planets 'cause she wants to be an astronaut."

"Hey, Jamie," Keisha said. Her face smiled all the way up to her large, brown eyes and thick lashes. She waved a thin plastic-wrapped package and practically skipped toward him. "I'm gonna paste these glow-in-the-dark stars on my bedroom ceiling."

Sometimes when Keisha smiled like that, Tony whispered to Jamie, "Man, oh man." Never to Keisha of course. Jamie liked Keisha too, but not that way. She was one of his best friends, kind of like Tony, but a girl best friend.

Tony spun the inner ring of a gyroscope before placing it on the counter. "Maybe I'll invent something cool like this gyro thing and be rich and famous."

Raj stepped in line behind Tony with a model-rocket kit and shook his head. "It is illogical how obsessed with money and fame you Americans can be," he said in his formal, Hindi-accented English.

Tony sometimes whispered comments about Raj to Jamie too, but not the complimentary kind. He once told Jamie he thought Raj sounded like Spock: cold and alien. Jamie happened to like Spock and wished Tony would be nicer, especially since Raj and his parents had only been in America a few years.

"Whaddya know about Americans, you Indian geek?" Tony said.

"I know what I see, and what I see is a lot of arrogant, shallow people."

"Oh, like people in India are so great." Tony grimaced. "What about all those young kids working their butts off in your country's factories?"

Jamie cringed. *Here they go again.*

"My parents and I detest child labor in any country, but we worship the deities, not money and power," Raj said.

"Before you go judging Americans you should try earning some coin." Tony raised the gyroscope in his hand. "I'm paying for this with my own cash."

Right, good for you, Tony. But why do you have to rub it in?

Raj lifted his chin. "I have not earned money but I have earned knowledge, and knowledge can be used to acquire money if that is all you care about."

"Yeah, yeah, yeah, now who sounds arrogant?" Tony said.

"Hey, guys, knock it off, okay?" Keisha stared them down until they obeyed and quietly placed their items on the counter for the store cashier.

Good going, Keish.

Tony never treated anyone else like he treated Raj. Well, except the bullies. When some of the kids in grammar school made fun of Jamie and tried to push him around because he was so shy, Tony always defended him. Nobody dared to push Tony around. And Tony always defended just about anybody who had a hard time defending themselves.

So what was bugging Tony? Up until Raj, Tony had always had Jamie all to himself, except for Keisha, but she was a girl, and Tony seemed to like her hanging out with them these past few years. Or maybe it was just because of Tony's ornery side. Whatever it was, Jamie wished Tony would give Raj a chance.

CHAPTER 3

After they all left the museum, Jamie walked in step with Raj down the sidewalk. He heard Tony and Keisha laughing behind them just before two African-American boys, who looked about fourteen, came around the corner of the museum at a fast clip. As the two boys barged past Jamie, he noticed a white skull tattoo on the side of the taller boy's neck. The tattoo boy crowded alongside Keisha and brushed up against her bare arm. "Yo, babe, you got some bad ash."

Before Keisha could reply, Tony scowled at tattoo boy. "What'd you say to her?"

"None'a your business, honkie."

Tony grabbed tattoo boy by his shoulder. The boy shoved Tony and Tony shoved him harder. The second boy grabbed Tony and pulled back his arms.

Jamie slinked back several yards away from the fighting. He partially hid behind a sidewalk museum kiosk and peeked around the edge, but he wanted to kick himself for it. *Get out there and help Tony, you coward. Now! Do it now!* His feet wouldn't budge.

Just as tattoo boy started to aim his fist at Tony, Raj leapt forward as fast as an overwound spring, blocked tattoo boy with the back of one hand, and flipped him down with one leg.

"Stop it," Keisha yelled. "All of you."

Raj dug his thumb and forefinger into the second boy's neck, pulled him away from Tony, then released him.

Raj, way to go!

Tattoo boy and his companion stood together and glared at Raj. "You're gonna pay for that," tattoo boy said.

Keisha inserted herself between the two boys and Raj. "Go, just go," Keisha commanded with a flick of her hand at the two boys.

They stood their ground.

Jamie willed his feet to move. *Keisha, please don't do this.* There was no way he was going to hide back here any longer. He came out from behind the kiosk and inched his way toward his friends.

Keisha stepped closer to the two intruders, tilted her head back and smiled. "Please go."

Jamie didn't exhale.

The boys gave Raj one last sneer, then swaggered away down the sidewalk.

"Are you crazy?" Keisha shouted at Tony once the departing boys were out of earshot. "He said *ash*. What my peeps call dry skin. They're my friends from church."

Tony's cheeks flashed pink and Keisha stormed off.

Jamie started breathing again, but when he saw Tony's face all he could think was *poor Tony.*

Tony and Raj stared after Keisha. Neither spoke for several seconds.

Finally Tony said, "Hey, Raj, you didn't have to do that."

"There was a fist coming at you and your hands were pinned behind your back. I thought I could help."

"I know, but I didn't expect you to take on my fight." Tony kicked at a small stone on the sidewalk. "Well thanks, man, for helping."

"You are welcome."

Jamie approached and averted Tony's eyes. "I'm sorry, Tony."

"Hey, nothin' to be sorry about, dude."

"But, Tony, I …" Jamie's upturned hands fluttered like wounded birds. Then he shoved them in his pockets. "I should have …"

"Forget it, Jamie," Tony said softly.

Jamie turned and trudged alone down the sidewalk toward the school buses.

Jamie didn't talk to his friends on the bus all the way home. How could he be such a rotten friend to the best friend he'd ever had? If Jamie was in trouble, Tony would never back away and hide like the worst kind of coward. Even after that terrible day, Tony had come to be with him. There was no excuse, nothing that would make his actions okay.

⁓

When Jamie got home he headed straight for his garden. He and his dad had carved it out in the far corner of the backyard, several feet from a natural privacy hedge that grew along the perimeter. He kneeled and began pruning his raspberry stalks.

The growing season in Alexandria usually extended through the fall, so he got to putter in his garden six to seven months of the year. Jamie had already harvested his bountiful summer yields of blueberries, butter beans, cucumbers, cantaloupes, and potatoes. But his peppers, tomatoes, and strawberries were going strong, and some squash and pumpkins on dark-green vines were almost ripe for picking.

Red and white impatiens, still in full bloom, framed his fertile patch of earth and offered up their nectar to hummingbirds that flitted from flower to flower. His recently planted yellow marigolds stood out like welcome newcomers to this colorful natural bounty. And as if to hint at the season's approaching end, a few early fall leaves skittered and cartwheeled across his carefully tended beds.

Jamie had been in love with gardening since the first time he planted seeds with his dad when he was seven years old and was rewarded days later with the emergence of carrot sprouts. That was the day he'd discovered he could draw life from the soil.

Most days his garden was a place of beauty and new beginnings. But today it was mostly a place to escape his shame.

Raj approached with a book tucked under his arm and squatted next to his friend. "Everything is okay, Jamie."

Jamie's eyes remained fixed on his raspberry plants. "I should have helped him."

"It is all right. We know you are not a fighter."

Jamie flinched. Yeah, another nice way of saying he was *sensitive*, which was how most of his family and friends described him. But he knew it was really code for *wimp.* He might as well have a big W stamped on his forehead.

Tony was the only one who never called him *sensitive.* He just told Jamie to get over himself. It was actually easier to deal with Tony's in-your-face, knock-it-off jabs than the polite excuses everyone else made for him. Tony never seemed to think of Jamie the way Jamie thought of himself. Like that time they'd seen bullies strutting toward them and Tony said, "Okay, dude, you get the one on the right and I'll get the one on the left." Then Tony got both of them while Jamie just ducked. Afterward Tony laughed like a crazy person and said, "All right! We made fast work of those two jerks."

Maybe Tony figured if he made believe Jamie wasn't such a loser, then Jamie would stop being one. If only Jamie knew how to do that. Before, he'd always had his dad to talk to about stuff that bothered him.

He twisted a cut raspberry stalk in his hands. "On my last camping trip with my dad he helped me get cuttings to grow these plants." Jamie finally forced himself to glance up at Raj. "I take good care of them and they survive each winter. But I'm not much good at saving anything else, Raj."

In crept the memory from two years ago of that terrible day. His dad suddenly collapsing on the kitchen floor, lying motionless, not breathing. Jamie's call to 911 and his frantic efforts to revive him with his Boy Scout CPR training. The taste of his tears streaming down his face as he pumped thirty times on his dad's chest. The rescue breaths he blew into his mouth. If only he'd been able to breathe his own life into his dad. But nothing stirred in that limp, sprawled body.

Jamie had clung frantically to a fragment of hope when the medical rescue squad arrived. They took his dad away on a stretcher. Later, they took his hope away too. A ruptured blood vessel, they said. Bleeding in his brain, they said.

An aneurysm, they said. It didn't matter what they said. His dad was gone.

When Jamie lost his dad it knocked out a piece of him, a piece of something vital. His grief was so severe it set down roots in his brain. It had been only six months since he'd managed to function almost like a whole person again, his pain buried under numbness. Buried, but not gone. It was always a shock when the old memory sprang up to the surface and tortured him. Only after he was able to tamp it back under could he move forward again. And live on the surface of his life.

Jamie tried to hide what was flashing through his mind. He knew Raj wasn't comfortable with such raw feelings. Good ol' Raj. How many times had he quietly stuck with Jamie at times like this? Always patiently waiting for the memories to pass.

A hummingbird flitted up in front of Jamie's nose and hovered there, its fast-beating wings emitting a familiar hum. It was so close Jamie squinted cross-eyed at the tiny creature. He and Raj laughed at their surprise visitor before it zoomed back down to Jamie's impatiens, foraging for nectar and insects. The two friends glanced easily at each other.

"I almost forgot," Raj said pulling his book out from under his arm. "I just finished reading this and I thought you might like it."

Jamie leaned back on his heels with the book in his hands and read the title: *The Hidden Life of Trees*.

"It is about how trees talk to each other and help each other," Raj said.

"Really?" Jamie flipped through the pages. "How do they do that?"

"Some of them send chemical distress signals through their root systems to warn their neighbor trees when they might get attacked by something like insects. They communicate about lots of different things and protect one another."

Jamie's eyes grew wide. "I look at a bunch of trees and I'd never guess they're all connected somehow."

"My Hindu religion teaches that there is unity among *all* created things," Raj said.

Jamie wasn't sure what that really meant, but it was so Raj to say things like that. Jamie knew Raj was a little older than he was, but sometimes Raj seemed a lot older.

He closed the book. "Thanks for this, Raj … and everything."

After Raj left, Jamie finished pruning his raspberry stalks. Out of the corner of his eye he thought he saw the sparkly mist in the air again, not far from the big oak tree. Maybe even more sparkles, this time. But as soon as he turned in that direction, it started to fade, then was completely gone. He stared at the spot. He knew it wasn't his imagination. But there was nothing to reflect the sunlight. Just grass and the tree. What in the world could it be?

CHAPTER 4

The walls of Jamie's seventh-grade classroom were covered with huge posters of rainforests, oceans, and mountains. Just two weeks back to Central Catholic and Jamie already liked his Earth Science teacher, Ms. Jean Tollhouse. Any teacher who started them off so soon with a field trip was his kind of teacher. Plus, he liked how sweet her voice sounded. But she also seemed like she wouldn't put up with any trouble in her classroom. Maybe Tony had caught on too. For his own sake.

Ms. Tollhouse came around to the front of her desk and tapped a pen against its side. When she turned her head, her shiny, light-brown hair swung all around her shoulders. "Class, I have some good news. The pope is planning a visit to the United States. He'll be in Washington, DC, later this fall."

Jamie knew a lot about this pope. That he was called "the peoples' pope" because he looked out for the needs of all people, especially poor and forgotten people. That he supported equality for everyone and preached against greed and abuse of power. And that he cared a lot about protecting the planet.

"I want you to do a report on one of the sections of the pope's encyclical that address the environment," Ms. Tollhouse said. "Leaders of many different faiths and countries and much of the scientific community have praised this work."

She rapped her pen again. "Okay, let's review what you've learned the past two weeks."

A boy in the front row blurted out, "Old fossils are blowing green gases into the sky."

Laughter erupted in the classroom. One of the students pursed his lips and made loud blowing noises.

"Not fossils," a female student said. "Fossil fuels. That's what they call coal, oil, and natural gas because they were formed over millions of years from fossils of prehistoric plants and animals."

The student who made blowing noises now made wild animal noises.

Ms. Tollhouse stared in his direction. "Mr. Sammy Sound Effects, that's enough, thank you."

When Jamie learned how fossil fuels got made, it was the first time he understood why scientists called them that.

Another student said, "We burn fossil fuels to run vehicles and planes and make electricity."

"That's right, now who's ready to demonstrate what else we know about fossil fuels?" Ms. Tollhouse said.

Keisha raised her hand. "Jamie and me."

Oh no, not the first ones! Public speaking was torture. Why had he ever let Keisha talk him into this by promising she'd give him pointers on shooting hoops? He didn't like basketball *that* much! But he couldn't let Keisha down, and it was too late to back out anyway.

Keisha handed Jamie their props and nudged him up from his chair, then they headed toward the front of the class.

Keisha led the way with a netless basketball hoop on a three-foot stand while she bounced a huge yellow beach ball with her other hand.

Jamie shuffled behind her carrying a black helium balloon, a dark-green baby's blanket, and a foot-wide, paper-mache Earth globe with raised continents. They'd glued a toy car and cardboard smokestack to the top of the globe.

Keisha nodded at Jamie, "You go first."

"No, you go first."

Keisha gently pushed Jamie forward and hissed, "NO, you go first."

Jamie lowered his head, and when he started talking in a quiet voice some of the kids in the back of the room yelled, "We can't hear you!"

See, this is why I should never let Keisha talk me into things. What was I thinking? He hated drawing attention to himself. It was so awful when everybody stared at him, just waiting for him to make a mistake.

"Come on, you can do it, you can do it," Keisha whispered out of the side of her mouth.

Jamie set the globe on Ms. Tollhouse's desk. He raised his head and took a deep breath. "We decided to do kind of a low-tech example of the greenhouse effect"—he paused, took another deep breath, and raised his voice a little— "which was in our last chapter and in part of the planetarium's show on our changing Earth."

Keisha used the basketball hoop and its stand to drape the green blanket above the Earth globe.

Jamie lifted the yellow beach ball three feet above the green blanket. "This is the sun, and that's a blanket of greenhouse gases. When the sun ..." His voice got lower, and the kids at the back of the room yelled again, "We can't hear you!"

Jamie's cheeks burned and he started over with a louder voice. "When the sun heats the Earth's land and water, this heat energy is carried into our atmosphere. Gases and water vapor in our atmosphere trap some of the heat and keep our planet from getting too cold. This is the reason it's called the greenhouse effect, which is a good thing." He caught a glimpse of Raj giving him a thumbs-up.

"But we can have too much of a good thing," Keisha said. "When we burn fossil fuels, they give off gases like carbon dioxide and methane that go into our atmosphere and trap even more of the sun's heat. Scientists named them greenhouse gases because they increase the greenhouse effect on our planet. The more greenhouse gases we pump into our atmosphere, the hotter the Earth gets."

"And the hotter the Earth gets, the more problems we have," Jamie said.

"Like glaciers and ice sheets melting," Keisha said. "NASA satellites show all this increase in water is causing the seas to rise and take over our coastlines." Keisha broke off the edges of some of the globe's continents and tossed them over her head.

"As the Earth heats up things are getting out of balance, so our climate is changing and becoming more extreme too," Jamie said.

Keisha pulled the black helium balloon down close to her. "Let's make believe this is filled with fossil-fuel gases."

27

She stuck a pin in the balloon and sent it weaving over the class, hissing as the helium escaped. The students ducked when it zoomed past until it petered out on the floor. "When we burn fossil fuels, we also pollute our air and water with toxins, and this can make people sick."

A few boys in the back of the room erupted into fake, loud hacking noises.

"So these are some of the reasons why countries all over the world are moving away from fossil fuels to energy that doesn't produce greenhouse gases," Jamie said.

Keisha stepped forward. "That's it for our demonstration." She bowed and pulled Jamie over by his hand with her.

"Jamie and Keisha, thank you for your imaginative portrayal," Ms. Tollhouse said and led the class in applause.

Jamie and his friend grabbed their props and returned to their seats. He couldn't get to his seat fast enough. *This must be what it feels like to escape from a burning building. And boy, Keisha's basketball tips better be really good.* But nothing could make up for the crazy way his heart was beating. He was never going to agree to anything like this ever again.

Without raising his hand Tony yelled out, "Hey, Ms. Tollhouse, my dad says people are just makin' up stuff about fossil fuels and climate change."

Jamie stared at his friend trying to decide if Tony was just being his contrary self. But he knew Tony's dad was a United States senator so Jamie figured people respected his dad's opinion.

"What planet does your dad live on?" one of the students said.

Well, maybe not everybody.

"Tony's right," Ms. Tollhouse said as she moved to the front of the class. "There are some scientists and others who don't believe there's a connection between human actions and climate change."

Two students blew raspberries at Tony.

"But many people do agree that we should use more clean, renewable energy to cut down on pollution. For your homework, I want you to research all the different kinds."

Raj leaned forward in his chair and said to Jamie, "My father knows a unique new kind. Come with me after school."

CHAPTER 5

Raj's dad opened the door to his laboratory for Jamie and Raj. Ultraviolet lights hung from the three-story ceiling over dozens of rows of large tanks. On the wall was a sign: *Arni Sanseria Innovations.*

Jamie was pumped. He'd never been in a research lab before.

"It is nice to see you, Jamie," Mr. Sanseria said. "Do you want a tour?"

Raj's dad led Jamie and Raj to knee-high, water-filled tanks where little green organisms floated on the surface. "My company is experimenting with algae to make biofuel. They can grow in almost any kind of water. Brackish, salt water, or even wastewater."

Jamie scrunched up his nose. "You mean that icky stuff on the pond near us?"

"Half the body weight of this icky stuff is oil," Raj said, "and it doubles in size overnight."

Jamie scanned the room. He still didn't understand why Raj and his dad were so excited about growing something most people were trying to get rid of.

Mr. Sanseria gestured with a sweeping motion around the lab. "The United States could grow enough of these hardy little organisms to completely replace our need for oil."

"No way!" Jamie said.

"Yes, it is possible," Raj's dad said. "When you turn algae into biofuel it can run cars, trucks, buses, even airplanes."

Jamie leaned over one of the tanks. "Gee, something so simple." He lightly touched the algae. "But how could we grow enough algae for the whole country?"

"They do not require land, or fresh water, or pesticides like the crops we grow now for biofuel," Raj's dad said. "And they produce more than seventy percent of the world's oxygen."

"We could grow all we need in algae ponds, right Father?"

Mr. Sanseria indicated for the boys to follow him over to racks that held stacked rows of glass tubes filled with water and algae. "Yes, and far fewer ponds if we grew it in hundreds of thousands of tubes like these."

Jamie scanned the high rows of glass tubes until his head tilted way back. It seemed like a scene from a science-fiction movie. Who knew this was even possible?

"My father started all this research because of what happened in Delhi," Raj said.

"Delhi?"

"Where we are from in India," Raj's dad said. "Not a good city to raise a family. Air pollution and smog caused irreversible lung damage in two million of Delhi's children."

Jamie's mouth hung open. "What? No. What?"

"Unfortunately, the air quality has not improved since we left, but I hope my work here will eventually help."

31

So kids in India suffer too. Like Katie. Two million kids in just one city.

"Even with the bad air it was not easy for us to leave our country, Jamie, and come to this foreign land," Raj said.

Mr. Sanseria nodded. "But I received a very good offer from some Indian-American investors to locate in your country and set up my own research lab. We now have our green cards for permanent residency."

"So I guess you'll be around for a while then, huh, Raj?" Jamie had never thought about what it was like for Raj to leave his country and his friends and learn a new way of life. Raj never talked about Delhi or if he missed his home or friends there. And he had no idea Raj was learning all this neat stuff from his dad about algae and replacing oil, of all things.

Jamie examined the tubes of algae again. "This is so cool! I bet a lot of people would want to use algae biofuel if they could get it."

"Maybe, but maybe not," Raj said. "Many Americans do not seem to care about protecting the planet." A sheepish grin cropped up on Raj's face. "I do not mean you, Jamie."

Jamie hoped Raj wasn't going to go off on a negative kick about Americans again.

"Son, the United States is our new home," Mr. Sanseria said. "We should not be so quick to criticize when our own country has much room for improvement."

"But, Father, many people here *do not care* about the planet. They act like they deserve to take whatever they want from the earth and treat our planet's air and water like global garbage cans."

"Well, yeah, but a lot of Americans aren't like that," Jamie said.

"Not enough," Raj said. "America is the richest country in the world, but it acts like a greedy, spoiled child gobbling up everything in sight."

"Who's doing all this gobbling?" Jamie said.

"The people who have the most, take the most, and waste the most," Raj said.

Jamie didn't understand why Raj was getting so flipped out when they just came here to look at what his dad was working on.

Mr. Sanseria placed a hand on Raj's shoulder. "There are people like that in many countries, not just the United States. But there are also billionaires in this country who are giving away their money to help others."

Raj and Jamie started to talk at the same time.

"Go ahead," Jamie said.

"But look what a lot of rich people do with their money," Raj said. "Buy big cars that burn huge amounts of gas. Have you seen those Homers that look like tanks? Who needs a car like that in a civilized place? Are their egos so big they have to drive to their offices in something that belongs in a war zone?"

"Hummers," Jamie said.

"What?"

"Hummers, Raj. Those big, tank-looking cars are called Hummers. But they don't make 'em anymore."

"I have seen them right here in Alexandria."

"They're older models," Jamie said.

"It is still a symbol of American waste and excess. No respect for the environment."

Jamie knew his friend always said what was on his mind, but he didn't want to hear any more bad things about his own country. "Hey, what about the Americans who got your dad to come here to do his algae thing?"

"Yes, there are many businesses here like mine working on developing new technologies for clean energy," Mr. Sanseria said.

Right, thought Jamie. *Look at all the good things.* "Raj, don't you like living here? Don't you like going to our school, and living in our neighborhood, and doing stuff with our friends?"

"Listen to Jamie," Raj's dad said. "Everything is not black and white. Our family has a nice life here. You have so much freedom and so many opportunities. In a few years you will go to a good college and maybe start a company of your own someday."

Raj hesitated. "I guess I like living here. But I still do not like all the dirty energy and pollution. We left Delhi to get away from that."

"I think attitudes in America are changing," Mr. Sanseria said.

"Come on, Raj, you know that book you gave me about trees?" Jamie said. "Don't you think it's possible we could all be more like them, protecting and helping each other?"

After a few seconds Raj said, "I guess anything is possible."

Most anything, thought Jamie.

CHAPTER 6

Jamie made Keisha follow through on her promise. They were shooting baskets with her dad in her family's driveway around the back of their house.

This was even better than Jamie expected because Mr. Taylor was still a player with the Washington Wizards. It was fun just watching him move. He was so confident and fast and graceful. Keisha was all that too. All the things Jamie wasn't.

"Okay, Dad, let's not wear out Jamie," Keisha said as she grabbed some towels for them to wipe off their sweat.

Jamie *was* worn out. Really, how could anyone keep up with the famous Sam Taylor and his daughter?

"At first I'd hoped my wife and I would have a son to follow me in the sport I love so much." Mr. Taylor cupped the ball with one huge hand and smiled down at Jamie from his six-foot-ten frame.

"But Keisha has exceeded anything I imagined for a boy. Her speed and skill are almost a match to my own when I was her age. And she certainly is much prettier. Just like her mother."

Jamie's dad used to brag about him too. Well, not the pretty part. But he didn't realize until after his dad was gone how much it meant to him.

A Lexus pulled into the driveway and out stepped Keisha's mom, a woman so beautiful Jamie always thought she could be a movie star. A movie star with fancy clothes.

"Speak of the devil," Mr. Taylor said as he dribbled the ball over to her, planted a smooch on her lips, and dribbled back to Keisha and Jamie. "Our girl's getting as good as her ol' man. She's gonna have recruiters after her one day."

"Jamie, you aren't being too hard on my cocky b-ball players, are you?" Mrs. Taylor said.

"No, ma'am. I'm trying not to."

"Now don't be mocking us, Mary, my love," Mr. Taylor said with a laugh.

"What would ever make you think that?" Keisha's mom said.

Jamie noticed Keisha's mom flashed that same kind of smile at her husband that gave Tony goo-goo eyes when he saw it on Keisha.

Mrs. Taylor turned to Keisha. "Honey, how was school today?"

"Jamie and I did our presentation on the greenhouse effect and fossil-fuel pollution. We did a super job, especially Jamie." Keisha grinned at Jamie, who rolled his eyes.

"You should talk to your momma's boss woman." Keisha's dad puffed out his chest, planted his hands on his hips, and swayed his shoulders from side to side.

Jamie thought Keisha's dad was a riot. He was always clowning around. It reminded Jamie of his own dad telling corny jokes in funny accents.

"Sam, will you please stop calling her my 'boss woman,'" Mrs. Taylor said. "You sound like you just came off a plantation."

"Well, she is your boss."

Jamie had seen that fake innocent look on Mr. Taylor's face before. It was just like him to call a United States senator *boss woman.*

"My love, you know she'd do it if you asked her."

Mrs. Taylor nodded toward Keisha. "Well, it might be good for you two to talk with her. She's been studying how burning fossil fuels affects our health."

"Talk to a … a senator?" Jamie said.

Mrs. Taylor smiled. "Yes, Jamie, she likes talking with kids. Why don't you come meet her at a cookout we're hosting?"

"You're the one who's hosting it," Keisha's dad said. "Me and my boys are just the lowly entertainment."

Keisha gave her father a quizzical look.

"My new group is playing," he said.

"I thought your saxophone was just a hobby, Dad."

"Well, it is, but we decided to form a little trio—Sammy's Sizzlin' Upbeats. And we're gonna do a few special gigs now and then."

"Your father always wanted to play in a professional jazz band, but he was better at basketball," Keisha's mom said. "So now he's testing out his little sideline with his buddies who teach public-school bands."

"Yep, your momma loved me when she thought I was just gonna be a mediocre sax player instead of the big-time, b-ball player she reeled in." Mr. Taylor winked at his wife.

Mrs. Taylor crossed her hands over her heart and fluttered her eyelashes. "Yeah, baby, you got that right."

She turned to Keisha. "And your daddy fell for me when I was just a part-time art teacher."

Keisha laughed at her parents. "You two are so silly!"

Jamie remembered when his parents used to flirt like that. When his dad got his mom to burst out her bubbly laugh. When he brought her flowers for no special reason. She always acted like it was the first time. She'd raise herself up on her toes and fling her arms around his neck real tight.

"Come on, Jamie," Keisha said. She pulled him near the basket. "Let's get in a few more hoops before my game."

"Yo, Jamie, please don't make me and Keisha look bad in front of my wife with your tricky moves," Mr. Taylor said. He dribbled the ball to Jamie, who, without thinking, took aim at the basket. To his surprise he made his first-ever rimless shot.

CHAPTER 7

Jamie had climbed up to the middle of the gym's bleachers to watch Keisha in that day's game between the seventh- and eighth-grade girls at his school. Tony and Raj were on either side of him. They were lucky to find seats in their favorite spot because a lot of other kids had piled into the bleachers before them.

Jamie loved watching Keisha play, especially when she showed off for them. That's what Tony said she was doing, anyway. It was easy to follow her around the court because she was the only black player on her team. And she'd always crack them up after a winning game with her funny little hip-hop dance.

Jamie checked out the scoreboard. Keisha's green-jersey team, the Shamrocks, was tied with the blue-jersey team, the Bluebells, at 54–54 in the fourth quarter.

"I think Keisha's team can break that tie if she lets loose," Tony said. "Look, the green's best shooting guard is setting up a shot."

A blue forward stole the ball and passed it to her team's shooting guard, who sprinted in the opposite direction. Keisha darted ahead and stole the ball.

"Gee, she's so fast," Jamie said.

"Man, she's like a ... like a gazelle," Tony said.

A blue defender tried to intercept Keisha, but she zigzagged, dribbled behind her back and between her legs, then changed from one hand to the other while she headed to the basket.

"Kei-sha, Kei-sha, Kei-sha," Jamie yelled in unison with Tony and Raj.

The blue team's forward lunged to block Keisha's shot. Keisha lost her balance but made a circus shot, firing the ball up and through the hoop as she fell to the floor. The buzzer signaled the end of the game with Keisha's team the winners.

Jamie, Tony, and Raj all jumped to their feet whooping it up along with the rest of the seventh-graders in the bleachers.

"Again! They won again!" Jamie said. "I'm gonna wait for Keisha. We'll meet up with you later."

"Tell her we thought she killed it," Tony said.

"She really did," Raj said.

Jamie made his way through the kids streaming out of the bleachers and down the corridor leading from the gym to the lockers. Several yards ahead he spotted Keisha taking a sip from a drinking fountain. Two of her teammates stepped behind her. He recognized Tiffany and Tara from when they were introduced at a past game.

"Seems our little African-American princess is a real hero," Tiffany said. Her sarcastic tone echoed down the empty corridor.

Tara tipped her head from side to side. "What-ev-ah would we do without her."

Jamie cringed as he watched Keisha turn around and face their sneers.

"Next," Tiffany said. She moved closer to the drinking fountain and jabbed Keisha with her elbow. "Oop-sie," she said in a high-pitched, sing-song voice.

Jamie made a dash to Keisha. "Hey, Keisha, what a game." He took her hand and pulled her away from her teammates. "Let's go. Everybody's waiting for you."

Once they got back inside the gym Jamie said, "Are you okay, Keish?"

"Yeah, I'm okay," she said.

But Jamie didn't think she looked okay.

Keisha sniffled and glanced toward the gym exit to the street. "Want a ride home with my dad?" she said. "Just don't tell him about … that."

"But you should tell him," Jamie said.

"There's nothing he can do."

"Yes he can."

"Like what?" She paused. "Jamie, he and my mom thought if they had graduate degrees, successful careers, lived in a really nice neighborhood, and sent me to a private school, then I wouldn't have to deal with bigots the way they did. But those things don't stop people like those two girls."

"You should tell the principal then."

"What's she going to do? They'll just say it's my imagination and it'll be my word against theirs."

"But I heard them. You can have me—"

"No, Jamie, thanks, but I'm not dragging you into this."

Outside, Keisha's dad was waiting for her in his classic Mercedes 380 SL convertible sports car. Jamie climbed behind the front passenger seat onto the little carpeted shelf in the back.

"Hope you're not too squished back there, Jamie," Keisha's dad said.

"No, sir."

"Hey, sport, how was the game?" her dad said.

"I did fine." Keisha's voice was flat.

"I saw your other buddies, and they seemed to think you did much more than fine."

"Yeah, I guess."

"So how'd those two teammates react?"

"The same."

"Taunted you again, huh?"

"Let's not get into it, Dad."

"Keish, tell him," Jamie said. "It's not right."

Keisha dropped her chin. "I still don't get it, Dad. I work hard at practice and try to be a good team player. I've never said anything bad about them. But Tiffany and Tara seem to get their kicks knocking me just because of my color."

Jamie reached between the bucket seats and gently squeezed Keisha's arm.

"Baby, it's not anything you've done," her dad said. "Some folks act ugly because they want to build themselves up by putting you down. Says something kind of sad about their sorry little lives, doesn't it?"

"Sure, but I just wish I didn't have to deal with their put-downs every time we play."

"Well, I hate to tell ya, but you're going to have to deal with people like that all your life. Just hold your head up and be proud of who you are. You don't need their acceptance or approval. The problem is with them. Not you. Remember that."

"Yeah, they've got a big problem," Jamie said.

Keisha stared out the window and didn't say anything.

Jamie thought about what her dad said, especially the part about being proud of who you are. He tried to remember a time when he'd felt like that. But he couldn't.

Chapter 8

J amie rode up to Tony's house on his bike and found his friend outside with his lawn mower. He seemed to be admiring the neat diagonal rows across his family's front yard.

"Hey, dude, good timing," Tony said. "This was the last of my nine lawns for the week. Best season yet for my little neighborhood business."

"Great, Tony. Did your dad say anything this time?"

"All he said was I better not spill gas anywhere when I fill up my mower. Which I've never done."

Jamie didn't understand why Tony's dad was always like that. He never knew what to say about it, so he was quiet for several seconds. Then, "Good game last night, huh?'

"Yeah, Keisha really is gonna be as good as her dad." Tony wheeled the lawn mower into the backyard shed, and Jamie followed.

"I made enough this summer to buy all the stuff I wanted. Hey, check out my new phone." Tony pulled the latest-model iPhone from his pocket and handed it to Jamie, who swiped the screen and tapped through a series of pages.

"Cool, Tony. Wanna trade?" He pulled out his beat-up phone and offered it to Tony with a grin.

"Not funny, dweeb." Tony grabbed back his phone. "Come on inside."

They scrambled through the back door to the kitchen and ran right into two grocery bags in the arms of Tony's mom.

"Oops, sorry, Mom."

"Honey, y'all try not to track grass and dirt into the house."

Jamie always liked hearing her Southern accent. To him it sounded musical.

"Hi, Mrs. Newsome. I took off my shoes." Jamie and Mrs. Newsome exchanged warm glances.

Tony's dad was leaning on the kitchen table, a newspaper spread out in front of him and a scowl on his face.

"Hi, Mr. Newsome," Jamie said.

Tony's dad didn't look up from his paper.

"Sweetheart, please don't be rude," Tony's mom said and nudged his dad. "Say hello to the boy, won't you?"

"What?" Mr. Newsome lifted his head from his newspaper. "Oh, Jamie. Good afternoon. I didn't hear you."

Then he turned to his wife. "I can't believe the garbage they keep writing. This damn columnist is tearing into me for trying to save the taxpayers' money. Get a load of this: 'US Senator Richard Newsome, chairman of the Committee on Appropriations, is urging his committee to submit a bill that would severely hurt the elderly.' That is total bull!"

When Tony's dad got like this Jamie always wished he could sneak out the back door.

"Everyone knows my committee has an outstanding track record for fighting wasteful spending," Mr. Newsome continued. "And this idiot is trying to make a case for protecting our bloated government bureaucracy. I'm sick of it."

"Maybe they should rename your committee the Senate Committee on Stinginess," Tony said.

Mr. Newsome glared at Tony. "Don't you make fun of my work, boy."

Jamie elbowed Tony in the ribs.

"Yes, sir," Tony said with a smirk and elbowed Jamie back. "Guess what, Dad? I earned enough money to buy an iPhone."

"It had better not interfere with your homework."

Tony shot Jamie one of his looks. He was up to something. "Our homework's on fossil-fuel pollution and climate change."

"How many times do I have to tell you that's a bunch of crap."

Tony stuck out his chin. "Even the pope says it's a problem."

"Don't throw the pope in my face."

Mr. Newsome's neck appeared flushed. Jamie hoped Tony would back off soon.

"Yes, sir," Tony said in his android imitation.

"I don't like our schools brainwashing you kids, either."

"Yes, sir," Tony-the-Android said.

Mrs. Newsome squeezed her husband's shoulder and he folded up his newspaper. "The only climate I care about is for our hunting trip." He held an imaginary shotgun.

"Dove season starts in Alabama next weekend. Make sure you're ready."

"Do I really have to go?" Tony said. Jamie noticed Tony's voice soften a little.

"What's wrong with you, boy? Yes, you have to go. I'm going to make a hunter out of you yet."

Tony turned to Jamie. "Come on."

Jamie followed Tony to his bedroom. "Why do you do that?"

"Do what?" Tony said.

"Try to irritate your dad."

"He gets himself riled up all on his own. You know he's always on my case … nothing I do is good enough. One of the reasons I started my lawn business was because money is so important to him. But he's never said one good thing about it. And get this: last week when I was weed whacking and I cut my toe open he didn't give a crap. Just told me not to bleed on the carpet when I came in the house."

"Oh, Tony."

"Hey, no big deal. I'm just going to do my own thing and forget about him."

Jamie wondered if Tony was trying to convince himself more than he was Jamie. "Well, what about your hunting trips together? How is he then?"

"That's *his* thing. It's always all about *him*. Let's not talk about this anymore."

"Okay." But Jamie thought at least Tony's dad wanted to do something with him.

Tony enlarged a photo on his phone. "Check this out. I got a pic of Keisha making that last circus shot. She's soooo good. Her dad's always telling her how good she is too.

She said he even introduced her to the guys on his team and bragged about how she's gonna be better than him someday."

Jamie was pretty sure how that made Tony feel even if Tony was glad for Keisha. "You should show her the photo."

"You think she liked that we were there?"

"I know she did." Jamie batted his eyes and grinned. "Especially you, Tony."

Tony rapped Jamie in the arm. "Cut it out."

Jamie laughed. When he saw the slight smile on Tony's face, he laughed harder.

CHAPTER 9

I n the kitchen at Jamie's house, red, yellow, and blue helium balloons bounced merrily on their strings above the backs of two adjacent kitchen chairs where his siblings sat. With three puffs, the twins blew out the yellow candles on a chocolate cake that said *Happy Birthday Katie and Billy*. Katie coughed several times and reached for her inhaler.

The twins pulled the candles off the cake so they could cut out their pieces. After they'd devoured their slices, their mouths still encircled with chocolate-frosting mustaches, they yelped with joy at the sight of the two new bikes their mom rolled in. A hot-pink one for Katie with a Miss Kitty medallion attached to the handlebars and a bright-green one for Billy with a Star Wars lightsaber emblazoned on its front fender. Big hugs for Mom.

Jamie slid papered boxes in front of the twins. Katie tore through hers and pulled out the stuffed Earth doll. She cupped the doll's head in her hands. "Ooooooh! She's got green eyes and yellow hair just like me."

"I got her at the planetarium, munchkin. You like?"

Katie nodded and cradled the doll's body to her chest, its droopy arms and head tossed onto her shoulder.

"I'm gonna name her Earthadilly." Jamie was relieved that her inhaler had done its job and the only sound now was a slight rasp in her voice.

Billy rummaged through the contents of his present from Jamie. A child's doctor's kit. He pulled out a stethoscope and wrapped it around his neck. "Just like Daddy's! Thanks, Jamie."

Katie offered Earthadilly to Billy. "Make believe she's sick."

Billy removed a thermometer from his kit and stuck it on the doll's mouth. "High fever," he said and held up the plastic stick.

"Give her something to make her well, please."

Billy searched around in his kit and pulled out a smiley-face Band-Aid that he slapped on top of Earthadilly's head.

Katie laughed. "Oh, thank you, Dr. Billy."

Jamie wished it were as simple as that for Katie.

Their mom's phone rang. She answered it and listened intently for a few seconds. Her face tightened just before she disappeared into the den. Jamie followed her and waited for her to hang up.

"Katie's test results," his mom whispered.

"Her asthma?"

"Dr. Abrams said her asthma is getting worse and now she has a lung infection."

"But she'll be okay, right?"

"She's going on an antibiotic and I have to keep her inside until the infection clears up." Her voice wavered. "We also need to sterilize everything she uses and give her plenty of liquids."

Jamie's body tightened. *With all the trips to the doctor's office, why is Katie getting worse? What's wrong with her lungs anyway? And now they're infected? Why can't they cure her?*

That old memory stirred inside him. How he'd failed to help his dad. Jamie absolutely couldn't bear to see anything happen to his sister. Especially when he knew he couldn't do anything about it.

When Jamie and his mom rejoined the twins at the kitchen table, he was determined not to let the news spoil their birthday. Katie stared straight at him, so he clamped down on his thoughts. Too late. She hopped out of her chair with Earthadilly, crawled into his lap, and cupped one of her small hands on his cheek.

"Jamie, you're the best big brother I ever had." There was that familiar swelling in his chest.

She put Earthadilly's face up next to his. "She has something to tell you." Katie pressed the doll's mouth against his ear. "Everything's going to be okey-dokey," she whispered in a throaty voice.

If only he could believe that was true.

CHAPTER 10

Jamie had just finished helping his mom clean up after the twins' birthday party when through the window he spotted his three friends coming up the front walk. He'd barely opened the door when Tony said, "Hey, dude, can you come out? I got some wild stuff to tell ya!"

A full autumn moon in a cloudless sky cast a flickering dapple of shadows through the majestic oak tree's fluttering leaves. Jamie sat cross-legged in a circle with his friends under the tree's outer branches.

He couldn't stop thinking about his sister. Then he realized Tony was waving his hand in front of him to get his attention.

"You're not gonna believe this," Tony said. "My father made me go dove hunting and this time we almost got wiped out by a tornado!"

"Are you making this up?" Keisha said.

"No, for real. We were out in this field in Alabama when a humongous tornado hit. I mean a real monster."

"Hey, even if you are bluffing, it's a good story," Keisha said.

"Keisha, I'm not making this up."

"Let him tell his story, Keish," Jamie said.

Tony sat up on his heels. "Yeah, Keish ... so first we heard this sound like a freight train roaring at the far edge of the field. We saw these gray streaks above us like they were churned by a giant eggbeater and then a dark funnel cloud on the horizon. The sky turned black and the wind whipped up so bad we looked like wash on a clothesline with our clothes and hair blowing straight out behind us."

"Geez, Tony, all this and you're in an open field?" Jamie said, crinkling up his face.

"Yep, no protection. Then that monster came barreling toward us. My father said to dive in a ditch on the side of the field so in we went." He cupped his hands over both ears. "Man, the closer it got the louder it roared. When it was almost near our ditch it whipped up a ton of dirt into my eyes and nose."

Jamie's eyebrows shot up.

"I thought it was gonna suck me right outta there. But then it sounded like it changed direction. We looked out and it had swerved away from us! Man, good riddance!"

"Whoa!" Jamie said.

Tony leaned back on his elbows and grinned. "So I just lived through the biggest twister Alabama's ever seen." He let out one of his goofy hyena laughs.

"Weren't you scared out of your mind?" Jamie said.

"Nah."

"Oh, sure, Tony, you big faker," Keisha said and poked his knee.

"Okay, maybe a little, but not as much as if it spun me around in a big loop de loop." Another hyena laugh. "It really was a shocker seeing how huge that thing was."

Jamie knew Tony was brave, but this was ridiculous. He made it sound like he enjoyed coming face to face with a tornado, as if it were just a bigger version of a bully. Jamie could not for one second sit out a tornado on the side of a field. He'd probably try to outrun it and get torn to shreds. They'd find pieces of him scattered all over the state of Alabama. He'd be delivered to his mom in a paper bag. And the TV station would report on the stupid boy who tried to run faster than a tornado and ended up like confetti. How embarrassing.

"What about your father?" Raj said.

Jamie winced at Raj's question.

Tony's face hardened. "He acted like he always does—with a big stick up his butt. He just bitched about how it drove off all the doves. I could've died out there. After the tornado just barely missed us, do you think he asked me how I was? No. My eyes were so clogged up with dirt I couldn't see, but do you think he cared? No. Think he even mentioned he was glad we survived? Heck, no. All he cared about was his hunting."

Jamie wished he could bring back Tony's hyena laugh. He couldn't imagine his own father being so cold. His dad had told him he loved him right up until the week he died. It seemed like another life. Back when Jamie was surer of himself. Well, maybe not totally sure. But with Tony's dad getting on him all the time, how come Tony had so much confidence?

"Gee, Tony, too bad you didn't get a photo of the tornado," Keisha said.

"Right, Keish, this monster's charging at me one hundred and sixty miles an hour, the wind's practically scalping me, and all I'm going to think about is how I can hang around taking photos so everybody can see me get splattered." The hyena laugh was back and Jamie was the first to join in.

Suddenly Jamie heard a *whoosh* like a strong wind blowing through a tunnel. A few yards from them, sparkly, crystal-like particles exploded into a thick mist. It looked like what he'd seen before, only bigger.

Once the mist cleared, there stood a white-haired old man with a weathered face holding a small, silver-colored box. With his white pants, white collarless shirt, and white spongy-looking shoes, he could have passed for an elderly ice-cream man. But no ice-cream man Jamie had ever seen arrived by way of sparkles.

Jamie scooted back a few feet. His friends did the same.

"Don't be afraid," the old man said softly.

"Who are you?" Tony said. "How did you appear like that? And what the heck are you doing here?"

"I'm Mr. James. A scientist from the future."

"I think we need to go," Jamie said. He stood up.

"Please don't go," Mr. James said. "I'm a friend, and I need your help."

"None of my friends appear out of thin air," Jamie said. "I'm sorry, Mr. James—we gotta go now." He inched toward the house and motioned to his friends. "Come on, guys, this is too weird."

"Just give me a chance to explain," the old man said. "What I have to tell you is extremely important for you and for our world."

"How do we know we can trust you?" Tony said. "Nobody in our world can do what you just did."

"Maybe if you hear what I want to share with you, it will help address your concerns."

Jamie hesitated, then lowered himself back to the ground. "I saw your sparkles in my yard a couple of other days. Have you come here other times—secretly?"

"No, you probably saw impressions of my vibration tests for entry from the future into this location at this point in time, but I haven't visited you from the future before."

"If you're from the future, where's your time machine?" Tony said.

"There isn't one. I use an energy vibrator."

"A what?" Keisha said.

Mr. James held up the silver box. Up close, Jamie could see a six-inch iridescent-purple rod attached in the middle. "All living things are made up of energy vibrating at certain speeds to create density."

Jamie studied the mysterious gadget. It looked too simple to do much of anything.

"This can make bodies vibrate fast enough to lose their density and slip through the time barrier," Mr. James said.

"It's true that subatomic particles vibrate," Raj said to his friends.

Tony rocked spastically from side to side. "So man, you just vibrated back through time?"

"Something like that. I can set it for any point in time." The old man gestured to what looked like a digital clock on the side of the box. "But I've come here on an important mission. May I join you?"

The tight muscles in Jamie's neck loosened a little. Maybe they should just hear him out. At least they were in Jamie's backyard with the door to his house close by. He stared at his friends.

"Okay, I'm curious," Tony said. "Let's see what this strange dude has to say. He doesn't look dangerous, so what do we have to lose?"

The old man slowly settled himself on the lawn across from them.

"What kind of mission?" Jamie said.

"To save Earth," Mr. James said.

Keisha smirked. "From what? Aliens? Meteors?"

"Earth as you know it is very different in the future."

"Whaddya mean? Tony said.

"I bet he means what's already threatening the planet," Raj said.

"It would be easier to show you."

"Show us how?" Keisha said.

"By taking you on a visit to the future."

"Cool," Tony said.

Jamie stared at Tony as if he'd lost his mind.

"Not so fast, Tony," Raj said. "We know nothing about this man who just appears out of nowhere."

"Yeah, we're not supposed to go with people we don't know," Keisha said. "And I'm pretty sure that includes people from the future."

"Some little box with magic powers?" Raj said. "Who ever heard of such a thing?"

"I understand how you all feel." Mr. James lifted his open palms toward the kids. "If you were my grand-children, I would want you to react the same way."

"You have grandchildren?" Keisha said.

"Yes, two of them are about your age."

"So how do they like living in the future?" Tony said.

"Well, to them it's the present."

Tony tapped the palm of his hand against his forehead. "Oh, right."

"But to answer your question, they don't like it at all. That's why I've come to ask for your help."

"Why us?" Jamie said.

Mr. James paused a few moments. "As children you will inherit the Earth of the future, where I live now. It's not a nice future. But from my vantage point I know you can help change it."

"Change it from what to what?" Keisha said. "Are you trying to scare us?"

"No, but I am trying to impress upon you how important it is that you believe me."

Keisha frowned. "If this is so important why don't you talk to the grown-ups?"

"The adults wouldn't believe me. I've already tried."

"Why do you think we would believe you?" Raj said.

"Because as children your minds are more open."

"Of all the kids in the world, why did you choose us then?" Jamie said.

Mr. James stared into Jamie's eyes. Jamie sensed something familiar, but he couldn't name it.

"I chose you because the four of you together have everything you need to be successful."

"If we went with you, how long would we be gone?" Jamie said. "I don't want my mom to worry if she can't find me."

"I can return you to this point in time when we've finished our visit."

Jamie started to feel drawn to this odd old man. His antenna didn't pick up anything to fear. There was kindness there. And sadness. Jamie couldn't bring himself to turn away. In fact, to his surprise, he had a strong urge to do what the old guy requested.

"I think we should let him show us the future," Jamie said. He knew if Jamie-the-Wimp was willing to go, they'd all be willing to go.

"I wanna see the future," Tony said. "What a kick. Let's do it."

Jamie turned to Raj and Keisha. "How do you feel about it?"

Keisha nodded slowly. "If you're okay with it, Jamie, so am I."

Raj stared at Mr. James for several moments. "Are you sure you will be able to return us safely?"

"Of course," Mr. James said.

Raj turned back to his friends. "I agree with Jamie."

Mr. James gathered them around him and punched some numbers into the clock on his energy vibrator.

Jamie's body seemed to dissolve into a zillion specks of light, his mind floating in the middle of them. Then the little lights rearranged themselves into his solid body with his mind back in his head. His backyard was gone. He found himself in a bizarre new place.

CHAPTER 11

J amie stood with Mr. James and his friends on a cliff overlooking a reddish-brown wasteland. Remnants of large, dead trees jutted from the earth like a long-forgotten forest cemetery. A thick, gray haze hung in the air, and red dust clouds whirled across the sterile landscape.

Jamie's nose and throat burned, and after a few breaths he realized the air was causing it. He couldn't stop rubbing his eyes and coughing. The heat made it even worse. He flicked away beads of sweat rolling down his face and checked out his friends. They were coughing and sweating as much as he was.

Jamie turned and saw behind him a big, round, silvery vehicle with a wide bubble window. It sort of reminded him of a helicopter with its huge horizontal propellers. Except it was mounted on three long, silvery poles and looked like it had a rocket exhaust at its base.

Why had Mr. James taken them to another planet? And what was wrong with this awful air?

Mr. James motioned to the vehicle. "Get in the heliojet where you can breathe safely." He activated the vehicle's stairs and ushered Raj, Keisha, and Tony into the back seat through a glasslike door. Then he seated Jamie in the front near the controls. Mr. James lumbered in next to Jamie and waved his hand over a smooth panel to close the doors. Air vents blew with a *hiss* inside the cabin, and after several seconds the kids' coughing subsided.

Jamie stared silently at the red, barren land below. After a moment he said, "Mr. James, are we ... are we on *Mars?*"

"This is Alexandria, Virginia, seventy years in the future."

"No way," Jamie said. "There's nothing here that looks like our city." He turned around to his friends for their agreement. They had disbelief written all over their faces.

"A lot has changed since you were children," Mr. James said. "That red layer is nitrogen dioxide dust." He gestured toward the eerie terrain. "It's from car exhaust, coal burning, and other industries. It's toxic to the lungs. So are the high levels of other gases here. You can't see them, but they're just as poisonous."

"You let us breathe poisonous air?" Jamie said.

"Don't worry. I didn't let you stay outside the heliojet long enough to cause any harm. But I wanted you to experience what it's like to breathe this air even for a few seconds."

Jamie stared at the ugly red landscape and couldn't believe his eyes. He pulled out his phone and started filming out the window.

"Is the whole country like this?" Keisha said.

Mr. James's face seemed to sag. "The whole planet is as polluted and barren as this."

Mr. James pushed a button and the propellers began to turn. The heliojet ascended quickly and cruised above the ground. Through the thick haze Jamie started to observe hundreds of rows of large, army-like tents. As the heliojet flew closer he saw people roaming around clothed in white shirts, pants, and shoes. But what really struck Jamie were the full-face respirators every person wore—see-through, glasslike masks that covered the eyes and attached to a large, black cup over the nose and mouth. Black canisters stuck out from both sides of the cup.

"Do they always wear those things?" Jamie said.

"Always," Mr. James said. "They wouldn't last long here without those respirators, and neither would you."

Keisha leaned closer to the window. "Where are their homes? What are they doing with all these tents?"

"Where do they get food and water?" Raj said.

The heliojet glided slowly. "Tent villages are everywhere," Mr. James said. "With so many severe hurricanes, tornadoes, and floods, many of our communities don't have a chance to rebuild before another one hits."

Mr. James maneuvered the heliojet far enough from the village so its propellers wouldn't stir up dirt near the inhabitants when they landed. "Would you like to go down for a closer look? I have enough respirators for each of you."

Jamie didn't want to get out of the heliojet in this strange place. What if the tent people thought they were dangerous and attacked them? What if a tornado appeared? What if the respirator didn't work right? This didn't seem safe at all.

"I totally wanna go down there," Tony said. "Just show me how to use the respirator."

"Maybe we should stay in the heliojet," Jamie said. "We can see okay from here, and it looks creepy down there."

"Knock it off, Jamie," Tony said. "We're going down there." He eyed Raj and Keisha who just shrugged.

Mr. James landed and gave each of them respirators. "Be sure to strap it on tightly so you get a good seal. You'll be able to talk through the round speaker over your mouth."

Jamie had trouble getting used to his respirator. The rubbery cup clamped over his mouth and nose weighed on his face, and it felt weird trying to breathe through filters. The eye mask pressed hard against his temples. It was like looking through a fishbowl. He thought this must be what it was like for deep-sea divers, except instead of being underwater they were trying to survive in poisonous air. And it was all over what used to be his hometown.

Jamie's breathing seemed loud to him and echoed in his ears. He nudged Tony and yelled, "Hey, Tony, can you hear me through this speaker thing okay?"

"Yeah, but your voice seems far away," Tony said.

Tony sounded like he was at the bottom of a barrel, and Raj and Keisha's conversation in the background came across like distant dueling foghorns.

Mr. James motioned for the kids to follow him. In the sky Jamie spotted a massive, military-like plane with propellers on top and a rocket exhaust similar to the heliojet, only bigger. It landed on the outskirts of the village, whipping up fine red particles all around it. Wheels descended from its base and it lumbered toward the village. As soon as it stopped, men and women wearing respirators and white uniforms marked with a brown badge disembarked, hauling large containers. Tent people headed toward the vehicle, pushing empty carts.

"Our water and food delivery service," Mr. James said. "We're very limited in what we can grow."

"Where are your gardens and farms?" Jamie said.

"We haven't had any open-air gardens and farms—or birds and animals—in many years."

Jamie didn't want to think about what it must be like to live in this kind of world. He just couldn't imagine it. Had these people ever even seen a garden? Did they have any idea what the planet used to be like, with its clear, blue skies, golden cornfields, and birds darting in and out of flowers?

"How do you grow your food then?" Jamie said.

"I'm going to show you on one of our stops, but it's not like any food you've ever seen before."

Jamie saw two young women adjust their respirator masks after they sat down on a forty-foot black square next to the tent nearest him. The square had large hinges on one side. "What's that square, Mr. James?"

"That covers one of the underground shelters. There's a shelter for every block of tents. When tornadoes or hurricanes are reported, that's where people go with their tents, equipment, and supplies until it's safe to come out."

"Why didn't they build underground cities if living on the surface is so dangerous?" Raj said.

Mr. James sighed. "Because of all the underground contamination and earthquakes."

"Earthquakes?" Jamie said. "Virginia hardly ever has any earthquakes, especially not big ones like in California."

"Well, fracking changed that," Mr. James said. "After they started fracking in Virginia, we've had as many man-made earthquakes as the other fracking states. Those states are full of tent villages now because they can't build underground and risk earthquakes tearing apart whatever they build."

"I thought fracking just pulled oil and gas out of the ground," Keisha said.

"It's the way they do it that causes the quakes," Raj said. "They inject fluids into the ground under high pressure."

Jamie's mind spun. Poisonous air, tent villages, and earthquakes in the same place where they lived now? How could this have gotten so bad? Jamie eyed Tony for his reaction, but Tony's eyes were empty.

Three children wearing respirators darted into Jamie's sight as they chased each other around the tents.

"There don't seem to be many kids here," Jamie said.

Mr. James stared at the three tent children as they whizzed by.

"So where are all ..." Jamie noticed a tall man and a red-haired boy, about Jamie's age, pushing a cart full of boxes and bottles from the food-delivery vehicle. As they got closer the boy stared at Jamie and his friends with curious eyes. Jamie was about to speak to him but changed his mind when the boy quickly turned his head away.

The man and the boy trudged over to one of the tents and distributed the cart's contents to the others. Once they'd finished the man approached Jamie and his friends and looked them over.

Jamie was suddenly aware how much he and his friends, in their colorful t-shirts and jeans, stood out among the villagers' white clothing flecked with red dust.

"You kids are pretty far from home, aren't ya?" the man said. "Never been outside your nice little sphere before?"

Jamie edged closer to Mr. James.

"This is all new to them," Mr. James said. "They're here to see what it's like to live in one of the villages."

"Oh, is that so?" the man said. He called out in the direction of the red-haired boy, "John, get over here. These kids from one of the spheres want to know what it's like to live in our little paradise."

John joined the man. His rail-thin body seemed to sag from the weight of his bones.

"This is my son, John, the only one of my kids who's survived," the man said.

A silent moment passed. Finally Jamie said, "We're sorry about your losses, sir ... and John." His friends nodded.

John lowered his eyes.

John's father said, "Guess you've noticed we don't have many kids around here." He sounded like he'd have spit out his words at them if he didn't have to talk through a respirator. "Their lungs were too undeveloped to survive this crappy air, even when we tried to keep respirators on 'em. Ever watch a baby try to breathe through a miniature respirator?"

The man's shoulders rose up so high they almost swallowed his neck. "But you wouldn't know about that, would you, being some of the *privileged* ones."

"Privileged?" Keisha said.

"We know how much better you all have it, all safe and cozy in your spheres," the man said. "If my children had been chosen, they'd be alive today."

The man flung his hand at Jamie and his friends as if to shoo them away. "Go on, get out, stop staring at us. We're human beings just like you, not something to gawk at." He shoved his hands in his pockets and trudged back toward one of the tents. Powdery puffs rose as each foot stomped the ground.

John started to turn to follow his father.

"John, we're not gawking," Jamie said. "We wish you didn't have to live like this."

John straightened a bit and heaved his chest. "You should probably go back to your sphere soon." He shuffled away.

A sandy-haired girl about six years old, the youngest child Jamie had seen so far, barreled out of a nearby tent and almost bumped into him. The second she looked up at him, Jamie's eyes met hers and they held a brief connection. The sight of the little girl peering up at him from behind a respirator pierced him. He started to kneel down to her level, but she bolted back to the tent. He wanted to call after her. To find out if she had any brothers and sisters. To ask her if she had enough food and water. If the children here had toys. If she ever felt safe.

"Why didn't people do something to prevent all this?" Jamie said.

Mr. James's face fell. "As scientists we thoroughly documented for years what we saw happening to the planet, and we warned over and over what the world needed to do to stop it."

"Like scientists do in our time," Raj said.

"Yes, but the world as a whole didn't do enough," Mr. James said. "Now every day all of us face an ugly truth— that the human race had the ability to save our common home but didn't have the will to do it until it was too late."

Jamie knew he wouldn't hold it together if he stayed in this bleak place much longer. "Maybe we should go, Mr. James."

The others wanted to leave too so they all piled into the heliojet. As the vehicle increased altitude and speed, more tent villages dotted the landscape below them. Jamie scanned the naked terrain searching for more children. Then everything disappeared beneath the clouds.

"What did he mean about a sphere and being privileged?" Jamie said.

Mr. James sighed again. "You'll see."

CHAPTER 12

After a short bolt through the air in the heliojet, they approached a flooded area around a river and tidal basin. Reddish-brown water completely surrounded what remained of the White House, the Capitol Building, the Supreme Court Building, the Lincoln Memorial, the Washington Monument, and all the Smithsonian buildings.

Tony pointed to the Capitol. "Hey, my father works there, uh … worked there."

"My mom worked there too," Keisha said. "But the Potomac River never flooded like this, not anywhere near this bad."

"Climate change caused heavy rain for weeks on end," Mr. James said. "Flooding is more frequent now and comes up higher, then takes months to subside."

Jamie couldn't see any trace of the long, grassy National Mall or any of the adjacent streets. From the air it looked like somebody had built a miniature replica of Washington, DC, submerged the whole thing halfway underwater, and pumped thick, gray haze above it.

"Is it always like this?" Jamie said.

"No, sometimes we have a drought that lasts for years and everything dries up," Mr. James said. "Not a pretty sight. Either way the area is no longer habitable."

It was hard for Jamie to see this place, so important to his country, destroyed. Or to know that kids in the future would never get to visit the Lincoln Memorial, climb the steps of the National Monument, or learn about space in the planetarium. He didn't understand how his country's powerful leadership couldn't even protect itself. If they couldn't, who could?

There didn't seem to be any hope for the future. It was like falling down a well and knowing there was no one to throw you a rope. He blinked several times trying to grasp what he saw, then reached for his phone and started filming again.

"But how could they—" Keisha started before Tony cut her off.

"Wait, does America still have a president and other elected people?"

"Yes, but they're in a place far from here," Mr. James said. "We'll head there in a little while."

Jamie shoved his phone back in his pocket and turned away from the scene below.

With a blast of air from its rocket exhaust the heliojet shot at high speed into a mass of gray clouds. In minutes it descended out of the clouds and hovered over what looked like a former military base next to a wide river. The area was even more flooded than Washington, DC, with submerged piers and rooftops.

"This is what remains of the Norfolk Naval Station on the Elizabeth River," Mr. James said. "It was once the world's largest naval station with seventy-five ships and one hundred and thirty-four aircraft. Sea-level rise and storm surges destroyed the whole base."

"My dad took me on a tour of this base just last year," Tony said. "This is crazy."

Jamie knew the base too. His dad had served as a navy doctor here. And his parents loved telling the story of how they met at a Norfolk Harborfest concert not far from the base. Now it was totally wiped out?

The heliojet flew slowly from one end of the submerged complex to the other. Jamie leaned closer to the side of the round window. He hadn't recovered yet from the last two scenes, and now this. It was still hard for him to accept any of it, and yet right there below him were ... he counted flooded remnants of fourteen piers and eleven aircraft hangers. It seemed impossible that the people back in his time had let this happen. He pulled out his phone to film.

"It's only one of the installations that were ruined," Mr. James said. "In just this southeastern region of Virginia we also lost Oceana Naval Air Station, Dam Neck Naval Base, and Langley-Eustis Army and Air Force bases. Our country's other coastline bases were destroyed too."

"Didn't they have any idea this was coming?" Jamie said.

"Well, as early as 2016 respected scientists issued a report warning Congress that sea-level rise would eventually swallow up these military installations, and the Defense Department created its own climate-change-adaptation plan. But the military couldn't convince Congress to take action."

"My dad's committee in Congress always supported funding the military," Tony said. "Where were their minds at?"

"They thought we should focus all our energies on fighting our foreign enemies," Mr. James said. "But it's kind of hard to defend your country when your military installations are underwater."

"But how does the military do its job now without these bases?" Jamie said.

"We really don't have much of a military anymore. After our bases were badly weakened, a long third world war destroyed most of the planet's military, including our own. Now our resources go primarily toward the basic necessities, just like in the other countries."

Jamie remembered some of the stories his dad had told him about all the people in his family who'd served in the military, dating back to his great-grandfather. In the future, no one in his family would know what it was like to serve that way, to feel the pride of defending their country. They would never experience the America he knew.

A knot twisted in his stomach.

~

The heliojet picked up speed and took only a few minutes to reach the Atlantic Ocean. As far as the eye could see, black waves clawed at the coastline like an army of angry panthers. White debris bobbed in the surf and littered the black sand.

"This was Virginia Beach, once the largest stretch of pleasure beach in the world," Mr. James said.

Mr. James landed the heliojet not far from the surf. The kids, breathing through their respirators, made their way through the gray haze toward the shoreline where they discovered the sand and waves saturated with oil. The white debris turned out to be the skeletal remains of sea animals, large and small, churning endlessly in the surf and stuck in the oil blanketing the beach. Jamie looked up and down the beach and realized there must be thousands of them.

This Virginia Beach didn't look anything like the one Jamie knew. His dad used to bring the family on vacations here. They stayed in one of the big hotels right on the oceanfront and spent the whole day with their boogie boards riding the waves and building castles on the beautiful, clean beach while little sandpipers landed nearby and poked around in the mud for food. At night there were bands, and rides on a Ferris wheel, and cotton candy and taffy, and walks on the boardwalk, and all the fresh seafood they could eat. Those were some of his greatest memories with his dad.

"You think of the Atlantic Ocean full of whales, dolphins, fish, crabs, so many other creatures," Mr. James said. "But the planet's oceans are too warm and polluted now. They're all dead—and so are all their sea and plant life."

"Oh, no, no, no!" Jamie wailed as he watched the waves roll skeleton shards up onto the beach and drag them back out in a hideous cycle.

Keisha dabbed her eyes and Tony wrapped his arm around her. Raj stared at the carnage, the muscles around his mouth tightening.

Jamie scanned the shoreline again and couldn't find even a trace of a boardwalk or buildings. "This is nothing but one long, oily graveyard!"

"Hurricanes have been off the charts, wiping out everything along the Atlantic Coast," Mr. James said.

"But we've had hurricanes in our time, and they never took away *everything!*" Jamie said.

"You never saw hurricanes like these. As Earth got warmer, the oceans absorbed eighty to ninety percent of that heat."

Raj grimaced. "Warm air and warm water fuel hurricanes."

Mr. James nodded. "The mega hurricanes also tore apart the offshore oil rigs, and nobody could stop the oil from gushing out for months on end. Between the rising ocean temperatures and the oil eruptions up and down the coastlines, the sea life didn't stand a chance."

Keisha released a feeble moan. "But my mom says there won't be any drilling off our Atlantic Coast because so many people are against it."

"Well, I'm afraid there will be."

"Right, because these idiots just didn't care, did they?" Tony said. "They should've plastered huge signs all over the country that said *We really don't give a crap.* Put it on a bunch of baseball caps!"

A wave washed up near Jamie's feet and deposited a small skeleton on the oily sand. He squatted down as if to examine it so he could curl himself around that increasingly painful knot in his stomach.

Everything he'd seen in the future raced around Jamie's brain in a dizzying, nauseating blur. This was worse than any nightmare he could possibly imagine. He started to consider the possibility that this really could be *their* future.

Jamie stood up, one arm across his abdomen.

"I think you've seen enough," Mr. James said. He'd started to usher them toward the heliojet when Jamie suddenly stopped and turned around.

"Please wait a second," Jamie said. He pulled out his phone and forced himself to film this last scene from the nightmare. He didn't know why. It just seemed like he should.

CHAPTER 13

M r. James gave the kids specially treated cloths for cleaning off their oily shoes and told them to remove their respirators inside the heliojet. As soon as they took off, the vents pumped out filtered air. Jamie stripped off the cumbersome equipment and smoothed the irritated skin around his mouth and nose. Then he massaged his stomach a bit because the tightness inside him still hadn't gone away.

They descended above a brown, flattened mountain dotted with traces of dead trees and enveloped in gray haze. A large, clear dome perched on the top.

"You wanted to know where the country's leaders went when the Washington, DC, area got so flooded out." Mr. James said. "That's the ecosphere compound for the president, the Congress, the Supreme Court, and what little is left of the Pentagon."

Jamie pressed his face against the window. As the heliojet flew closer to the mountain he could make out white multilevel buildings inside the dome clustered among young trees.

"Most of the federal government offices moved to this Appalachian mountain."

"How nice for them, all safe and tucked away up here," Tony said.

Mr. James steered the heliojet along miles and miles of the mountain range, most of which was flattened and browned out like the mountain with the ecosphere.

"The Appalachians used to be one of our country's most beautiful regions," Mr. James said. "But these mountains were also loaded with coal."

The aircraft swooped down closer to where big, ugly grooves ripped through the mountains.

"They leveled thousands of mountains, digging up coal and wiping out hundreds of forests," Mr. James said. "Coal burning was our worst polluter."

He steered over a barren valley and riverbed filled with miles of rock, dirt, and gray sludge. "They turned our valleys, rivers, and streams into landfills for their waste. It caused flash flooding in towns below and poisoned our water and fish."

"My mom says they're doing that now in our own time," Keisha said.

Mr. James nodded. "It got worse."

Jamie shook his head. "How were they allowed to trash everything like this?"

"I guess some thought digging the coal out was good for the country," Mr. James said.

The aircraft descended above another large, clear dome on a mountaintop. "We're approaching the Blue Ridge Mountains, and that's one of our supply-center ecospheres," Mr. James said.

The dome covered a white, twenty-story pyramid with terraces extending from each floor. People moved in and out of the doorways opening onto the terraces. A road curved around smaller buildings and led to a lake and forest. All under the clear dome.

"It's a big job keeping the outside of our ecospheres clean from all the pollution," Mr. James said. "But if we didn't do it regularly, we'd lose our access to sunlight."

Mr. James waved his finger over some of his controls. "Get ready for landing. You won't need your respirators down there because the air inside is purified by a large filtering system."

The heliojet zoomed down and landed on the roof of a building attached to the dome. The roof opened and the vehicle descended inside.

Mr. James helped the kids out of the vehicle into a dimly lit structure that resembled a small airplane hangar. He swiped his hand over a wall panel and heavy doors slid open to a closet-sized chamber. "These passageways protect our living environment from pollution."

The kids followed him into the chamber and the doors closed behind them. Mr. James again swiped his hand over a wall panel and led them from the chamber into the ecosphere.

People dressed in white, like Mr. James, bustled throughout the dome. No one wore a respirator. "We grow food and purify water here. Other ecospheres grow cotton and make clothing and herbs for medicine."

He escorted the kids to a vehicle that looked to Jamie like a six-seat golf cart with big wheels and solar panels on the roof. They drove past several multilevel claylike buildings.

Mr. James stopped the vehicle outside a long, white, two-story building and led them through the door. Hundreds of rows of glasslike tubes about a yard long and filled with green liquid were stacked in racks from the floor to the ceiling two stories above. People in white uniforms with handheld devices seemed to be monitoring the contents, rising up and down the stacks in small, individually operated forklifts.

Jamie was sure he'd seen something like this before. "Hey, Raj, don't these tubes look like the ones in your dad's lab, only bigger?"

"And the green stuff looks like algae," Raj said.

Mr. James gestured toward the tubes. "That *is* algae. I'm in charge of growing enough of it for the southeastern United States."

Jamie looked more closely at the tubes and saw algae blooms floating in the water.

Mr. James headed toward the end of the rows. "Our algae production line starts here at the algae press."

At the end of each row of tubes, liquid containing the algae poured through a black pipe into a huge metal barrel. A technician operated controls that forced a round metal plate to press down on the algae-rich liquid, separating the algae from the liquid.

On one side of the algae press, green, oily glop dripped out into a funnel that drained into a smaller pipe, which then ran along the wall to the far side of the building.

"This is algae biofuel that hasn't been processed yet," Mr. James said. "We use it to power some of our vehicles. But we should have started using it decades ago. Your father was right, Raj."

Jamie wondered how Mr. James knew about that.

Raj nodded and leaned over to inspect the raw fuel.

On the other side of the algae press Mr. James gestured to a dark-green solid dropping into a big vat. "Here's what's left after we press the fuel out of the algae. Our food. It's rich in micronutrients."

Mr. James donned a white glove from a dispenser next to the vat and picked up a small piece of the solid algae. He offered it to the kids. "Want a taste?"

Jamie put some in his mouth and chewed slowly. "Tastes like lettuce."

"We also use algae to gobble up the carbon dioxide from our human waste." Jamie quickly spit out the algae into his hand.

Mr. James chuckled. "Don't worry, Jamie, there's no human waste in that food. But one of the other things that makes it a good biofuel is that it absorbs carbon dioxide and releases oxygen like trees and other plants do."

Mr. James ushered them out of the building to the vehicle and drove along a narrow road. They passed a small, round, blue lake framed by a clay edge. "We pump this water from contaminated underground springs and remove the pollutants here."

"What about the real lakes?" Keisha said.

"All polluted, just like the oceans. Lakes, rivers, oceans. Nothing survives in them."

"Can't you build enough of these ecospheres for everybody?" Jamie said.

"The United States has hundreds of millions of people. We don't have the money or resources to house them all." Mr. James rubbed the back of his hand across his forehead. "We have all we can do to supply enough food, water, and clothing. And fuel for the vehicles to make the deliveries. Other ones like these are building more ecospheres, but not nearly enough yet."

"So you spend your days helping people get just enough food and water to stay alive?" Keisha said. "That's all there is? People on the outside have to spend their lives wearing respirators in that bad air, watching their kids die from it, hiding from horrible weather disasters, and struggling just to *exist* in this insane future place?"

"Unfortunately, it's the best we can do until we have a whole lot more ecospheres."

"Is that what that man in the tent village meant when he said we were privileged?" Jamie said.

"He thought you were some of the children chosen to ensure the human race will survive. We have ecospheres devoted to raising those children."

"With their parents?" Keisha said.

"Sadly, not all live with their parents. The government has trained people to raise them. If the parents have other children who are not chosen, those parents take care of them in tent villages like the ones you saw today."

"Who decides which kids are chosen?" Jamie said, his voice quivering.

"They're selected based on their stronger intellectual and physical genetic makeup."

"So you just let the weaker kids die?" Tony said.

"We try very hard to prevent them from dying, but since we don't have enough ecospheres for everybody, the government wanted the brightest and healthiest children to live in the ecospheres. Many of our scientists, myself included, preferred a lottery system that would keep the whole family together and give every family an equal chance, no matter how strong or weak their children. But we had no say in the government's decision."

Jamie couldn't believe his ears. Who in the government came up with this mean idea of deciding which kids got saved and which got left behind? Didn't all kids deserve the same chance? What if those government people had children with weak lungs? Would they make their children live in the tent villages while they lived in the nice, unpolluted ecospheres?

"How does the government decide which other adults get to live in the ecospheres?" Raj said.

"Healthy adults who have expertise in the fields we need are chosen to live in the ecospheres," Mr. James said. "That's why I get to live here." His face sagged. "But it's hard knowing that some of my grandchildren have to live on the outside."

"What do you know about us and our families?" Jamie said. "What's going to happen to all of us?"

"It doesn't matter what I know because your time travel has influenced your futures."

"What do you mean? Jamie said.

"I think he means that because we have come here and learned about all this, our futures will be different than if we had not come," Raj said.

"Yes, that's correct," Mr. James said. "And my knowledge of your futures is based on what would have happened before you came here. But I don't know how your experience here will affect your lives and the lives of those around you."

"But you said you chose us because together we had what we need to be successful. So you must have known something," Keisha said.

Mr. James sighed. "I know that the four of you have the *potential* to change the future, but I don't know what you will do with that potential."

"Look, Mr. Scientist-from-the-Future, I can tell you how all this affects me right now," Tony said. "I don't want anything to do with it."

Jamie didn't want to know any more about this demented place either. He wished he'd never agreed to come.

"Mr. James, this is a nice ecosphere, and I guess you're doing everything you can, but we're just having a hard time accepting what we've seen as our future," Jamie said softly.

Raj cocked his head. "Jamie, my father had a hard time accepting that air pollution damaged two million kids in Delhi, but he's trying to do something about it."

"That's great, Raj, but this is a whole planet full of pollution," Keisha said. "How can we do anything that would change that?"

"Keisha's right, but if we do nothing we already know how things will turn out," Jamie said.

"We cannot make believe we never came here," Raj said.

Jamie nodded.

"This future sucks," Tony said. "I want outta here."

Jamie looked at Mr. James. "I guess maybe we should go home now."

Chapter 14

The heliojet landed back at the hill where they had first arrived in the future. Jamie stared out the window at the barrenness below. Tony, Keisha, and Raj had escaped into sleep, all slouched against each other in the back seat.

"Jamie, it doesn't have to be this way," Mr. James said.

"I'd like to believe that. But we're just kids, there's nothing we can do."

"Yes, there is."

"How? We have no power."

"Jamie, everyone has power. The mind is the most potent force in the physical world. Our thoughts act like magnets, attracting what we focus on."

"I don't understand how that can save our planet."

"If you want to have a healthy planet, you start with that thought and release all doubts or fears around it."

"I don't know about all this, Mr. James. I've never felt anything but powerless as long as I can remember."

"Just give yourself a chance."

"Please, if you think there's something we can do, why don't you just tell us?"

"I can show you what's coming, but I can't direct your actions. The decisions you make must be your own."

"But it's just me and my three friends. Is it all up to us?"

"Once you keep your mind focused on what you want to accomplish and release all doubts, you will be guided in the right direction."

Jamie thought all this stuff sounded good, but how could thoughts be so forceful they could change the world? Mr. James seemed sincere, but what he was asking them to do wasn't possible. If what they saw actually was just seventy years away, they'd have to live in that terrible world in their lifetime. So that meant things would get worse pretty fast.

"How long do we have before it's too late to change the future?"

"If you start worldwide changes soon to replace fossil fuels? About ten years."

"Ten years! That's so little time."

"But it's possible. You must believe me."

"I'm sorry, Mr. James, but I don't think there's any way we can make that happen, no matter what you say."

"Let me give you a simple example. You know how water streams through your garden hose? But if the hose gets clogged up with dirt then the water can't flow very well? See, our minds are like that … there's powerful energy always streaming through us. But if we hold onto negative thoughts, they clog up our minds so it's harder to use our power and harder to receive guidance."

"But who turns on the hose?"

"Our Creator."

"Really?"

"That's my understanding … our Creator is always with us, always moving powerful energy through us and providing guidance whenever we need it. We just have to be open to receive it."

Whoa! Jamie figured he needed time to mull this over. He always thought God was far away up in the sky in heaven … wherever that was.

"I need to warn you, though," Mr. James said. "Even after you open up to that energy and guidance, you'll still have to deal with forces that will oppose you at every turn, the same forces that stopped my generation from saving the planet. But, Jamie, you all have the potential to overcome those obstacles."

Mr. James pulled out his energy vibrator and adjusted the dial. "I'll take you home now."

Jamie peered up at the old man's face. What was it about Mr. James that made Jamie trust him? No one had ever seemed to have this kind of confidence in Jamie before. Okay, his parents and teachers always said he could do whatever he set his mind to. Never that he could save the planet. But then he thought about what he'd seen and he thought about Katie's lungs. That was his last thought before his body dissolved into a zillion specks of light with his mind floating in the middle of them.

~

Jamie tapped the ground with his foot to reassure himself they were standing in his yard. Everything looked the same as when they left. He stared in silence at Mr. James along with his friends.

"I know this was a lot for all of you to absorb," Mr. James said. "Just give yourselves time to think about what I've shown you, then see how you feel about it. Thank you

for coming with me … I have to go now … goodbye."
He activated his energy vibrator and vanished.

"I think we need to talk about this," Jamie said.

Tony crossed his arms and dug in his feet as if he were planting himself in the ground. "No, we *don't*."

"Come on, Tony."

"No, Jamie. See? They're all the same."

"Who?"

"The grown-ups. I knew we couldn't depend on them for anything. They trash the planet, and it's like, oh well, why don't you kids come and clean it up."

"That's not fair. Mr. James said they tried."

"Yeah right—and look how great that turned out."

"But Mr. James said we can change how it turns out."

"You don't really believe that do you, dude?"

"Well, I don't know. He came all the way back in time to pick us, didn't he?"

"Big deal. We don't know anything about that strange old guy."

Keisha gave Jamie's arm a gentle tug. "We're all tired and sad, Jamie. Maybe we should get some sleep and talk about this another time."

"We need to decide if we believe what we saw is going to happen," Raj said. "And if we think it is, then we need to decide if there is anything we can do. Strange old guys do not normally appear out of thin air to ask us to save the planet, no?

"Don't you get it, Raj?" Tony said. "They don't care about us."

"That is not what we are debating," Raj said. "It does not matter."

Tony rapped his fist against his chest. "Well, it matters to me. Why should we care if they didn't?"

"Because we are not them," Raj said. "And we would be cleaning up their mess for *us.*"

"Tony, we care about you," Keisha said.

Jamie tapped Tony's shoulder. "Yeah, Tony."

Tony's mouth softened, and a light crimson glowed on his cheeks. "Okay, okay, enough already. Are we done?"

"Maybe this isn't such a good time to talk," Jamie said.

"Maybe not," Raj said.

After his friends left, Jamie crouched on the edge of his garden. He inhaled all the good, rich earth smells, and surveyed the colorful bounty before him.

This earth gives life. The thought helped comfort him.

CHAPTER 15

J amie's sleep was filled with nightmares. He kept waking up in a hot sweat and gasping for air. But the next day he shoved all the images of the future to the back of his mind and focused on the present. He insisted that his mother bring Billy and him to Katie's doctor's appointment.

It seemed like it was taking a long time for their mom and Katie to come back to the reception area. The receptionist told Jamie the doctor was still with their mother and Katie was with the nurse in the examination room. He was anxious to find out about their sister, so when the receptionist started searching in a cabinet behind her desk he snuck down a hallway with Billy until he spotted their mother in a small office. She was seated across from Dr. Dorothy Abrams, who was looking down at a tablet.

Dr. Abrams had taken care of their sister ever since her first asthma attack. Their mother had told them that Dr. Abrams was a children's pulmonologist, a special kind of doctor who treated kids with breathing and lung diseases.

As soon as Jamie approached the office with his mom and Dr. Abrams inside, he signaled to Billy for them to flatten their bodies against the wall next to the open doorway where they stayed out of sight. He strained to hear the softly spoken words and felt a little guilty about their eavesdropping.

"Unfortunately, Mrs. Sawyer, asthma is a chronic condition that has no cure, but we can reduce its effects much of the time."

"Then why is Katie getting worse?" their mom said.

"We aren't certain. Her allergy tests didn't turn up anything. We know air pollutants can badly aggravate or damage children's lungs and make them more susceptible to infection."

"So what can be done to help her?"

"You can treat Katie at home with a medicated breathing machine called a nebulizer," Dr. Abrams said. "It's less stressful for young children if they're in a familiar environment with a visiting home nurse to check on them instead of in a hospital. The nebulizer will help her asthma, but her lung infection hasn't responded to the antibiotic so I'm going to put her on a different one."

"Does she have a good chance the new one will work better?"

"The bacterial infection is severe and is complicated by her asthma. I'm concerned she could develop pneumonia."

"Pneumonia? But isn't that treatable?"

"Generally, yes. However, the bacteria in her lungs seem to be resistant to antibiotics. The last one had no effect."

"What are you saying?"

"If we can't get the infection under control it could mean critical damage to her lungs."

Silence.

"But, Mrs. Sawyer, we're hoping the new antibiotic will prevent that."

"And if it doesn't?"

"Let's not think about that right now."

"Doctor, I need to know."

"You're asking me about a worst-case scenario, and it's too soon to be talking about that."

"Please, I don't want to be unprepared." His mom's voice trembled. "Worst-case scenario, if you can't get rid of the infection, how long does Katie have?"

Dr. Abrams paused for a few seconds. "Mrs. Sawyer, it's hard to give you a number of days or weeks. It can only be a rough timeframe based on past resistant cases and the extent of Katie's compromised lungs. If we can't knock out this infection …"

Jamie held his breath and peeked with one eye around the doorway.

A cluster of leaves sailed past the window and Dr. Abrams glanced over. "Worst case … she could be gone by the time all the leaves have fallen."

Jamie slid down the wall onto the floor next to his little brother and started shaking so hard he thought he would never stop. He peered into Billy's watery eyes and pulled him into his arms.

~

Jamie hovered in the doorway of Katie's bedroom, watching his mother tuck Katie into bed. His sister's face was flushed, her breathing labored. Jamie still shook inside from what he'd heard about his little sister.

"Am I very sick, Mommy?" Katie said in a raspy voice.

"You're going to get well, honey."

"Will you ask Billy to stay next to me a little while?"

Jamie ran through the house calling out for Billy, then spotted his brother through a window. He was almost hidden among the leaves, halfway up the oak tree in the backyard. Jamie rushed outside.

Moonbeams streamed from a clear sky, bathing the whole yard in a white light. Jamie peered up from under the tree and saw Billy straddling a thick branch. He was holding a ball of string and reaching for a leaf.

"Billy, what are you doing?"

"I'm tying the leaves. So they won't come down." Billy's voice cracked, "So Katie won't go away."

~

Jamie slouched in his bed sobbing: deep, gut-wrenching sobs, head hung low.

"I wish you were here, Dad," he whispered. "I wish you could help Katie. She's so little. Like those future kids who didn't make it. I'm sorry I couldn't save you, Dad, but I have to save Katie. I just don't know what to do."

Jamie lifted his head to rub his eyes. He noticed Earthadilly slumped against the wall outside his doorway where the doll had slipped from Katie's hand during her recent asthma attack. He shuffled out to pick up Earthadilly and carried her back to his room.

A gentle breeze blew a gathering of leaves by his window. Some of them plastered themselves like tiny brown hands against the glass. Others twirled past as if propelled by fairy wings. He peeked outside at the oak tree and the long shadow it cast in the bright moonlight.

Jamie leaned back against his bed's headboard, his mind worn out. Just before closing his eyes he noticed on his nightstand the book Raj had given him. The book he'd been reading about the community of trees, how they protected each other. Then his lids lowered and he became very still.

In the void between consciousness and the onset of sleep, a seed of an idea began to take root in Jamie's mind. The seed slowly sprouted and grew. He sat upright and wiped his nose on his sleeve. Over the next hour his mind nurtured and harvested a crop of possibilities before he chose what he thought would be the most fruitful one.

Jamie pulled out his phone and sent a text to Tony. "Please meet me in the park and bring the others."

CHAPTER 16

In the neighborhood park near Jamie's house, several large maple trees teased onlookers with subtle flirtations of orange, yellow, and red. Young mothers watched their tots tumbling on the ground like puppies while other children competed for the highest altitude on a couple of swing sets. A teenage boy on a park bench inched his way closer to a teenage girl and wrapped his arm around the back of her shoulders.

Jamie sat cross-legged across from Tony, Keisha, and Raj on lush, green grass. All his energy was back and zipping through his body. "We can work together to save the planet. Kids all over the world."

"Dude, you gotta stop reading so much Captain America," Tony said.

Jamie wondered how he was going to get through to his friend. "Please listen, Tony. We can stop what we saw in the future from happening. Look at all the kids out there who already care about the planet, and they haven't even seen what we've seen."

Keisha leaned against Tony and flashed her special smile up at him. "Come on, Tony, give Jamie a chance."

Just keep those smiles coming, Keish.

Tony's cheeks flushed. "Okay, fine. But how can a bunch of kids do anything when our leaders can't even agree?"

"That's why it's up to us," Jamie said. "All the kids. Create our own plan. A really urgent plan to stop fossil-fuel pollution and climate change. And get all the leaders to support it."

"But kids all over the world?" Keisha said.

"Yeah, everybody has to help or it won't work," Jamie said. "We all need to be connected … like the trees."

Raj eyed Jamie and Jamie nodded.

"Say what?" Keisha said. "The trees?"

Jamie smiled. "Never mind. Mr. James asked us because he thought we could do a better job than the grown-ups."

"But he told you we'd need to replace fossil fuels in ten years," Keisha said. "How is that even possible?"

"Mr. James said they did not do enough soon enough," Raj said.

"Yeah, so we'd have to do a whole lot better," Jamie said.

Boy, a whole lot better was right. Jamie wanted to believe they could do it. But save the whole planet in just ten years? This wasn't one of his superhero movies. Plus, they didn't have money or anything really. They were just kids.

Then he remembered what Mr. James said about the garden hose. About not clogging up your mind with negative thoughts … so powerful energy and guidance can flow through.

"It has to be possible or I don't think Mr. James would have come back here to ask for our help," Jamie said.

"My father says *it is* possible to replace most fossil fuels with renewable energy," Raj said.

Jamie leaned forward. "I think we need to make switching to all clean energy in ten years our goal and figure out with the other kids how to get the world to do it."

"We can create a plan for radical change," Raj said. "A revolution. We can call it the children's revolution."

"Or maybe something that sounds less violent," Jamie said.

Raj nodded. "How about Children Against Pollution?"

"What about climate change?" Keisha said.

Raj nodded. "Burning fossil fuels is causing climate change. If we can stop fossil-fuel pollution soon enough, we can stop climate change."

"Okay, then how about Children Against Polluting Earth?" Jamie said. "C … A … P … E … the CAPE for short. What do you guys think?"

Keisha fisted her hand, thrust her thumb at her chest, and said in a gruff voice, "Hey, I'm with the CAPE."

"I can create our own website where as many kids who want to can sign up to join us," Raj said. "And we can tape a video message to post on Facebook, Twitter, Instagram, YouTube, Weibo … and create a CAPE Facebook page too."

"Don't you have to be thirteen?" Keisha said.

"I turned thirteen this summer," Raj said. "With your parents' permission I can get us signed up."

"Maybe we could also contact the websites of other kids who want to protect the planet," Jamie said. He was psyched that his friends were jumping on board. Things were going great.

"We should buy a respirator for you to wear, Jamie, when you tape our message," Raj said.

Maybe everything wasn't going so great. No way he was going let them post him all over the internet. Jamie did a time-out signal. "Uh, Raj, I don't think I'm the one—"

"Ooooh I like that respirator idea too, Raj," Keisha said. "That'll be the perfect thing for Jamie to wear for our message."

Jamie waved his hand back and forth. "Wait, let's hold off on who's going to do the message. But I'm glad you're all with me on this."

He stared at Tony to try to read him. But Tony was wearing his poker face.

"What do you think, Tony?" Jamie said.

Tony grimaced. "Well, what I think is … if we don't want to end up living like primitive life-forms, we better clean up after the grown-ups. And maybe then they'll … never mind. Anyway, I'm in."

Jamie resisted the urge to hug Tony in front of the others.

"You can use my lawn money to buy the respirator," Tony said.

Raj looked at Tony and tipped his head a little. "That is very generous, Tony."

"No problem, dude."

Jamie looked at each of his friends. "I knew I could count on you. It means so much to me … I just … thank you."

PART TWO

CHAPTER 17

About eight miles away, across the Potomac River in Washington, DC, someone else was hatching a plan. Colton Slone, a lobbyist for the fossil-fuel industry, waited in the reception area of his largest client, Thomas Mandel, president and CEO of King Fuel.

Colton's dark-gray designer suit was perfectly tailored to his tall, muscular frame. Slick, black hair hugged his scalp in the style popular among certain businessmen in their forties. Penetrating eyes stared out above hollowed cheeks on a face that looked chiseled from granite, and a three-inch scar ran along the right side of his forehead.

Coal miners, two hundred feet underground, stared down at him from a large, black-and-white photograph on the facing wall. It reminded him of how far he'd come from that wiry, sooty kid who grew up in the mountains of West Virginia.

Colton knew all too well what it took to scratch out a life underground. He started at fourteen right after his dad died from a mine explosion. Passed for the legal age of sixteen because he was tall for his age. Summers he labored ten-hour shifts, six days a week in the bowels of the earth, wading in cold, muddy waters, bent low, endlessly shoveling coal onto the conveyor belt. When summers ended he worked shorter hours at the mine, but it was the same scene every day after school.

With his dad dead he was powerless to do anything else. Colton was the oldest and there wasn't anybody but him to support his mother and siblings. All the while he knew he was busting his back for some rich guys off in a distant city who didn't care whether he lived or died. Rich guys like Thomas Mandel. But that was then.

Now he thought of Mandel, another former coal miner, as one of his own kind. And Colton's kind were a dwindling breed—threatened with extinction by the arrogant elites who looked down their noses at men like Colton and tried to replace their coal-mining livelihood with new sources of energy.

But after working in the mine for ten years he'd inhaled enough coal dust to last a lifetime and had the lungs to prove it, and when the mine closed he vowed he'd never go back. He was the first in his family to leave the mountain. The first to get a college degree. The first to get a high-paying job in the city. During his twenty years as a lobbyist he'd accumulated a level of wealth that his family couldn't even imagine. Much of that wealth grew from the fees he charged Thomas and his other clients.

Thomas's assistant came out to the reception area and told Colton it would be a few minutes before he could go in. The delay gave Colton more time to plan how he'd handle the meeting. Colton had been hearing stories recently about an increase in renewable energy cutting into King Fuel's profits. As a national coal, oil, and natural-gas conglomerate, King Fuel had long tentacles that reached into every area of energy production. If any one of those tentacles was threatened, Thomas mounted an attack with the ferocity of a pit bull.

That's why he'd hired Colton. To be his pit bull. Colton knew he was one of several lobbyists on Thomas's payroll, but he'd also heard through the grapevine that Thomas considered him the most cunning and, okay, a little volatile. But so what. That's why he succeeded at intimidation. All good traits to get the job done.

The assistant finally motioned for him to enter the office, where Thomas had to tilt his head back when they shook hands to meet Colton eye to eye. Thomas looked his age with loose jowls, a paunch, and gray, thinning hair. But Colton knew that beneath that worn exterior was a mind like a steel trap.

"A new assignment?" Colton said.

Thomas plunked down behind his desk. "Good to see you, Colton." Thomas pushed several booklets toward the front of his desk. "These are reports from organizations we've funded to do research on fossil fuels, pollution, and climate change. They prove there's no connection. Get them distributed to the news media through the right people."

Colton shoved the reports into his briefcase.

Thomas gestured toward some documents. "I've had two bills drafted this time. The first one eliminates the rest of those ridiculous regulations for so-called clean air and water. They're affecting our bottom line."

"You know we're going to have to deal with the usual battles from the environmentalists in Congress and in the courts," Colton said. "Those lunatics never let up."

"But we've already done a great job making 'regulation' a dirty word, right?"

"Yeah," Colton said. "I think our best bet is to go after our usual Congressional targets and choose one of our long-time senators to sponsor it."

Thomas nodded. "Okay, next. Even though we've slowed competition from solar and wind energy, they're still a threat and they're generating too many jobs. Too much job growth in those businesses gives more weight to the argument that they're good for the economy, and we end up losing more of our edge and our market share."

Thomas slid more paperwork toward the front of his desk. "So this next bill places tariffs on solar panels and wind turbines that have any parts made in foreign countries."

"Another headache dealing with the environmentalists," Colton said. "But I'll make the right calls to the administration, then to sponsor this one I'll tap our legislators who've benefited the most from our generosity."

Colton picked up the documents. "You've made the deposits in the account for my contact with them?"

"Yes, keep me informed," Thomas said.

On his way out of the building Colton calculated who was going to get in his way and who he could use to help him navigate around or through the opposition. This was why he loved his job. It gave him a sense of power and control in fighting off those who wanted to destroy his kind. It didn't matter that he didn't work in the mine anymore. Coal mining was still his roots, and the miners were still his people. And every time he got to make someone bend to his will, it helped him bury the old remnants of the powerless mountain boy he'd left behind.

~

Colton took a cab to the Capitol where he checked in with security for Senator Richard Newsome's office, his first appointment. The senator's assistant offered him a glass of water while he waited, and after she was gone he used it to swallow his bronchodilator medication. He treated his emphysema with pills instead of an inhaler. People with inhalers always looked weak to him.

Richard's reception area was nothing like Thomas's. No black-and-white images of dirty coal miners here. Only beautiful color photographs of Washington, DC, mansions during cherry-blossom season. Also one of Richard in a tux, shaking hands with a former president, and another of the senator with a movie star. Colton was sure Richard had no idea what it was like to work all day with coal dust coating his face, caking his eyes and nostrils, ground into his fingernails and hair. Or to live in fear of a methane-gas leak that could demolish an entire mine. Or to cower under a foreman.

Colton shoved all those thoughts aside when the assistant ushered him into Richard's office. Colton was used to the way Richard always glared at him, but as long as Richard did what he wanted he could glare until his eyeballs popped out.

"Which client is it this time?" Richard said the minute Colton stepped into the room.

"King Fuel," Colton said.

"Haven't I helped Thomas enough this year?"

"This is a big request, but King Fuel's level of financial appreciation will match it."

"All right, all right. What is it?"

Colton handed Richard a copy of the documents Thomas had given him. "These are the two bills we want you to sponsor."

Richard flipped through the pages of the first document. "The bill eliminating regs on air and water might be possible," he said. "But what are you going to do when all the environmentalists come out of the woodwork and threaten legal action? They're getting a lot more support these days."

"Doesn't matter. We've got the votes and we're getting more judges on the bench who see things our way."

Richard considered the second document more intently. "This one for tariffs is going to be tough. Most of our people support a free market."

"We're sure you and your colleagues will find a way," Colton said. "We know your campaign chest for the next election is running a little low."

"That's what I admire about you, Colton. You're so subtle."

Colton just stared at Richard.

"Fine, I'll do the best I can," Richard said. "But don't underestimate one of our most problematic senators. You know she doesn't toe the party line."

"Lydia Pattern. That woman is a walking hornet's nest."

"But she's sharp and has a lot of influence, and most of the bipartisan legislation she's sponsored over the years has passed. She's also blocked a fair number of bills that ran against her principles. A real maverick, that one."

"I'll deal with her if she gets in the way."

Colton headed out the door and down the hall. He always liked to start with the easiest ones. Especially the longtimers who had become so dependent on his clients. It felt good knowing he owned guys like this.

CHAPTER 18

J amie had let Keisha talk him into coming to her parents'
backyard cookout by promising him he'd meet someone
who could help them with their cause. After he entered
Keisha's yard through the back gate, he tried to hide in the
shadow of the home's overhang.

This had better be good. Chit-chatting in groups,
especially adult groups, was almost as painful as public
speaking. There had to be at least forty grown-ups here, all
talking and laughing and drinking and having a good ol'
time.

He pressed his back against the side of the house. As
soon as Keisha spotted him, she ran up and gave him a little
hug.

"I'm glad you came, Jamie. Want a hamburger?"

"Yeah, thanks." He wasn't hungry, but he figured it
would give him something to do. If he stayed right where
he was, maybe none of them would even notice him.

Keisha's dad and his buddies were playing jazz. Or
what Jamie thought was jazz. Not really his kind of music.
He'd hoped that some of the players on her dad's team
would be here, but he didn't see anybody who came close
to her dad's height. Just a lot of average-sized people.

Wait, but who's that? Not an average-sized person, that's for sure.

Keisha's mom approached him with a woman who seemed as big as a grizzly bear. She was at least a foot taller than most of the men in the yard. A few strands of gray ran through her short, red hair, but it was hard to guess her age. There were hardly any lines on her almost pretty face.

"Hi Jamie," Mrs. Taylor said and turned to the big woman. "Lydia, this is my daughter's friend, Jamie Sawyer. And Jamie, this is Senator Lydia Pattern."

Keisha scooted next to Jamie, her hands full with his hamburger and soda. Nice timing. He wasn't very good at meeting new adults, especially important people like a senator.

The senator shook Jamie's hand with a grip like Keisha's dad. "Ah yes, Jamie." She spoke with a deep voice, too. "I understand you want to replace fossil fuels."

Jamie couldn't tell if she thought that was a good thing or a bad thing. Tony's father was a senator too, and he went ballistic whenever Tony even brought it up.

The two adults and Keisha looked at Jamie as if they expected him to say something. So he did. "Well, we're worried about the pollution, ma'am."

"So am I," the senator said. "In fact, I've scheduled a Senate public hearing on what fossil-fuel pollution is doing to public health."

Relief washed over Jamie like a sprinkler on a hot day. Whew, nothing like Tony's father. And then came the realization that this must be the person Keisha told him about. Good ol' Keisha.

"Jamie, Senator Pattern is chairman of the Senate Committee on Energy and Natural Resources," Mrs. Taylor said. "She knows a lot about fossil fuels and clean energy. I work for her."

Jamie suddenly remembered that day at Keisha's house when Mr. Taylor had said they should talk to Mrs. Taylor's *boss woman* about their school studies on climate change. So this was the actual *boss woman*!

"Think maybe you could help us once we get our plan together, Senator?" Keisha said just as easily as if she were talking to the mailman.

"Just let me know when you're ready. I'd be delighted to help."

Jamie looked up at the senator with the same awe he'd felt the first time he saw the Washington Monument. But he said nothing. Then Keisha gave him a little nudge with her foot.

"You'd really help us? That would be terrific, Senator," Jamie said, trying not to jump up and down right there in front of everybody.

"I'm glad I met you, Jamie. It's encouraging to see our young people involved."

Mrs. Taylor escorted the senator to meet two men laughing near the bar. Keisha turned to Jamie with an I-told-you-so look.

"Keish, a United States senator! You're the best!"

"See, I knew you'd be glad you came."

"Yeah, oh, yeah!"

But then old familiar doubts scratched at the edge of Jamie's mind. He stared straight ahead at the mingling crowd.

"What?" Keisha said.

"Nothing."

"Spill it."

Jamie turned back to Keisha. "What if we can't get this off the ground? I've never, ever done anything even a little bit like this, and now we've got a senator who's going to be watching how well we do."

"You can't be thinking like that. Mr. James wouldn't have come to us if he didn't think we could do it."

Jamie shifted his weight. "Right."

He just wished he could be half as sure as Mr. James.

CHAPTER 19

J amie was in his tidy bedroom researching asthma and pollution on his computer. Superman, Batman, Spiderman, Ironman, and the Defenders of the Galaxy congregated around him on the movie posters all over his walls. A large poster of Captain America, his favorite superhero, took the place of honor above his bed.

Books on Earth Science and gardening filled half the shelf above his desk. Below that, a small corkboard neatly displayed a year-at-a-glance planting calendar and two ribbons for his science projects.

On the flat-screen TV mounted on his bedroom wall, a news anchor gave an update on plans for the pope's visit to the United States that fall. It reminded Jamie that he needed to finish his report on the pope's encyclical on the environment for Ms. Tollhouse's Earth Science class.

He muted the volume when Keisha bounced into the room with the package of glow-in-the-dark stars she bought at the planetarium. "How's Katie doing?" she said to Jamie. "I thought she might like these stars on her bedroom ceiling."

"She's still wheezing a lot ..." He swallowed hard. "But, thanks, Keish, she'll love these."

"Maybe it's just taking a little time for the medicine to work."

"Yeah, I hope that's all it is," Jamie said.

Raj and Tony appeared in his doorway. Tony carried a black, full-face respirator, and Raj had white poster-board signs tucked under his arm.

"I made cue cards of the message we all decided on, and Tony used some of his lawn money to buy the respirator," Raj said.

"Will you have enough left to buy that iPod you wanted?" Jamie said to Tony.

"Not really. So what."

"But you've been saving up for it."

Tony shrugged. "No big deal. Are we gonna get this thing started or what?"

Jamie grinned at his friend. "Whatever you say, Tony."

"There is something on YouTube I think you all should see first," Raj said. He pulled up a video on Jamie's computer monitor titled *Turning Green*. "An environmental group interviewed kids about what their countries are doing with clean energy," he said as he fast-forwarded the video.

A girl appeared on the monitor with an "Oslo, Norway" banner across the bottom of the screen. "My country gets almost one hundred percent of its electricity from green energy," she said. "Most of it comes from hydropower, but we also use wind and thermal energy."

"We get almost all our electricity from green energy," a boy from Montevideo, Uruguay said. "We're using wind, hydropower, and biomass."

Next, a girl from Orkney, Scotland spoke. "This year we received more than one hundred percent of our electricity from wind power."

"More than one hundred percent!" Jamie said.

"My country is the only country in the world that gets one hundred percent of both its electricity and heat from clean energy," a girl from Reykjavík, Iceland said. "Geothermal plants and hydropower make our electricity, and a volcano heats our homes. We draw out steam from thousands of hot springs at its surface and molten rock underground."

"Wow," Keisha said. "Can you imagine heating your home with a volcano?"

A boy from San Francisco appeared next. "The United States gets only seventeen percent of its electricity from renewable energy, but here in California we're at over thirty percent and moving fast to increase that. Almost five million of our homes are already powered by solar."

"Our country plans to eliminate all fossil fuels in just a few years," said a boy from San Jose, Costa Rica. "Even for transportation. We already get ninety-nine percent of our electricity from hydropower, wind, and geothermal."

Raj stopped the video. "So it is possible. My father says even though the United States is much bigger than these countries there is something he called 'economies of scale,' which means the more you produce of something, the lower the cost."

"Dude, this is like a good-news-bad-news thing," Tony said. "Great to know all these countries are using so much clean energy. But how are we ever going to get our country to one hundred percent when that one kid said it's only at seventeen percent now?"

"I think we need to find a way to pressure the world's leaders, especially our own," Keisha said.

Jamie nodded. "How about we research this and talk about it with the other kids? But Raj is right. If these countries can go one-hundred-percent green, then they prove it can be done, especially if states in our country acted like some of these small countries."

"Let's get on with the taping then," Tony said. He adjusted the straps on the respirator. "Jamie, when people see the CAPE message on websites and apps, this will help get their attention. So wear it when you first start talking."

Raj handed Jamie a small poster. "And when you get to the part of the message about our one-hundred-percent goal, you can show this. But I'll edit in our website address at the end."

Jamie's entire face twisted into a frown. "I never agreed to tape the message. I'm a lousy speaker."

"Hey, you did that thing with Keisha in class and nobody threw spitballs," Tony said.

Jamie chuckled. "Oh, like Ms. Tollhouse would let anybody get away with spitballs."

"But you got up and did it, dude, and it wasn't bad. Anyway, this whole save-the-planet thing was your idea, so you're the best one to do it."

Jamie recoiled at the thought of being taped and posted on the internet where the whole world could see him. Why was Tony pushing him when Tony knew he hated drawing attention to himself? It made him feel exposed.

It was easy for Tony to say *just get up and do it*. He barreled through life like a steamroller. Never showed any fear. Gushed his opinions right out of his mouth like a waterfall. Jamie had hoped over the years that some of

Tony's confidence would rub off on him. But Jamie was still a skittery little mouse.

Tony was the one who should be their spokesperson. He'd be great at it. The only hitch, though, was his dad. That was a pretty big hitch. If Tony taped their message, his dad would probably take away his mowing business and ground him for life.

Raj would be good as their spokesperson too, except Raj told them that because he wasn't an American citizen he should stick to the technical stuff. That left Keisha. Yeah, he'd ask Keisha to do it.

Tony finished adjusting the straps on the respirator and threw it to Jamie. Just then Jamie saw Senator Newsome talking to a reporter on TV. He motioned toward the screen. "Look, Tony, your father." Jamie turned up the sound.

"… Climate change is the biggest hoax ever foisted on the American people," the senator said. "The Earth has been heating up and cooling off for eons due to changes in its tilt and orbit around the sun. Human behavior has nothing to do with it. Cheap fossil fuels are the backbone of our economy, and we need to protect them from needless regulation."

The reporter turned the newscast back to the newsroom anchor. "That was Senator Newsome reacting to the upcoming Senate committee public hearing on fossil fuels."

Jamie shut off the TV and turned to Tony. "What if he finds out you're doing something to try to replace fossil fuels?"

"He doesn't like anything I do anyway."

"But this is different," Jamie said.

"Yeah, so what? I follow all his rules *under his roof* where he gets to be the big dictator. But when I'm not under his roof I have a right to do what I want … if I'm not breaking the law."

"You really think he's going to buy that?" Keisha said.

"He can rant all he wants," Tony said. "I don't care. He doesn't have to know what I'm doing anyway."

"You know he's going to find out," Raj said.

Tony stared up at the ceiling and tapped his foot. "If he finds out, he finds out. I'll deal with it."

"But what about—" Jamie said.

"It's my father and my problem. I said I'll deal with it, so I wish you'd all quit bugging me."

The only sound in the room was the clicking noise Jamie made as he fidgeted with the respirator.

Keisha gave Tony a little shove. "But Tony, you're so buggable."

Tony threw up his hands. "All right, I know you guys are just trying to look out for me, but I need for you to chill, okay?" He half-smiled at Keisha. "No matter how buggable I am."

"Okay, Tony, we'll chill," Jamie said.

Keisha gestured toward the respirator. "Jamie, have you tested it out for taping your message yet?"

"I'm not doing the message," Jamie tried to hand the respirator to Keisha. "You do the message … please, Keish?"

"Nah, I don't want to do it," Keisha said. "I agree with Tony. This was your idea, and you're the best one to do it."

"See!" Tony said. "Come on, Jamie, quit stalling."

Jamie felt his heart speed around his chest like a supersonic jet.

"I'll do it on two conditions. If I can be invisible, and if I can use someone else's voice."

"Don't try to be funny," Tony said. "You're only funny when you're not trying to be."

Jamie was trapped. A little mouse in a big mouse trap. But they were right. It was his idea, and if their plan was going to work, he'd have to push himself to do things he'd never done before whether he liked it or not. *Just suck it up,* Tony would say. Jamie didn't know exactly how one did that. It always made him imagine sucking on a gigantic straw from a dark, mucky hole in the ground.

So Jamie did the thing he usually did. He surrendered. "Okay, but I warned you I'm not good at this."

Raj handed the white boards to Keisha. "Can you hold up these cue cards for Jamie when we are ready to start filming?"

"Hey, what about using the video Jamie shot when we were in the future?" Keisha said. "Let's check it out on Jamie's computer."

Jamie rummaged around in his desk drawer and pulled out a cable that he connected between his phone and computer. After a moment they were watching footage of the reddish-brown wasteland, tent cities, adults and children wearing respirators, the submerged Capitol and naval base, an oil-covered shoreline with thousands of sea-life skeletons, and flattened brown mountain ranges with miles of dead trees.

"Those scenes are just as horrible as when we were there," Keisha said. "We should include them with Jamie's message."

"But we can't let anybody know we traveled to the future," Tony said. "They'll think we're nuts and won't listen to anything we say."

"Tony's right," Jamie said. "I think we need to promise not to tell anyone about our time travel. Okay?"

"But this stuff is such a scary warning," Keisha said.

"Remember how we did not believe the old man when he came to us?" Raj said. "We would have to spend all our time trying to convince people we traveled to the future."

Tony shrugged. "And they'd still think we're nuts anyway."

"Well, I think it would be more real for everybody if they could *see* what's gonna happen." Keisha said.

Raj raised his index finger. "What if we say it is computer animation based on projections by climate scientists?"

"Oh, I like that," Keisha said.

Jamie and Tony nodded.

Raj wrote on a white cue card and added it to the group he'd handed to Keisha. "I can edit the video into Jamie's message later and post it all on our CAPE website and the social-media websites and apps."

"Are you ready now, dude?" Tony said to Jamie. Before Jamie could answer Tony started strapping the respirator on Jamie's head. "Make sure you talk loud so we can hear you through the mask."

Raj pulled out his phone and focused it on Jamie. "Say anything first for a test."

Jamie lowered his chin and slouched. "I still think I'm a lousy choice for—"

Tony tapped Jamie on the back of the head. "Come on, man. Get a grip."

Jamie straightened up and strained to see Raj's phone through the respirator mask. "This is a test, testing, testing." His voice was slightly muffled behind the bulky equipment. But there was a weird sense of protection in wearing it. Like it hid his identity. A little bit like, well, almost like being invisible.

"3 … 2 … 1 … go," Raj said.

Jamie thought about Earth in the future and all the kids who would never get to have a future. He thought about Katie. He thought about Billy tying leaves to the trees.

Jamie swallowed hard, stared at the cue cards, and forced out the words: "We all know that burning fossil fuels is poisoning our planet, creating climate change, and making a lot of us sick. We need to stop it or we'll all be wearing these to breathe. If we don't act now, here's a look at our future."

Raj signaled for Jamie to stop. "Good, Jamie, so here is where I will edit in your video while you keep talking."

Jamie nodded and continued. "This computer animation is based on what scientists are warning us about. In our lifetime, fossil-fuel pollution will make it impossible for us to breathe our planet's air, get clean water, or grow food. It will cause severe weather to destroy our homes and cities, the oceans, and life as we know it."

Jamie pulled the respirator down from his face. "We're running out of time. It's up to us kids to fight for our future. We need our world to phase out fossil fuels in the next ten years and replace them with clean, renewable energy."

He flipped the small poster Raj had given him in front of his chest. It said *100% Green —10 Years.*

"If millions of us all over the planet unite behind our own plan, we'll be unstoppable. Please join our global group, the CAPE ... Children Against Polluting Earth. You can sign up today by going to our web address you see here. We need your help right away."

Raj stopped filming and gave a thumbs-up.

"Way to go," Tony said.

Jamie's skin was tingling. He couldn't believe it. He got through the whole thing the very first time. How did he do that? It was like somebody flicked a switch in his head and he went on autopilot. It must have been a fluke.

"See, Jamie, you nailed it," Keisha said. "We knew you could do it."

"But all I did was read a bunch of cue cards. Any dummy could do it." Jamie glanced at Raj. "Thanks for making me look good with the cards, Raj."

"What about me," Keisha said. "Don't you think I did a good job holding 'em up?"

"Yeah—"

Keisha laughed. "I'm just kidding ... what's next?"

"After we get a bunch of sign-ups we need a way for some of them to help us with a plan," Tony said.

"I can direct sign-ups to our new Facebook page and create a Facebook group from our new CAPE friends," Raj said. "Everyone there can download a translator app since we hope kids from other countries will want to share ideas."

Jamie was looking forward to chatting with kids from all over the world to create their plan. And since he'd made it through the taping the very first time, he wondered if maybe he could do more than he thought he could.

CHAPTER 20

After his friends left, Jamie brought Katie the gift from Keisha. She was propped up on her pillows in bed talking to Earthadilly in a raspy voice. It seemed to Jamie like it was taking an awfully long time for the antibiotic to work. He hauled that thought around like a ton of bricks. Now the sight of her pale-green eyes and the sound of her voice pressed the weight down harder. He tried to hide his thoughts from Katie, but as usual, he wasn't very good at it.

"Oh, Jamie, I've been telling Earthadilly what a fun time we're going to have when I get well and how you're going to take us to the planetarium," Katie said. "And Earthadilly was really happy, and she said she wants to sit in your lap and watch the planets spin around with you. Okay? Won't that be fun? And maybe on the way home we can stop at the mall play center. I like Super Saturday, but anytime is good, really. Earthadilly's never been to Super Saturday and I know she'd love to go with us sometime. Earthadilly is my very best friend, and I'm so glad you gave her to me." Katie coughed but then beamed at Jamie and lightened the load on his mind.

He showed her the package of stars he'd brought with him. "Look what Keisha got you, munchkin. Can you get up for a second?"

He helped her slide out of bed and into a chair. After he'd gathered her pillows in piles, climbed on top of them, and affixed the stars to the ceiling, he helped Katie back into bed and propped her and her pillows against the headboard. Then he turned out the light on her nightstand, put his arm around her, and gazed up at the glowing stars in the darkened room.

Katie whispered, "I feel like an astronaut."

Matching his sister's whisper, he said, "Maybe I can stick some planets up there too."

"But I can't be a wheezer if I'm gonna fly up to the stars."

"You're going to be a wonderful astronaut, munchkin," he said.

Jamie hoped it was true. He hoped Katie would grow up to be an astronaut or a pilot or even a flier of hot-air balloons. As long as she grew up healthy.

He recalled the little girl in the future, the one with the eyes staring up at him from behind the respirator mask. What kind of a life was that for a little girl? No trees to climb. No running barefoot on soft, green grass. No flowers to pick. No balloons or cake or huggable dolls. No clean air to breathe. How did it feel not to be able to take a deep breath? Katie already knew. To gasp for oxygen and inhale toxic gases instead? What was it like for the kids who didn't make it? Did they suffocate to death?

Jamie wished he could blot out the horrible scenes from the future. But they were burned into his memory. When the images snuck out from the back of his brain, they always jolted him. But then he'd remember. Those scenes hadn't happened yet. It was up to him and his friends and all the other kids to make sure those scenes never happened.

He gazed at his sister. She was asleep, her blond, curly head resting peacefully against his shoulder. He raised her hand to his lips and softly kissed it as if to seal a promise.

CHAPTER 21

After school Jamie rode his bike to Keisha's house where his three friends were playing basketball in the driveway.

"Did you guys check out our website today?" he said as he lowered his kick stand. "At first I was worried because there were only about two hundred sign-ups the first day, mostly from our own country. But every time I look this week, tons more kids have signed up from all over the world!"

Keisha dribbled over to the side of the driveway to her gym bag and pulled out her phone. "Yeah, I checked right before school and there were more than eighty thousand kids from seventy countries!" She tapped on her phone. "Geez, now one hundred and seventy-five thousand kids from … ninety-two countries!"

"Big jump!" Jamie said. "That counter at the top of the page was a terrific idea, Raj."

"I think it is good for everyone to see how quickly interest is growing," Raj said. "Did you notice that kids from India signed up right away?"

"I hope we get a lot more from those other big, polluted countries like ours," Jamie said. "And did you see all the hits and comments we're getting on social media for our video of the future?

"Some dude even offered to do more animation for us," Tony said. "Hah, if he only knew!"

"Yeah, I'm glad now we included that," Jamie said.

"Come on, you guys," Keisha said. "Let's celebrate all our sign-ups and supporters with a little two-on-two. Jamie, you can be on my team."

Jamie joined his friends, but his mind wasn't on the game. When they took a break, he pulled out his phone and checked out their website. "Wow, wow, wow, we just passed the three-hundred-thousand mark and we're up to one hundred and five countries! This is amazing!" He imitated one of Keisha's funny hip-hop moves and waved his arm like a helicopter propeller.

Keisha joined him, and Tony and Raj chuckled at their antics.

Jamie didn't care how goofy he looked. They'd gotten kids all over the world to sign up to save the planet!

"Hey, propeller boy … land," Tony said, grinning. "We're just getting started, remember? Government leaders are going to laugh at us when they hear our goal. We still need a way to put pressure on 'em."

"How?" Keisha said.

"I've been thinking about this," Tony said. "There's one thing I learned from my father that's worth anything and it's called leverage. Sometimes he gets the votes he needs for his bill because he has something that can pressure other senators into it, like not supporting their bills if they don't support his."

"But what do we have that can pressure the adults into giving us what we want?" Keisha said. "We don't have any power."

Tony pulled out his new phone. "We have economic power. You know how much money gets spent on stuff for kids, like phones, games, sports equipment, and a zillion other things? What if kids boycotted and all that spending stopped for a while? I bet it would give us lots of leverage."

"I think he is right," Raj said.

"Yeah," Keisha said. "Every time my mom buys me a new pair of sneakers she says, 'What would the economy do without kids?'"

"But you think our CAPE members would agree to that?" Jamie said.

"We need to explain to them why this is a good way to get the adults to do what we want," Tony said.

Jamie didn't want to be the one to ask the other kids not to get new stuff. But it might be their best chance to pressure the world's leaders. Maybe enough kids would be willing to boycott that they really could have a big impact. "I think Tony's right too and we should talk to our members about it."

"When do you want to do it?" Keisha said.

"How about this Saturday with our Facebook group that Raj set up?" Jamie said.

The more Jamie thought about it, the more he liked the idea that they had this thing called leverage.

"Sounds okay to me," Tony said and bounced the ball toward Raj. "So, wanna get back to our two-on-two?"

Raj scooped up the ball and dribbled toward "center court." Suddenly he made a quick glance over his shoulder at the basket behind him, looked away from the basket, and tossed the ball over his head with one hand. It went straight through without touching the rim.

Jamie gaped at his friend. It was as if Raj had eyes in the back of his head.

"You got good focus, dude," Tony said.

"I learned from yoga and Adithada, one of the Indian martial arts."

"Cool," Tony said. "I always wanted to learn to fight like that. Can you teach me?"

"And me?" Keisha said.

"I can teach you, but it is not so much about fighting as being centered and disciplined," Raj said.

"So you in, Jamie?" Tony said.

"I guess." Jamie wasn't real big on martial arts, but if he was going to change he should try things like this.

Jamie followed Raj as he led them off the driveway to the lawn. Raj kicked off his shoes and stood barefoot on the grass with legs spread. Jamie, Keisha, and Tony lined up in front of him.

"First thing to remember," Raj said. "All your power is here." He pointed to his head. "Not here," he said clenching his fists.

Raj stood on the toes of his right foot and bent his left knee so the bottom of his left foot pressed against the inside of his right knee. He held his posture perfectly still. "We will start with this yoga pose to practice balance."

Jamie stood on his toes, swayed back and forth, and fell over. His two friends didn't do any better.

"Again, and this time stare at a single leaf on that tree," Raj said, gesturing toward one of the maples in Keisha's yard. "Hold your attention there. Breathe deeply. Feel the stillness of your body's center. Feel your mind in connection with your body."

Jamie tried and tumbled, tried and tumbled, tried and tumbled. He was the last one to finally hold his balance.

Raj then demonstrated arm thrusts, plunges, and kicks. Jamie did his best to imitate Raj's movements. Raj partnered with Tony and told Jamie and Keisha to practice on each other.

Tony executed a chop toward Raj's knee that Raj blocked.

Keisha kicked Jamie's legs out from under him and he landed on the ground. She leaned over him. "I'm sorry, Jamie. You okay?"

"Yeah, I'm fine. Nice kick." Jamie jumped to his feet and thrust his elbow at Keisha's forehead, but she ducked out of the way.

"When you finally gain control of your mind your body will follow," Raj said.

Jamie brushed some grass off his knee. "Raj, my body doesn't seem to want to listen to my mind."

"You all just need practice," Raj said. "If we practice every day it will become part of you."

Well, Adithada might be a good thing to learn. But even if he did Jamie was sure he'd never use it.

Chapter 22

While Jamie read the comments streaming in from their Facebook group, he felt like doing another little hip-hop dance. The other kids really liked their goal of one hundred percent clean energy in ten years, and when Tony suggested boycotting to get government leaders to support the goal, they liked that too!

Jamie had asked members posting to the group to type in their cities and countries along with their comments so everyone knew where they were posting from. Now the live feed updated steadily with ideas from kids all over the world.

"We shouldn't boycott businesses that support our plan."
—Tokyo, Japan

"That's right. If businesses say in writing they commit to our plan, we keep them off our boycott list."
—Halifax, Nova Scotia, Canada

"We wouldn't have much to boycott because a lot of us don't have enough money to buy things. How can we help?"
—Mexico City, Mexico

"Any countries that can't boycott could picket their dirty-energy companies. We can use it to get stories on the telly for our cause."
—London, England

"We want to help too. But a lot of kids in our country work in factories that make some of those things you want to boycott. Kids in other countries do also."
—Delhi, India

Jamie didn't think kids should have to work in factories. He wondered if they got to go to school.

"Do you work in a factory?"
—Dublin, Ireland

"No, but it is how a lot of poor kids here help support their families."
—Delhi, India

"What if we raised enough money to pay their wages so most of them could strike at those factories?"
—New York City, United States

"In our country we could collect pennies. Call it something here like 'Pennies for the Planet.'"
—Fort Lauderdale, Florida, United States

"If all the richer countries did their own collections maybe we could raise enough money to support any factory-worker kids who want to strike."
—Quebec City, Quebec, Canada

"I think we need to be cautious, but it might work. We would have to make sure we can collect enough money to replace their low wages for what could be many weeks.

Once we see a steady stream of enough donations, they could strike."
　—Alexandria, Virginia, United States

Jamie noticed that comment from Alexandria was Raj's.

"I will take that back to the others and see if they agree."
　—Delhi, India.

"So now we have boycotts and pickets and maybe even strikes! We shouldn't stop until they agree to meet our goal."
　—Paris, France

"What about the rainforests? They absorb tons of carbon dioxide, and we need to include them in our plan because they're being destroyed so fast."
　—Manaus, Brazil

"We should get everybody to reduce how much energy we all use too."
　—Algiers, Algeria, Africa

"Yeah, we sure don't need to keep our stores and offices in the USA so freezing cold in the summer."
　—Atlanta, Georgia, United States

"Yes, we must save the rainforests, and we all know there are a hundred ways to do better at energy conservation, so we should make them part of our plan."
　—Asuncion, Paraguay, South America

"No new coal plants."
　—Seoul, South Korea

"No new pipelines, fracking, or mountaintop mining."
　—Charleston, West Virginia, United States

"Switch to non-polluting farming."
—Canberra, Australia

"No more access for fossil-fuel companies to public lands, especially national parks."
—Phoenix, Arizona, United States

"Require manufacturers to make vehicles that run on biofuels or electricity."
—Frankfurt, Germany

Jamie's spirits were flying high from following the steady stream of kids in other countries and across the US who continued to voice their support and ideas. When the comments petered out, he thanked the group and said his team would post their plan on the CAPE website and Facebook page.

That night while he was brushing his teeth before bed, Jamie thought about all the fantastic stuff that had happened that day. They still had a lot more to figure out, but they already had hundreds of thousands of kids behind their goal, and they had come up with a plan.

He looked at himself in the mirror. Not bad, wimp. Not bad at all.

CHAPTER 23

Jamie and Tony headed to Jamie's house after school and talked all the way there about the CAPE. As they approached Jamie's yard, a car pulled up with a local network TV logo on the side. A man in a blue blazer with boyish features and perfectly groomed hair got out with another man in jeans and a t-shirt who carried a TV camera and a microphone.

"Hi, I'm Steve Headley with WRG-TV and this is my cameraman, Chris Rane," blazer man said. They both shook hands with the boys. "Are you Jamie Sawyer?"

Jamie wasn't sure if he wanted to tell him.

"Yeah, he's Jamie Sawyer," Tony said. "What's up?"

"People are commenting all over the internet about your group the CAPE and that video of you in a respirator, Jamie, with the animated scenes of the future."

"That was him all right," Tony said, grinning. "And I'm Tony Newsome."

"Are you one of the CAPE founders, Tony?"

"Yeah, I guess you could say that," Tony said.

"I'd like to interview you both," Steve said. "Would you like to do it inside or out here?"

"Oh, right here would be fine," Tony said.

Jamie scrunched up his face at Tony.

"Okay, good," Steve said. "I'm going to do a little intro and then I'll ask you a few questions."

Steve held up the mic and faced the camera. "I'm with Jamie Sawyer and Tony Newsome, two of the young people right here in Alexandria who started the newly formed international group Children Against Polluting Earth. The group goes by the acronym 'the CAPE,' and they've been devising a plan with their global counterparts to save the planet from the effects of burning fossil fuels."

Steve moved his mic in front of Jamie while Chris focused the camera on him. "Jamie, how are things going with the CAPE?"

Jamie turned his head away. Chris followed Jamie's face with the camera and Steve repeated his question, moving the mic a bit closer to Jamie's mouth. Jamie felt his throat and jaw lock up. He stared down at the mic like it was going to leap up and bite him. He'd never spoken to a reporter before, and certainly not with a camera rolling so thousands of people could gawk at him. He wished he could melt into his shoes. Just when he thought he was leaving behind wimpy Jamie, that Jamie popped right back into his head.

Tony lightly elbowed Jamie in the rib.

Well, okay, so he wasn't exactly Captain America, thought Jamie. But what was he going to do, just keep wallowing in his puddle of panic? With everyone watching?

Jamie lifted his head slightly and glanced up at Steve. "Well, uh, we uh … we kids from all over the world …" he said in a very quiet voice and felt another jab to his rib. He raised his voice a little. "We've joined together to stop fossil-fuel pollution and climate change … we want to replace these dirty fuels with clean energy in the next ten years."

"*Ten* years?" Steve said.

"Yes, sir," Jamie said. "The planet is already in so much danger ... we also want stricter energy conservation and protection for the rainforests ... we put a list of what we want on our website."

Steve motioned for Chris to include both boys in camera view. "How do you kids think you can get the world to give up fossil fuels?"

"We're going to pressure the world's leaders with a boycott," Tony said. "Our CAPE members are gonna boycott all kids' products, entertainment, and food places, except the businesses that support us."

Jamie swallowed hard. "We have other plans to pressure our leaders that we'll talk about later." Jamie didn't want to say anything about kids striking at factories until they knew they could pull it off.

"We're also gonna picket wherever we can to get attention for our cause," Tony said.

"You kids seem pretty determined," Steve said then faced the camera. "This is Steve Headley, Alexandria, Virginia."

While Chris packed up the equipment, Steve said to him, "Let's file this with the desk for tonight's newscast."

After the reporter and his cameraman drove away, Tony said to Jamie, "Hey, dude, way to go!"

Jamie hummed—with dramatic fanfare—the movie theme song from *Captain America: The First Avenger* and made Tony explode with his crazy hyena laugh.

After they had dinner with Jamie's family they started on their homework. But when Tony looked in his backpack, he realized he'd left one of the assignments they'd been working on this week at his house. "What do you want to do?" Tony said. "We have to turn it in tomorrow."

"Let's just go over there and finish it," Jamie said.

Jamie hummed the same movie theme song again on the way to Tony's house. He followed his friend through the kitchen toward the family room as Tony called out, "Hey, Mom, we're home."

Jamie stopped short when he saw Mr. Newsome and the look on his face. But Tony was already charging through the room. Tony's dad was on the edge of his big chair across from the TV. His eyes blazed.

"Hold it right there, boy," his dad said. "I just saw the news. What the hell have you been up to behind my back?"

Jamie slunk farther back in the dark hallway.

"Where's Mom?"

"She's out. I want an answer."

"I was going to tell you."

"Tell me? You have no business getting involved in this garbage to begin with."

"Dad, listen."

Jamie didn't want to desert his friend. But he couldn't say anything to Tony's dad. So he just stayed hidden.

"Do you know how this is going to look for me? My own son contradicting me. Fighting against me. Out in public. In front of television cameras!"

"It's not to fight you. It's to protect our planet."

"Save the planet. Superman to the rescue. All this CAPE crap is ludicrous! Why don't you just buy yourself a cape and run around the neighborhood like a little damn superhero."

Jamie blanched.

"I'm not trying to be a hero. We're trying to help clean up the big mess you grown-ups made."

Geez, Tony, maybe not the best thing to tell your dad right now.

"Don't you dare lecture me, boy. If it weren't for us *grown-ups* you spoiled kids would be living like wild animals. How long do you think you'd survive without coal, oil, and natural gas?"

"A lot of us won't survive with 'em."

Hey, good one. But ouch for your dad.

"Bull. I've had enough of this. Now listen to me, you're going to drop out of this little rebellion and keep your mouth shut."

"But I have a right to speak up for my future."

"A right? You're a kid. Living in my house. You have no rights!"

Tony stomped his foot. "I have a right as a human being to be heard!"

Uh-oh, Tony, bet he's going to make you pay for that.

Mr. Newsome jumped up from his chair, grabbed hold of Tony's t-shirt, and pulled him close to his face.

"Don't you dare sass me, boy. You ... will ... not ... be involved in this CAPE thing. Period. Now shut up and go to your room."

Tony stomped down the hall and slammed the door. Jamie slipped quietly out the kitchen's back entrance and called Tony on his cell phone from the sidewalk.

"Are you okay, Tony?"

"Did you hear him? What a jerk he is! I'd like to run away from here and never come back! I'm glad you left or you'd have to deal with him too."

"Just lie low. Please, Tony, lie low."

"I'll email you the homework assignment. See you tomorrow." Tony ended the call.

This was just what Jamie was afraid of. Their fight was all his fault. And it would be just like Tony to run away and make things worse. That would be Jamie's fault too.

CHAPTER 24

Jamie's neighborhood park was awash with early autumn colors as its mighty, mature trees heralded the new season. Some of the first fall castaways scudded across the grass and danced merrily down the sidewalk. Dozens of pumpkins in rows of threes and fours huddled around a wooden kiosk where a thin, older woman was selling one of the larger pumpkins to a young couple.

Perched cross-legged on top of a picnic table, Jamie watched a male and female cardinal land near him. He wondered why the male was the colorful one, with its beautiful deep-red feathers, while the female was just a plain light-brown. Kind of like the sacred peacocks of India that Raj talked about. Jamie wished he could see a male peacock, its royal-blue body fanning out its tail with hundreds of green feathers and eyespots. Raj said the drab, brown peahen didn't even have a tail.

Jamie chuckled at the difference between the flashy males and their unflashy female partners, the ones who had the most important job of producing their offspring.

The cardinals took off when Tony plunked down on a bench next to the picnic table. "Look, let's not make a big deal out of what my father did yesterday, okay?" Tony said.

Jamie nodded. "I don't want you to get—"

"He's always yelling at me anyway."

"What are you gonna do?"

"Nothing."

"It's okay that you can't be part of the CAPE," Jamie said. "It doesn't change anything with us."

"I know that, you dweeb."

"But it's my fault and I don't want you to run away and then I'll feel even worse and—"

"I'm not gonna run away, and don't be an idiot, it wasn't your fault. You know what he's like. So just forget about it. Okay?"

"Okay, Tony." Jamie knew he wouldn't forget about it. But there wasn't much he could do.

Raj and Keisha dashed across the park and up to the picnic table.

"Hi, guys," Keisha said. "Wasn't it fun reading all those comments from the kids in our Facebook group?"

"It was a wonderful feeling of unity," Raj said.

Tony tapped two twigs on the table like drumsticks. "Yeah, but it has to be all the countries, especially the biggest polluters. I'm glad our CAPE members bought into our boycott idea and added pickets and strikes." Tony broke the twigs in half. "The adults are going to be sorry if they try to mess with us."

"Did you see yourselves on the news?" Keisha said. "You both sounded great."

"Well, I probably won't be doing any more interviews," Tony said.

Keisha giggled. "Oh, right, Tony, you suddenly shy?"

"Yeah, Keish, that's it, I'm switching places with Jamie."

"No, really, whaddya mean?"

"My father doesn't want me involved with the CAPE."

"And that's okay, right everybody?" Jamie said.

Keisha grimaced. "Yeah, Tony, we understand."

"Sure," Raj said.

Tony pulled his chin up. "Well, I'm still going to help no matter what he says. I'll just stay in the background for a while."

"Hey, at least you got to do that one interview, Tony, and I bet the news people interviewed CAPE kids in other countries too," Keisha said. "So we're already getting the kind of attention we want."

Jamie noticed a few young women carrying pumpkins and several young children trailing along behind them in single file. "I just got an idea to kick off our plan." He paused briefly, testing it out in his head. "A parade."

"A Halloween parade?" Keisha said.

"Yeah, but a really different kind of Halloween parade."

~

After Jamie shared his thoughts for the parade, his three friends jumped in and built on the idea with the same synergy as when they first created the CAPE. By the time they were done, they were so pleased with their brainstorming they were eager to get to work.

"I think this'll be a big boost for our cause," Keisha said.

Jamie nodded. "Yeah, but we're going to need help from some grown-ups."

"My mother and her yoga classes organized an Earth Day parade in April," Raj said. "Maybe she can get them to help us organize ours."

"My dad's a wannabe musician, and his buddies teach school marching bands," Keisha said. "I think he'd love to work on the music. And my mom was a former art teacher so she can help us create a lot of the stuff."

"That's great," Jamie said. "My mom is staying home with Katie for a while, but she can make phone calls to get some parents working on whatever else we need ... Oh, and I'll also ask Ms. Tollhouse to help us get the other schools involved."

"The public schools should be in on this too," Keisha said. "My dad can help with that through his buddies."

"My father offered to do more for us," Raj said. "Many of his clean-energy employees volunteered too."

"And my dad can volunteer to muck up the whole thing," Tony said.

"Let it go, Tony," Keisha said softly. "We'll have plenty of help."

"Plenty of help from everybody's parents but mine," Tony said. "My father just wants to go on TV and say stupid crap."

"He has a right to say stupid crap on TV if he wants to," Raj said. "This is the United States of America."

Tony broke out his hyena laugh. "That's right, Raj, 'cause America is the world leader in people saying stupid crap on TV." Another burst of laughter.

"I am glad I could entertain you," Raj said and flashed his bright white teeth.

"Hey, Raj," Keisha said. "If we're done talking about the CAPE for now, why don't you give us another Adithada lesson?"

Raj got to his feet and sauntered a few yards from the woodsy picnic-table area out onto a large, open expanse of freshly mowed grass. He gestured for Jamie to stand in front of him. Then he positioned Jamie's arms and legs in a pre-lunge stance. "Close your eyes, Jamie. Focus on your core."

With eyes closed Jamie focused as hard as he could. But he knew his posture looked dorky. Raj's hands guided Jamie's elbows and slowly alternated bringing his arms around in a circular motion. "Feel the energy pouring through you," Raj said.

There was energy all right, but it was the old familiar kind that made Jamie want to retreat. *This isn't gonna go well. I can tell already.*

"Where is your focus, Jamie?" Raj said. "You are resisting my direction."

"I'm sorry, Raj, but this all feels so weird to me."

"It will stop feeling weird when you stop thinking it feels weird."

Raj nudged Jamie's right leg. Jamie tried to remember what he was supposed to do next in this stance. He lifted and bent his right leg in a kicking motion and lost his balance. His frame folded over like a blade of grass in the wind.

"Jamie, you need to have control of your mind so you can control your body," Raj said. "How about if you go over to the picnic table and try to calm your mind by focusing on something else, like one of the trees. I will work with Keisha and Tony, then just come back when you are ready and we will try again. I know you can do it."

Jamie moped over to the picnic table and dropped down on the bench with a sigh. *What a dud I am. Can't even do a simple stance.* He watched Keisha and Tony mimic the moves Raj had taught them and successfully carry them out on each other, lunging, kicking, and blocking. Maybe he just wasn't cut out for this martial arts stuff. He didn't know how to focus, he didn't know where his core was, and he really didn't know how to calm his mind. He folded his arms on the table and rested his head on them. All he could think was *dud, dud, dud.*

But then little pieces of what Mr. James had said started floating around in his head. Something about the mind, the most powerful physical force, and magnets. *That's it! Our thoughts act like magnets attracting what we ... focus on.* But here he was focusing on being a dud. No wonder he felt like a dud.

Hmmm ... if my thoughts act like magnets, then every time I think I'm a dud, that's what I attract ... the experience of being a dud. I attract ... dudness!

Okay, so he needed to stop thinking like that. Instead, he should focus on what he wanted, like being a good Adithada student.

But what about the dud thoughts already stuck to the inside of his brain? He imagined himself tying a helium balloon to the dud thoughts and letting go of the balloon. *There it goes ... higher and higher into the sky ... taking my dud thoughts with it.*

Oh nice. His head seemed lighter. Jamie relaxed with his eyes closed, picturing himself doing the moves Raj had taught him. It was a much better feeling than the feeling of failure.

After a while Raj tapped him on the shoulder. "How are you doing, Jamie?"

"I think I'd like to try again, Raj."

Jamie did his warm-up poses, then took his position with Raj behind him. This time when Raj nudged his leg,

Jamie kicked backward at Raj's thigh. Raj blocked Jamie's leg with his own. "Now let your energy flow through you and into me."

Jamie circled his left arm back for momentum, jabbed his right elbow toward Raj's forehead, then kicked toward Raj's left knee in a fluid motion. Raj blocked all his moves. "Much better, Jamie. You just need to be able to sense my moves before I make them."

For the next hour Jamie concentrated on their lessons, trying to think of himself as a good Adithada student while he practiced the correct moves. He imagined his mind opening up to a power he never knew he had. After a while he realized his body was easily responding to his thoughts.

The minutes flew by as if propelled by a slew of fluttering peacocks, and Jamie was disappointed when Raj said it was time to go home.

"You are all doing very well," Raj said. "We can practice again tomorrow."

Yes, I am *doing very well.* Jamie headed home wondering what it would be like to fly.

Chapter 25

Colton had just received his latest marching orders from Thomas Mandel and was getting ready to leave when Thomas brought up some kids he saw on the TV news talking about getting rid of fossil fuels.

"Yeah, I saw it," Colton said. "What a joke."

"I don't know, Colton. I have a bad feeling about this."

Colton laughed. "You must be getting paranoid in your old age. They're just some crazy kids. And did you see that skinny one? You think he's going to lead a world crusade of kids?" Colton laughed again. "He was too scared to even look at the TV camera. If somebody said *boo!* he'd probably head for the hills. What a pathetic little worm."

"Well, just watch out for them. The news media loves to make a big deal out of sappy do-gooder-kids stories like these."

"Sure, Thomas, whatever you say."

Colton said goodbye and charged out of the King Fuel offices eager to get started on his next assignment. This one was going to take a lot more hustling, but he thrived on stuff like this. Kind of like a hunter stalking his prey. And the best part was when he got to go in for the kill.

Colton arrived at Richard Newsome's office on time for his appointment, but as usual Richard made him wait thirty minutes. *Guess that makes the big shot feel important.*

By the time Richard's assistant showed him into the office, Colton had his ammunition ready. There stood Richard like a deer in an open field.

"Now what?" Richard said. "I haven't even finished working on the last bills."

"Thomas has two more bills you need to sponsor and an offer you'll want to accept," Colton said.

"I don't need to accept anything from you two," Richard said.

"That's fine," Colton said. "It's up to you."

Colton tossed some documents on Richard's desk. Richard didn't even glance at them.

"Thomas's company needs new investment opportunities," Colton said. "You've campaigned on taking advantage of this country's large, untapped oil reserves. A perfect match."

Richard had a blank expression.

"So Thomas's first bill will approve more offshore drilling," Colton said.

"You know very well that most of those coastal communities have already voted against it," Richard said. "And we just got a report that says all our coastal national parks and seashores could be harmed by offshore drilling."

"When have you ever let something like that stop you? This is the best opportunity to make good on your campaign promise."

"I never said we should go after oil on the ocean floor."

"Doesn't matter," Colton said. "You've got no excuse. Your constituents are too far inland to be affected by offshore drilling, and if you don't sponsor this bill, Thomas will make sure your constituents know you reneged on your promise. And it goes without saying there won't be any more campaign contributions."

Richard's eyes narrowed.

"Speaking of national parks, this last bill opens up more public lands for drilling, including national parks and national monuments."

"You can't be serious. I cosponsored legislation to help protect our national parks."

"Well, now you can sponsor legislation to help make them a good investment and create more jobs," Colton said.

"You can't throw the jobs argument at every bad bill and expect voters to swallow it."

"Why not? They always do."

"Thomas must be off his rocker. Do you realize how many lawsuits will tie this up in the courts?"

"Don't play stupid," Colton said. "You know the administration is already trying to remove safeguards against oil and gas drilling in more than forty national parks, so you've already got tremendous support for this bill."

Richard turned and looked out his window.

"Richard, you can do what you want. But these bills are going to go forward with or without you. I have others who will buy in. So either shore up votes with your constituents and fill your campaign chest ... or find a new career because Thomas doesn't forget people who don't play ball with him. There's already a young, promising guy ready to run against you if Thomas says the word."

Colton waited. He knew he had him. The sound of a single gunshot went off in his head.

Richard sunk into his chair and pulled the documents on his desk toward him. He beeped his assistant and said, "You can escort Mr. Slone out now. He has what he came for."

Colton started whistling as soon as he stepped into the hall outside Richard's reception area. Then he almost choked on his last note when he saw Lydia Pattern farther down the hall heading in his direction. He was determined to avoid her. He hoisted up his briefcase and pretended to rifle through it. But she was too busy flipping through her phone, and she ran into him and almost knocked him down. Despite his height, she towered over him with the bulk of a football lineman. If that wasn't bad enough, she'd grabbed hold of his shoulder to help steady him.

"Sorry about that," Lydia said, voice booming. "Well, well, well, if it isn't Colton Slone."

"Senator," Colton said and tried to shake his shoulder free from her grasp.

Lydia let go but said, "Hold on. What nasty deeds are you up to today?"

"Nothing I care to share with you."

"Of course not ... I'm surprised I didn't smell you coming. I've always had a nose for rats."

"Everything I do is completely legal." Colton stiffened his spine. He was not going to let her get under his skin this time.

Lydia laughed her big, obnoxious laugh. "Oh, aren't we touchy? I just want to know what you're peddling and who you're buying off? You know I'm going to find out, especially if it gets in the way of my committee's work."

Colton gave her his best smirk. "Think I'm scared?"

Lydia glanced down the hall. "Was that Newsome's office you just left?"

"I don't think that's any of your business."

"We'll see if it's my business or not. You can tell your clients I'm going to shake things up. I'm tired of them trying to run this country."

"You can't scare them or me. You got nothing."

"Oh, I definitely do have something. But, hey, that's a subject for another day. It was a pleasure bumping into you, Colton. Give my regards to Thomas." Lydia grinned before striding away.

Colton would give anything to find something on her so he could get her to fall in line like the others. *What's she scheming this time?* She was one of the worst ones here, pushing so-called clean energy down everybody's throats, trying to wipe out his kind.

Did she even care what happened to people when a coal mine closed down? He'd lived through it in his mining town. The bowling alley was first to go. Then the movie theater. The five and dime, the only clothing store ... then the shoe-repair shop, drugstore, barber shop ... until finally all that were left were the post office, the church, and the sheriff's office. Enrollment dropped so low at the grammar school and high school that the remaining kids had to be bused to the next town. The bank foreclosed on many of the homes and moved to a town twenty miles away.

Colton felt his chest tighten. He removed his bottle of bronchodilator meds from his inside coat pocket and swallowed two.

He was glad his dad hadn't lived to see it. His dad was a proud miner. *You take away a man's livelihood and his town, and what does he have left? A wife and a house full of kids and no way to feed 'em. But does Ms. High and Mighty Senator care?* He promised himself he'd find a way to make her pay for trying to plow them all under.

Chapter 26

J amie rode his bike up to the bottom of his long driveway and screeched to a halt. An ambulance was parked at the other end near the front of his house. He threw down his bike on the lawn and sprinted diagonally across the front yard, his chest pounding. Men in white uniforms rolled a gurney out of the house with his mother walking alongside. Jamie dashed to the gurney. He peered down at the little face tucked above a blanket. It was Billy. "What happened?" Jamie said.

Billy looked dazed. "I fell out of our tree."

"Jamie, thank goodness—you're home," their mom said. "We're taking Billy to the hospital. Please look after Katie until I get back."

Hours later Katie was propped up on the den sofa with pillows, her own pale face poking out from under a colorful afghan. Strewn on the coffee table were a pill bottle, water glass, tissue box, and inhaler. On the side table perched a portable nebulizer: a square, plastic box with a thin tube extended to a flask that attached to a clear, plastic mouth and nose mask. Jamie just called it a breathing machine.

Jamie was carrying in two peanut-butter-and-jelly sandwiches when their mom came through the door, Billy hobbling along on a crutch in front of her. One cut-off pant leg revealed a bandaged knee and thin, red scrapes on his calf. Katie flung back the afghan, ambled over to her brother, and hugged him so hard he almost toppled over. Billy hugged her back and steadied himself as Katie began coughing.

"Billy has a sprained knee," their mom said in a weary tone. "I hope there will finally be no more tree climbing."

She headed for the kitchen and called back to Billy, "Please stay put, Mr. Tarzan. I'm getting you some baby aspirin."

"Oh Billy, I wish I was with you in our tree," Katie said. Her cough started up again, and she reached for her inhaler. "I could have grabbed you so you didn't fall."

"Nah, I slipped and went down fast."

Jamie tousled Billy's hair. "Well, Billyboo, looks like now you two can get well together."

"Come sit with me, Billy, and Jamie will give you a sandwich," Katie said. She plopped back down on the sofa and gazed up at her older brother with a dimpled smile.

"Here, take mine," Jamie said, and placed both sandwiches on the coffee table.

As soon as Billy lowered himself next to his sister, she rested her head against his shoulder. "Maybe we shouldn't climb our tree like Mommy says until we're older and bigger." She paused, then giggled. "Mr. Tarzan."

He grasped his sister's hand and held it in his own. "Maybe. Or at least until you're all better, Miss Monkey Girl."

A sudden warmth filled Jamie's chest.

Katie lightly touched Billy's bandaged knee, which he'd propped up on the coffee table. "Did they give you a needle in the hospital? Did you wear one of those little backwards dresses with your bum hanging out the back? Were the nurses nice? Whenever I go to the hospital the nurses are really nice. How long do you have to use that stick? Does your knee hurt?"

"No needles. Nice nurses. Knee hurts. No bum hanging out."

Jamie didn't think there was anything funnier than his brother and sister when they were together.

A text came in from Keisha. *They're about to interview Senator Pattern on TV! Turn on channel 9!*

He joined the twins on the sofa, turned on the TV with the remote, and scrolled through to a network channel. Senator Pattern appeared on the screen. "Hey, Mom, come quick. The senator I met at Keisha's house is on some show."

Charles Wilson, moderator for a network TV news program, introduced his guests, both seated across from him at a large, glass table. "We have with us today US Senator Lydia Pattern, chairperson of the US Senate Committee on Energy and Natural Resources, and Thomas Mandel, CEO of King Fuel, an international conglomerate for oil, coal, and natural gas."

The TV camera zoomed out to a wide shot of the two guests.

"Senator, you've been a strong proponent of renewable energy," Charles said.

"Everyone should be," Lydia said. "The United States is the world's largest fossil-fuel polluter per capita, but we trail way behind other large, polluting nations in our use of renewable energy."

"Are you familiar with this new kids' clean-energy movement called the CAPE?"

Jamie's mom appeared in the doorway. Jamie turned to her and said, "Did you hear that?"

His mom nodded with a smile and took a chair near her children.

"Yes, I've been impressed with their commitment to cleaning up the environment," Senator Pattern said.

"Then you know they're pushing some pretty drastic measures to replace fossil fuels," Charles said.

The senator leaned forward. "Yes, but we need extreme measures for extreme problems. Air pollution is creating health hazards for more than half the people in our country. I'm glad these CAPE kids are taking a stand."

Jamie pumped his fist.

"But what about complaints that the fossil-fuel industry is overregulated?" Charles said.

"Look, Charles, the Americans at greatest risk are our children, who have much smaller, undeveloped lung capacity, and many of them are suffering with lung ailments due to polluted air from dirty energy. Why would we want to water down or reverse clean-air laws when we're already basically poisoning our children's lungs?"

Jamie nodded. "You tell 'em, Senator."

Charles turned to his other guest. "Mr. Mandel, what's your reaction to these CAPE kids and their fight against fossil-fuel pollution?

The King Fuel man flicked his hand as if waving away a pesky fly. "If those kids got their way, we'd see the biggest global depression in the history of the world. Millions and millions of people would be out of work. Those kids have no idea what they're doing. They see other kids coughing and they want to get the whole world to stop using cheap, reliable, job-producing energy. Come on. How crazy is that? So there are kids with weak lungs. Are we going to shut down some of our most important industries all because of some weak-lunged kids?"

Jamie blew raspberries at King Fuel. So did Katie and Billy. Billy kept blowing raspberries so loud Jamie had to signal him to stop so they could hear the people on TV. Billy sucked in a big gulp of air and blew an even longer raspberry while shaking his head. Then one last short one before stopping.

Charles arched his eyebrows. "Mr. Mandel, are you saying we shouldn't care about how air pollution affects children?"

"Of course we should take care of our children," Thomas said. "Give them what they need to be healthy— nutritious food, good healthcare, plenty of exercise, and all those kinds of things. If we did a better job spending money on all that and not wasting it by throwing millions of dollars at alternative energy that we don't even need, then the world would have healthier kids."

"Mr. Mandel, but what about the impact of burning fossil fuels on human health?" Charles said.

King Fuel puckered his lips. "Look, the atmosphere is like a big purifier. No matter what we pump into the air, our planet's atmosphere is so big that if anything nasty gets in there, it just gets filtered out and it's released into outer space, gone forever."

Jamie looked at his mom and crinkled his forehead.

"I see," Charles said. "So Mr. Mandel, why do you think then that our nation's Air Quality Index keeps registering such increasingly high rates of pollutants?"

"Of course it's registering pollutants. People are burning wood. Are we going to stop using wood? Cows digest their food and expel methane gas. Are we going to stop raising cows?"

The senator placed her two elbows on the table and stared at King Fuel. "Mr. Mandel, there is substantial, documented, medical evidence on the negative impacts of fossil-fuel pollution on human health."

"Well, I can show you reports by real scientists that prove fossil fuels are not the issue," Thomas said.

"We'll see about that," Senator Pattern said. "I'm sponsoring a Senate public hearing on that very topic."

"I can promise you two things, Senator," Thomas said. "One, I will be there to refute your findings, and two, there's no way people in my industry are going to let this group of CAPE kids get to first base with their crazy plan. You can bet money on it."

Jamie glanced at his mom with a frown.

"That's all the time we have for today," Charles said. "Thank you Senator Pattern and Mr. Mandel for joining us. Tune in to our network's local affiliates for other reactions to the children's campaign to fight fossil fuels."

"Holy cow, Mom, can you believe it? We made a national news show."

"That's extraordinary, Jamie!" his mom said. "So that's the senator you met? She seems like an excellent person to have in your corner."

"Yeah, but that King Fuel guy is scary, huh?"

"You know, Jamie, a lot of people make a lot of money off fossil fuels, and they're going to protect their interests any way they can. You need to be careful."

"But we have more important stuff to protect. I think my friends and I should go to that thing ... that public hearing thing."

"Well, you're part of the public too."

"Keisha can probably find out from her mom about it. She works for Senator Pattern you know."

"Yes, sweetie. Mary's been around Congress a long time."

Jamie was a little worried about that King Fuel guy, but he couldn't believe their good luck with Senator Pattern. And they hadn't even had their parade yet. Wait 'til Mr. King Fuel got a load of what they had planned.

CHAPTER 27

It was one of those clear, sunny, fall days in Washington, DC, crisp and crunchy as a McIntosh apple. The invigorating nip in the air and the clean scent of freshly mowed grass on the National Mall washed over the spectators who gathered four and six deep along Pennsylvania Avenue to wait for the parade to start. News media and the parade participants' relatives and friends packed the bleachers of the viewing stands.

Just a few blocks away, young people found their assigned positions and each group lined up in formation. Band members tuned up their instruments. Parents helped with last-minute costume adjustments. Someone directed latecomers to their places. Someone else did a countdown to the parade start time. The excitement built like a huge wave rolling through the mass of youthful bodies.

Someone blew a whistle. They all came to attention and began marching.

They wound their way to the main route down Pennsylvania Avenue, many of them sporting long, green capes and blue pants, their white t-shirts emblazoned with the group's emblem: *CAPE* in green letters above an image of the Earth.

Jamie wore the same CAPE attire, but he sat in the reviewing stand with Steve Headley, whose local TV station was broadcasting the parade. Steve had asked Jamie to serve as commentator for the parade, which Jamie had turned down at first. He may have made it through that first interview with Steve in his front yard, but he didn't know the first thing about being a commentator, whatever that was, and he didn't like the idea of everybody watching him try to do it on TV.

But his friends had ganged up on him until he agreed, so here he was sweating in the cool fall air and twisting his hands into pretzels. Well, at least he'd get to see the whole parade … and it was coming into view!

There were Keisha and Raj at the front carrying the CAPE's new banner with *Children Against Polluting Earth* in big letters. Jamie waved like crazy at them, and the hair on his arms stood up when the spectators loudly applauded.

The TV station's camerawoman in the reviewing stand focused on the parade as it came closer, and a cameraman focused on Steve and Jamie. "If you're just tuning in, this is Steve Headley with WRG-TV in Washington, DC, covering the CAPE Halloween Parade. The CAPE is a global kids' group fighting fossil-fuel pollution. Joining me is the leader of the CAPE, Jamie Sawyer, our commentator …" Jamie forced a smile. Steve continued, "And as you can see, the parade has just started."

Behind Raj and Keisha, a kids' honor guard marched in unison waving an American flag, another flag with the CAPE emblem, and a third flag that said *Save Our Planet.*

Jamie knew Tony would be somewhere watching. He was such a good guy to use the last of his lawn money for the CAPE banner and flags. If only he could be with them.

But Tony was probably getting a kick out of knowing he'd secretly helped them. And now he'd get to see how nice the banner and flags turned out.

A school marching band behind the honor guard played "We Are The World" while eighty young voices behind the band sang the lyrics.

"Tell us where these kids are from, Jamie," Steve said.

"That's the Northern Virginia Schools Marching Band and three choral groups from the DC area," Jamie said.

A huge helium Earth balloon bobbed along attached to ropes guided by dozens of kids. "We had so many kids who wanted to march with the Earth balloon, we had to have them draw straws," Jamie said. "I saw the guys blow it up, it was awesome, it *is* awesome. It was in the Earth Day parade in April so my friend's mom got them to loan it to us."

Three girls with a banner marked *Global Ghouls* introduced the next wave of the parade as an Arlington school band played Frederic Chopin's "Funeral March." Dozens of children marched encased in huge paper-mache chunks of coal. Other children wore black top hats with Lego-constructed drilling rigs glued on top. Another group twirled fake tailpipes like batons. Several rows of children wore four-sided cardboard boxes with huge photographs of smokestacks. Others carried large, cardboard models of oil tankers.

Some of the spectators booed. Which was fine with Jamie.

"You consider these types of energy 'ghouls'?" Steve asked Jamie.

Jamie nodded. "Yeah, because they prey on live bodies and can turn them into dead bodies."

A hush permeated the sidelines when dozens of kids wearing black respirators came into view. Several toddlers in the crowd clung to their parents and buried their faces. "We could all end up wearing these," Jamie said.

Kids in white uniforms carried stretchers with child-sized lumps covered by blankets. Other kids with black-hooded cloaks and skull masks rode bikes in circles of five each, black streamers waving from their wheels. Several rows of children wore large, cardboard tombstones with only their heads and feet visible. Emblazoned on the tombstones were the words: *R.I.P Mother Earth and Her Kids.*

Steve gestured toward the tombstones. "Seems like you all are trying to send a pretty strong message."

"Well, we want people to think about what's happening," Jamie said.

"But don't you think the fossil-fuel industry is going to put up a strong fight to protect their interests?"

Jamie tried to ignore the question by focusing all his attention on the parade.

"Jamie?" Steve said. "What about the coal, oil, and natural-gas businesses fighting you?"

"Sir, we're just trying to do what's right for the planet, and I think these businesses can too by switching over to clean energy."

A third school marching band shifted the mood with a rousing new rendition of the musical tune "I'm Gonna Wash That Man Right Outa My Hair." A choral group sang along, but with the new lyrics "We're Gonna Clean That Junk Right Outa Our Air."

Jamie laughed. "My friend's dad rewrote that song for our parade, and he rehearsed that band and choral group from Alexandria." Jamie suddenly realized he was hardly nervous anymore about being on TV. He gestured to the next leg of the parade. "Here's another good part coming up."

Three boys carried a banner that said *Clean Energy to the Rescue.* The onlookers cheered loudly. Jamie couldn't resist clapping.

Six rows of kids marched in formation with small replicas of wind turbines attached to helmets on their heads.

More cheers erupted at the sight of kids carrying miniature solar panels. Other kids drove pint-sized battery-operated cars. Dozens of kids pulled little red wagons with hand-painted, three-dimensional cardboard replicas of water pouring off dams and the word *Hydropower.* Another group of youngsters carried large posters of geothermal plants.

Fifty kids flapped above their heads long strips of silky lightweight fabric painted to look like ocean waves. "This represents electricity from wave power," Jamie said. "It's another clean-energy source we'll never run out of, and we hope there'll be more efforts to use wave power."

Dozens of children dressed up like trees filled the street. "We need to save and plant more trees and especially the rain forest," Jamie said. "Trees are so important because they absorb carbon dioxide and help stabilize the Earth's climate. They also release oxygen, which we depend on to survive."

Suddenly out of the corner of his eye Jamie noticed a man, all in black, who seemed to be trying to stay out of sight behind the bottom edge of the bleachers. When Jamie turned to look, he saw that the man held a camera with a really long lens—aimed right at him. He had a hoodie pulled over his head, but a sudden breeze blew it off long enough for Jamie to realize the guy was bald. He couldn't see his face well enough to make out his features, and as soon as he focused on the man, the man pulled his hood back on and disappeared into the crowd. Jamie wondered why a photographer would be so secretive.

Steve interrupted Jamie's thoughts. "What's going on with this next part of the parade, Jamie?"

Two boys and a girl carried a banner that said *Children's Boycott to Save Our Planet*. Dozens of children marched by with large, cardboard signs atop four-foot poles. Each featured a product or brand name, encircled in red with a red line slashed diagonally through it: video games, iPods, iPads, cell phones, TVs, Rollerblades, skateboards, bikes, jeans, sneakers, entertainers, pizzas, cheeseburgers, and movie posters.

"That's a lot of boycotting," Steve said.

"Well, we aren't old enough to vote, so we're using the power we do have. We won't boycott businesses that support us, but we're doing everything we can to get change to start soon."

Three girls marched into view with a banner reading *Pennies for the Planet*. "Here's something else we're doing," Jamie said.

Dozens of kids with CAPE t-shirts and green capes carried large, clear plastic bottles labeled *Pennies for the Planet*. They scattered along the parade lines and offered spectators the chance to donate pennies. The clinking of coins echoed all along the street.

"We just started our pennies collections here today." Jamie said. "Kids in other counties are also collecting coins to help support another part of our plan."

The end of the parade featured another school marching band playing the "Kids for Saving Earth Promise Song" with three choral groups singing the words. Jamie hummed the tune as he watched the last line of kids head down the street.

"Well, Jamie, that was quite a unique event," Steve said. "You must be pleased with the big turnout of kids in the parade and all the people who came to see them."

Jamie grinned. "It was way better than we even hoped. But this is just the beginning. We now have millions of CAPE members all over the world and we're all working to get our countries to replace dirty energy with clean energy as fast as possible."

Steve shook Jamie's hand. "Looks like your group is on a roll." Then Steve faced the camera and said, "Thank you for tuning in for the CAPE Halloween Parade. This is Steve Headley at the nation's capital."

Jamie's whole body buzzed. It was almost too much to take in. So many kids marching for the planet. So many people along the parade route. So many volunteers who helped make it possible. And the whole thing broadcast for everyone to see.

He wished he could share it all with his dad. His dad would smile his biggest smile and they'd go home and talk about it half the night. He made believe his dad was really there with him. "Good one, right, Dad?" he whispered into the breeze. It was a little phrase his dad used a lot. "Yeah, good one!" he heard the breeze whisper back.

CHAPTER 28

A week after the parade Jamie asked Raj to ride around with him on their bikes to check out the early impact of their campaign in their city. They stopped outside a video-game store where a picket line on the sidewalk slowed passing drivers. A group of children marched in a circle, singing and holding hand-drawn cardboard signs that read *Support Our Plan—Save the Planet.*

"Hey Raj, there must be thirty kids just at this one store," Jamie said.

Raj cupped his hand to his ear. "Listen to what they are singing."

A small boy at the head of the marchers was shouting phrases in cadence like a drill sergeant. "Adopt our plan or we won't buy."

The other children repeated it in unison.

"Our planet needs help. It's not a lie," the boy sang.

The others repeated it.

"They made up their own little picket song," Jamie said, laughing. "They seem like they must be in the lower grades too."

"And they are getting a lot of attention," Raj said.

"Let's check out the store a few blocks down," Jamie said.

Jamie led the way to a large costume store with only a few cars parked in its lot. "Why don't we look inside," Jamie said. "They should be packed on a Saturday so close to Halloween."

Inside the store the aisles were almost empty except for a few kids and their parents. Jamie sauntered over to the racks near three sales clerks who seemed to be just hanging around. Raj joined Jamie within earshot of the clerks.

A clerk dressed like a witch said, "Can you believe it? Three days 'til Halloween and sales are still so slow."

"My grandson loves boycotting," said a clerk in a green fairy outfit. "Says he feels important."

A clerk in pirate garb donned an eye patch. "Yeah, they're making their own Halloween costumes. Don't be surprised if your trick-or-treaters show up as lumps of coal."

"My daughter's going nuts with her kids boycotting fast food," the fairy clerk said with a chuckle. "She's tired of cooking every night 'cause they won't eat nothing but home cooking,"

The witch clerk adjusted her pointy hat. "You gotta hand it to the little buggers," she said. "They mean business."

Raj grinned. Jamie stifled the urge to let out a whoop right there next to the SpongeBob SquarePants costumes. He whispered to Raj, "So far so good!"

~

After school Jamie did his weekly check on the pennies collections. At the entrance to the cafeteria the two-foot-high plastic jar on prominent display was filled to the brim with pennies. Taped to the wall above the jar was a sign with the CAPE emblem and the words *Pennies for Planet Earth*. It was a treat for him to see the jar full by the end of every week.

Inside the cafeteria dozens of students bent over long tables stuffing thousands of pennies collected from other sites around town into paper rolls. The sound of clinking pennies filled the room. He approached a girl who sat at one of the tables entering figures into her laptop. She worked with other CAPE coordinators to keep track of all the collections in the United States and other CAPE countries.

"Hi Ginny," Jamie said. "I just found out somebody's getting us some of those coin machines so we can do this a lot faster."

"Great!" she said. "We can barely keep up." She turned her laptop monitor toward Jamie. "Check it out."

Jamie leaned over and peered at the numbers. "Whoa, more every week."

"Everybody's collecting from their family and friends, and we started a big competition with some of the other schools," Ginny said.

"I know. Of course we'll have to beat them."

"Oh, we will! Hey, there's a pickup in two days from the rec center, and we expect another big haul after the game tonight."

"You're all doing a terrific job!" Jamie glanced around the cafeteria at all the kids. "Do you have the latest from our other CAPE coordinators?"

Ginny tapped on her laptop and showed Jamie another report.

"This is even better than last week!" Jamie said.

Ms. Tollhouse appeared in the doorway and joined Jamie and Ginny.

"Hi, Ms. Tollhouse. Guess what? The way these collections are going in our country and some of the other countries, I think we'll be able to support the kids who want to strike at their factories."

"Are you sure you still want to do that, Jamie?"

"Why wouldn't I?"

"It's a much bigger and more complicated job than you and your group can handle alone."

"But look at all the money we're collecting in lots of countries."

"I know, but that's much different than getting all that money to the factory kids on a regular basis."

"What do you mean?"

"For example, you'd need some kind of organization that can legally set up a global network to gather the collections, record them, convert them into foreign currency, and distribute them somehow."

"Oh, I hadn't thought about that ... but there must be a way."

"Well, let me think."

Jamie fidgeted with his hands. Ginny sat down and went back to working at her computer. The clinking of the pennies started to sound louder in Jamie's ears, much louder.

Finally Mrs. Tollhouse said, "I have an idea. I belong to a nonprofit based in the United States that has offices overseas—the Planet Defense Council. I could ask them if they would take this on since supporting your group would fall under their mission of protecting the environment.

Maybe they could distribute the money through some of the charities they work with in other countries."

"Perfect!"

"I'll see what I can do and let you know."

"Thank you! Thank you!"

Jamie hummed a tune all the way home. It was from a song his mom used to sing back in the days when his dad did something to make her happy. It was called "We're in the Money."

CHAPTER 29

J amie joined Keisha at the gymnasium before her game to help her set up a small folding table with one of the penny collection jars and a *Pennies for Planet Earth* sign at the gym entrance.

Keisha seemed to be tapping her foot to a silent rhythm. "Hey, Jamie, weren't the bands and choral groups in the parade super? And didn't all the banners and homemade props and flags look really nice?"

"Yeah, and that Earth balloon was fantastic!"

"I'm used to cheering crowds at my b-ball games, but the way the people along the parade route sounded you'd think we were winning in the big leagues."

"Yeah, I loved seeing all those people." He paused. "But this one guy kind of spooked me. He lurked around the bleachers and took pictures of me with a long lens."

"Not a news photographer?"

"I don't think so. He was being all sneaky about it, and he ran off when I stared at him."

"What did he look like?"

"All in black, hoodie pulled over his head—except when it slipped off for a second I saw he was bald."

Keisha's mouth dropped. "I saw a bald guy like that at the parade, all in black, with a long lens. He was shooting photos of me and Raj from a couple of rows back in the crowd. Raj said it looked like a telephone lens ... no, a telephoto lens, like the kind you see in those spy movies."

"Creepy."

"Yeah, creepy is right. What do you think that was all about?"

"I don't know," Jamie said. He unfolded the table and set it up.

Keisha placed the jar on the table, then glanced up at the gym clock. "Uh-oh. I don't have much time before I need to get ready for my game. I'll tape up the sign and then go."

While Keisha arranged the sign, Jamie spotted Tiffany and Tara sauntering into the gym. Well, here was another creepy sight. He nodded their way and whispered to Keisha, "You don't have to talk to them if you don't want to."

Jamie noticed Keisha's back stiffen the way it did every time those two teammates came near her. Maybe they'd just ignore her this time. Keisha had told him she'd given up hope that they'd ever treat her like the other members of the team.

Jamie slid closer to Keisha, and Keisha busied herself at the folding table as if she hadn't seen them come in. But Jamie thought you'd have to be deaf not to hear them laughing so loud, like a couple of cackling hens. *Geez, who laughs like that. They could probably break a windowpane if they shrieked any louder. But ... oh wait ... they're passing right by and ignoring Keisha. Good.* Now she'd only have to see them during the game if she got out of the gym fast enough afterward.

Tiffany stopped and turned back toward Keisha. Tara copied her.

"Hey, was that you I saw carrying a CAPE sign with some other kid at the Halloween parade?" Tiffany said.

Slowly Keisha faced Tiffany. "Yeah."

"So you're all about the environment now, huh?"

"Yeah."

"No, really, what's with you and this CAPE thing?"

Keisha hesitated. Jamie could tell she was trying to read what Tiffany was up to.

"I'm interested for a reason, okay?" Tiffany said, her voice softening.

Tara raised her eyebrows.

"Well, I've been helping my friend Jamie here and our whole group try to stop pollution from dirty energy," Keisha said.

Tiffany glanced at Jamie. "You're the kid that started it, right?"

"Yeah, me and Keisha and my other friends."

Tiffany faced Keisha. "And these penny jars?"

"We're raising money as part of our plan," Keisha said.

"You know much about air pollution?"

Keisha nodded. "Enough."

"My little brother has horrible asthma," Tiffany said. "It's much harder on him when the air is bad. The other day he barely made it into the house."

"A lot of kids are suffering from all kinds of lung diseases," Keisha said. "Jamie's little sister, too. And things are going to get much worse if we don't do something."

Tiffany frowned and sadness seemed to creep into her eyes. "Do you really think a bunch of kids can get rid of dirty energy?"

Jamie waited. Keisha hesitated again. Jamie hoped Tiffany wouldn't make one of her snide remarks.

Keisha raised her chin. "Yes, I think a bunch of kids *can* get rid of dirty energy. We've got kids all over the world working on this who've joined the CAPE."

Keisha started to say something else, then stopped. She jiggled her left knee a little. Jamie realized he'd seen her do the same thing when she was trying to figure out her next move on the court. Finally, she said, "Would you like to join us?"

Tiffany focused intensely above Keisha's head for several seconds as if preparing to leap off a diving board. Then she looked directly into Keisha's eyes. "Yeah, Keisha. I would."

Jamie did a silent little cheer inside for his friend.

Keisha's eyes widened. She had never heard this strange mellow voice from Tiffany before. "Good, Tiffany, just go to our website."

Tiffany nodded, then reached in her purse, pulled out some pennies, and dropped them into the jar. "For my little brother."

Tara stared at Tiffany for a moment and made her own contribution.

"Thank you," Keisha said warmly to the two girls.

Jamie nudged the back of Keisha's sneaker. She nudged him back.

CHAPTER 30

J amie, Keisha, and her parents were discussing Keisha's good day over dinner at the family's kitchen table, with the countertop TV on in the background. Mrs. Taylor had told them there was something they'd want to see on the TV that night, and she turned up the volume when news anchor Kalyn Roberts came on reporting the national evening news.

"The newly formed international group, Children Against Polluting Earth, known by the acronym CAPE, have ignited widespread interest in their mission to save the planet from fossil-fuel pollution and climate change," the anchor said. "The group was launched by youth in Alexandria, Virginia." Scenes from the kids' parade filled the screen, including a close-up of Keisha and Raj carrying the CAPE banner. "They kicked off their campaign with a well-attended parade in the nation's capital."

"Keish, Keish, there you are!" Jamie said. "See how they zoomed right in on our banner and the Earth balloon?"

"Hey, look at you, the big commentator in the viewing stand!" Keisha said.

Jamie's cheeks flushed. "Yeah, right."

Jamie's video footage from the future followed the parade scenes. "The internet is buzzing about the group's YouTube video depicting a future Earth so polluted it's turned into a wasteland devoid of any plant or sea life and its inhabitants have to wear respirators to breathe," the anchor said.

"Was it Raj who created that horrific video of the future?" Mrs. Taylor said. "What an imagination you all have."

"But what if it turns out to be not just our imagination, Mrs. Taylor?" Jamie said.

The report continued. "Please rejoin us after this commercial break for our exclusive interview with a member of Congress who is adding her clout to their cause."

"Keish, what a big story on us!" Jamie said. "On the *national news again!*"

~

While Jamie and Keisha were clearing the dishes, Mrs. Taylor said, "I think there's another surprise coming up." The network resumed coverage, and Jamie riveted his attention on the TV.

"If you were with us before the break, you heard about the drastic measures being proposed by an international kids' group to counter fossil-fuel pollution and climate change. They're not alone."

The screen cut to file footage of Lydia Pattern speaking before Congress. "US Senator Lydia Pattern, chairman of the US Senate Committee on Energy and Natural Resources, has sponsored a bill supporting the kids' goal for phasing out fossil fuels in ten years."

Jamie choked on his glass of milk. "Holy moly!"

Keisha laughed. "Pretty rad, huh?"

"You knew?" Jamie said.

"Mom told me."

Back on camera the anchor said, "Initial reactions at the Capitol have mostly run from lukewarm to strongly opposed. Efforts are already underway to stop the bill from reaching the senate floor. Here's Steve Headley, our Washington, DC, affiliate correspondent reporting on this highly controversial bill."

"I hate to say this," Mrs. Taylor said, "but I have my doubts about Lydia's bill ever getting passed,"

"Geez, Mom, then don't say it," Keisha said.

Steve was with Senator Pattern in her senate office. "Senator, given the extensive use of fossil fuels, how is it possible to switch over to clean energy in only ten years?

"Many American and foreign utility companies are already switching over to clean energy," the senator said. "We just need them to move faster, and we need to remove the subsidies for fossil fuels in our country that encourage their use."

"Aren't we going in the opposite direction now by weakening our environmental-protection regulations and opening public lands for drilling?" Steve said.

"Yes, absolutely," the senator said. "But the biggest reason we haven't made a faster transition by now to clean energy is because the powerful oil, coal, and natural-gas companies have spent millions in campaign contributions to convince lawmakers to ignore decades of science and research so these companies can line their pockets with dirty-energy profits."

"But aren't you concerned about the cost to consumers and businesses?"

The senator shook her head. "Utility companies that are making wide-scale infrastructure investments have already proven that clean renewable energy can be cheaper than dirty energy."

"In what way?" Steve said.

"Think about renewables for a second—the concept of an energy source that's not used up," the senator said. "If your electricity is powered by wind, solar, water, or the Earth's internal heat, that means you don't have the high cost of removing oil, coal, or natural gas from the ground or ocean floor, converting it, storing it, transporting it long distances, using it up, then constantly repeating the whole process and polluting the environment more each time you do."

"Yeah, why would you want energy from stuff that gets used up when you can have energy from stuff that never gets used up?" Jamie said.

"Senator, don't you think it's going to be almost impossible to convince enough legislators that they should get behind phasing out fossil fuels, especially since much of your own party is against it?"

"Well, people have short memories," the senator said. "Some of the earliest, most important environmental laws were passed with the support of my party. And now there are several bipartisan groups devoted to reducing fossil-fuel pollution. One is made up of equal numbers from both parties in the US House of Representatives called the Climate Solutions Caucus. Another is the US Climate Alliance, a bipartisan coalition of American states committed to reducing greenhouse-gas emissions."

Senator Pattern counted off on her fingers each group as she mentioned them. "Over thirty-five hundred businesses, investors, US governors, mayors, faith leaders, university presidents, tribal leaders, and cultural institutions representing all fifty states have signed the bipartisan 'We Are Still In' pact to reduce emissions and stem the causes of climate change. Another active group, RepublicEn, is a growing movement of conservatives and libertarians—the 'EcoRight'—who want to solve climate change through free-enterprise solutions.

"Polls show sixty percent of American adults support dramatically reducing the country's use of fossil fuels in favor of clean energy, and that includes independent voters and voters across all parties," the senator said.

"Wow, so many people already on our side," Jamie said.

"But what about the people who say humans aren't causing climate change?" Steve said.

"What different deniers have in common is that they don't believe the scientific evidence of human-caused climate change presented by over ninety percent of the world's active climate scientists from eighty countries."

"Geez, Keish, if they don't believe scientists, they're not going to believe us," Jamie said.

"So what?" Keisha said.

Steve rubbed his chin. "Senator, what do you say to those deniers?"

"To be honest I've found it rarely helps to say much to them about climate change," the senator said. "But I do ask them to consider the possibility that these toxic gases are having a devastating impact on peoples' health. Air pollution is measurable, and the health professions have verified over and over again that fossil-fuel pollution is responsible for sickening and killing millions of people."

"Did you hear that, Keish? Millions of people already—not just in Delhi." Jamie said.

Keisha flinched.

"But with our country being so polarized, how are you going to get enough Americans to come together to support your bill?" Steve asked.

The senator leaned forward in her chair. "Tribal politics is what's dividing our country. When people identify with a certain tribe, then the tribe's identity becomes that person's identity and the tribe's opinions become their own, so they shut out any other views. Well, we're never going to solve our country's problems that way, are we?"

"Is she talking about like American Indian tribes?" Jamie said.

"No, she's talking about how when people hear anything that goes against what their group believes, they feel personally attacked," Mrs. Taylor said.

"Why do they feel personally attacked?" Jamie said.

"You know when you're watching your team play b-ball for your school and your team gets beat?" Mr. Taylor said. "Well, don't you feel like you yourself got beat even though you're not actually on the team?"

"Yeah, I do," Jamie said.

"Well, that's how a lot of people feel if you try to tell them something that their group doesn't agree with," Mr. Taylor said. "They've programmed themselves to feel so much a part of that group that they can't or won't believe you because they feel like you're beating up on their tribe … and that's like beating up on them."

"Like a tribe of robots," Jamie said.

Mr. Taylor chuckled.

"Shush," Keisha said. "Let's hear what they're saying."

Steve was asking Senator Pattern another question. "So given the controversial nature of this bill and the extremely short timeframe for the phase-out, do you realistically think it can ever pass?"

"I realize today I'm faced with a whole lot more noes than yeas. But as my mother used to say, 'No is just a comma on the way to a solution.'"

"Thank you, Senator," Steve said. "Looks like you're really heating things up here at the Capitol."

Keisha hit the off button on the remote.

"You know what this means, Mrs. Taylor?" Jamie said. "Now we have a way to get our government leaders to support our plan!"

"Oh, Jamie, I don't want to dampen your spirits, but I think what they were saying is that Senator Pattern is going to try hard to get a bill passed, but there's a lot going against her."

"Your boss woman really knows her stuff, though," Mr. Taylor said.

"Will you please stop calling her that, Sam," Mrs. Taylor said. A smile seemed to tug at the corners of her mouth. "But she does, doesn't she?"

Jamie was still absorbing what he'd just seen on TV. When the senator said she'd help them, he thought she was just going to give them some advice. "Mrs. Taylor, this is much better than what we expected."

"Senator Pattern has been passionate about replacing fossil fuels with clean energy for years, and you kids came along at just the right time," Keisha's mom said. "But some of her colleagues from the coal, natural-gas, and oil states have already accused her of being a traitor to her party and stirring up trouble."

"They have to do right by the people they represent," Keisha's dad said.

Mrs. Taylor nodded. "She understands that, but she also wants to do what she thinks is right, and she thinks there's a better way for everybody."

"Just my little ol' opinion, but I think they're up against one tough cookie," Mr. Taylor said.

Keisha's mom laughed. "Yeah, she is!"

That's what we need, thought Jamie. A tough cookie.

"The senator prides herself on being assertive, clever, and persevering even though she knows a few of the senate good ol' boys call her bossy, conniving, and pushy behind her back," Mrs. Taylor said. "But she doesn't care. When they try to stick her with those worn-out put-down labels for strong women, she just shakes them off."

Jamie wondered how Senator Pattern got to be so strong. Was she like that when she was a kid?

"I've seen her in action when she tries to get them to consider the facts," Mrs. Taylor said. "She comes to them well prepared for any rebuttal, a smile on her face, with sound reasons why things need to change and how each senator would benefit from supporting her bills. More often than not, eventually she gets their votes."

"So she'll be able to get the votes for her bill then, right?" Jamie said. He was liking Senator Pattern more and more.

Keisha's mom frowned. "I'm sorry, Jamie, but this time is going to be different. Not only is she going up against a lot of people in her own party, but much worse, she's taking on some of the most powerful industries and lobbyists in the country."

"But, Mom, you just finished telling us how good she is at getting votes," Keisha said.

"Well, she is usually," Mrs. Taylor said. "But I don't want to give you kids false hopes. This is one big hot potato with a long treacherous road to roll."

"What long road, Mrs. Taylor?" Jamie said. *See there it is again, just when you think things are going go well, bam, you find out they're not.*

Keisha's mom looked over at her dad, who shrugged his shoulders.

"Please, just be straight with us, ma'am," Jamie said.

Mr. Taylor raised his hand. "Mary, my love, before you get into all that, how about we take a little break and have some of that deeelicious chocolate-pecan pie you made?"

Keisha jumped up. "I'll get it. Wanna help me, Jamie?"

Jamie followed Keisha into the kitchen.

"Look, no matter what my mom says, don't worry, okay?" Keisha said.

"Yeah, sure," Jamie said. But he was already worrying.

CHAPTER 31

Jamie finished off the last bite of his chocolate-pecan pie at Keisha's house and sat back in his chair. He divided up the night in his head. Good news: A national TV news show reported on the CAPE. Good news: Senator Pattern has a bill to support our cause. Bad news: Her bill is a hot potato. Good news: Senator Pattern is a tough cookie. Good news: That pecan pie *was* deeelicious. Bad news: Coming up next?

Jamie helped Keisha clear the dessert plates and they both joined her parents in the family room.

"Okay, Mrs. Taylor, we're ready," Jamie said. "What's it gonna take to get Senator Taylor's bill passed?"

Mrs. Taylor sighed. "I don't want you kids to get discouraged, but I think it's important that you understand how tough it is to get a bill, especially this bill, through Congress."

Jamie nodded.

Mrs. Taylor sighed again. "Well, in a nutshell, after the executive agencies give their comments on Senator Taylor's bill, and her committee holds public hearings, then meets to do changes called *amendments*, then you have to hope the bill will actually make it out of the committee at all."

"But if Senator Pattern is chairperson, why wouldn't it make it out of her committee?" Keisha said.

"Sweetie, voting the bill out from her committee to the full Senate will be tough because there are so many on her committee opposed to the bill."

"Well, make believe they agree to vote the bill out," Jamie said.

"All right, but then the senate majority leader decides whether or not the full one-hundred-member senate can vote on it, and I expect he won't. But we'll make believe he allows it to be debated and voted on. As a result of the debate, there will probably be more changes to the bill."

"How many changes?" Jamie said.

"Usually whatever it takes to get enough senators to vote in favor of the bill. But, Jamie, I have to tell you that even if the bill got this far, which remember is highly unlikely, I think there wouldn't be nearly enough votes for the Senate to pass this bill."

"Crap," Keisha said.

"Right, but please don't use coarse words," Mrs. Taylor said.

"Can we make believe again, Mrs. Taylor?" Jamie said. "Then what happens?"

"So, then the House of Representatives gets a shot at it if the Speaker of the House will allow the bill to go to the full membership. There you're dealing with four hundred and thirty-five votes if it makes it out of the House committee."

"Keep making believe, Mom."

"Okay, let's say by some miracle—and I do mean miracle—the bill survives both the Senate and the House. There's no telling if it will remotely resemble what it looked like in the beginning. Usually the House and Senate pass different versions of the same bill, so then members from each house try to work out a compromise. And then it goes to the president for approval or veto."

"Double crap," Keisha said.

"Yes, but please stop with that word, Keisha," Mrs. Taylor said.

Jamie thought *double crap* summed up things pretty well.

Mrs. Taylor continued. "See, by then Senator Pattern would have needed enough votes in both the Senate and the House to get a veto-proof majority."

"Say what?" Keisha said.

"That means she'd need to get enough votes to make it impossible for the president to stop her bill."

"Mary, you're painting such a dreary picture," Keisha's dad said.

Jamie dropped his chin. "Yeah, now I wish I hadn't asked." This bill wasn't just a hot potato, it was a nuclear-active potato.

"I'm sorry. You kids said you wanted me to be straight with you. But you know what? Maybe I've been around Congress too long and maybe what we need are young people like yourself who believe anything's possible. And maybe anything *is* possible."

"She just wants you kids to know the odds," Mr. Taylor said. "But listen, remember when you kids were little and you wanted to play basketball with me, but you could never make a basket? You remember what I told you?"

Jamie and Keisha nodded in unison.

"You said just focus on how great it will feel to get that ball in the basket," Keisha said.

"And not think about all the times we missed," Jamie said.

"That's right. Focus only on what you want, not on what you don't want. It's good to know the odds so you understand what it's going to take to make this next basket. You've got a much higher hoop to aim for this time. But there's a lot more power in feeling like you'll make it than feeling like you won't."

Jamie thought this Congress stuff was like trying to run the obstacle course at the rec center with your knees tied together. How would Senator Pattern ever get enough votes? And it didn't seem like he and the CAPE could possibly help her.

But he used to think he'd never be able to shoot a basket either. Or do Indian martial arts. Or get millions of kids to join the CAPE. So maybe, just maybe, it *would* be possible if they did like Mr. Taylor said and only thought about how great it would feel to make this higher hoop.

CHAPTER 32

C ardinals crisscrossed the sky as a curtain of clouds parted to showcase a shimmering sun. The trees were at their autumn peak. When the wind tousled their branches, leaves swirled through the air in a floating ballet while others descended and blanketed the ground in a colorful patchwork.

Jamie and Tony huddled on picnic-table benches at their neighborhood park, waiting for Keisha and Raj to arrive so they could do another Adithada lesson.

Some anxious little thoughts swooped around the edges of Jamie's brain. He tried to dwell only on all the great things that had happened, but he was always on the alert for something bad to come along—even when things were good. Ever since his dad was fine one minute and gone the next.

No, no, no, he'd promised himself he wouldn't think about that anymore. But it seemed like everything with the CAPE was too good to be true right now, and there were so many things that could go wrong. Hadn't his mom warned him to be careful because a lot of people made a ton of money off fossil fuels? What about Mr. King Fuel and his threats? Or what if this whole thing went on for a long time and the kids got tired of boycotting and picketing? What if the money collections for the factory-worker kids dried up?

Well, this was exactly what he wasn't supposed to do. *Why am I such a thickhead?* Did he think he could keep bad things from happening if he worried about them? Didn't he learn anything when he stopped telling himself he was a dud that day during the Adithada lessons and saw himself as being good at it instead? *So, okay, snap out of it. Think about all the good stuff instead of making your brain hurt with bad stuff that hasn't even happened..*

Jamie felt an acorn ping against his forehead. It was Tony trying to get his attention.

"What's goin' on in there, dude?"

"Oh, not much," Jamie said. "I was just worrying about all the things that could go wrong."

"See, now that is the exact opposite of being cool." Tony let out his hyena laugh.

Jamie laughed with him, then got quiet again for a few moments before speaking. "Don't you ever worry … like even about what your dad might do when he's ticked off?"

"Let's see … umm … no. Not even for a nanosecond."

Jamie stared at Tony. He was afraid to say what he was thinking.

"What?" Tony said.

"It's just that sometimes I think you're lucky to even have a dad, cranky and all."

Tony glanced down at his index finger as he ran it back and forth between two of the boards in the picnic table. "I know you miss your dad, Jamie," he said softly.

"I'll be okay."

Tony turned his head and stared out at the park. "I used to miss when my dad was more like yours." His voice was barely a whisper.

Jamie's eyes misted. "What do you think happened?"

"I don't know. Could never figure it out. I heard him talk to my mom sometimes about how much power he was getting in the Senate. How important people were donating more money to his campaigns. You'd think that'd make him happy, right? But the weird thing was he became *un*happy and it seemed like he took it out on me. It got worse every year."

"Geez, Tony, that doesn't make any sense."

"I know." Tony shifted in his seat and the tone of his voice shifted too. "But who cares, it doesn't matter anymore. I'm used to him the way he is now and I won't let him get to me."

Jamie tried not to let his face show how bad he felt for Tony. And all this talk about their dads made Jamie miss his own dad that much more. Jamie may have crawled out of his cocoon of grief, but the emptiness his dad left was always there. He still wracked his brain trying to figure out how he could have saved him. Nothing he could have done, they said. But there must have been something.

"Hey, wonder who that guy was parked next to the curb," Tony said, gesturing behind Jamie toward the street that ran parallel to the park.

Jamie turned toward the street in time to see a car driving away. "What guy?"

"When he pulled up he looked like he was staring at us. Only sat there a couple of minutes, then drove off."

"What did he look like?" Jamie said.

"Couldn't really tell from here."

"Maybe he just had the wrong park."

Tony held his hand up to his eyes to shade them from the sun filtering through the trees. "Maybe. I've never seen him around here before."

CHAPTER 33

J amie expected this to be a special night because Keisha's mom said there was going to be another story on the CAPE, only bigger. Keisha had invited Jamie, Tony, and Raj to watch the news on her father's ninety-inch TV while he was out with his band buddies.

Jamie got a kick out of Keisha acting like they were in a movie theater with her sodas and bowls of popcorn and little bags of chocolate-covered raisins spread out on the coffee table. It was a fun place to watch anything, really, because of the way her dad had his den set up with two-person leather recliners and a surround-sound speaker system.

"Are you all comfortable?" Keisha's mother said when they settled in.

Tony and Raj grinned. "Oh, yes ma'am," Jamie said.

"Well, I'll be upstairs watching on my humble TV, and I know Keisha will take good care of you."

Keisha joined Tony on one of the big double chairs. "Hey, when I checked our website today we had reps from over one hundred and twenty-five countries signed up," Keisha said.

"I know!" Jamie said. "And Ms. Tollhouse told me the Planet Protection Council is still doing a great job getting the money collections to the striking factory-worker kids."

"It is a good thing we have that group helping us," Raj said.

"That's for sure," Keisha said. She grabbed the remote. "Are we ready now?" She turned on the TV to the news show.

Network anchor Kalyn Roberts introduced the top stories of the night and led with a report on the pope's visit to the United States. Video streamed of the pope riding in his popemobile, speaking to crowds outside the Vatican, blessing the poor, and visiting a children's hospital.

"One of the pope's most important stops in the United States will be his address to a joint meeting of Congress," the anchor reported. "He's expected to include comments from his encyclical on climate change and environmental pollution. Senate sources tell us it was Senator Lydia Pattern, a Catholic and Jesuit university graduate, who encouraged her party's Congressional leaders to extend the invitation to the Jesuit pope. Organizers are erecting a massive stage and jumbotron on the Capitol West Front Lawn so the throngs of people who want to see the leader of the Catholic Church will be able to watch and hear him on the giant screen."

"I think we should get there early so we have good seats in the bleachers when he drives by in his popemobile," Keisha said.

She passed around the bowl of popcorn. "Have any of you done your report for the pope's encyclical on the environment yet?"

"I've read most of the parts I'm writing my report about," Jamie said. "I think sometimes he sounds like a scientist. He seems to know a lot."

"Well, he used to be a chemist," Keisha said.

Raj nodded. "Even in India there is much respect for the pope."

"Yeah, he's … oh, wait, the story on the CAPE is starting," Keisha said.

At the anchor desk, Kalyn said, "Our foreign correspondents on several continents are reporting reactions to the CAPE, a worldwide children's group that's fighting fossil-fuel pollution and climate change. Here's Chin Min in Beijing, China."

An Asian reporter stood in front of a coal plant, its stacks emitting vast black and gray billows of smoke. "Members of the CAPE in China are trying to generate support for phasing out fossil fuels like the kind produced at this coal plant," he said.

Coal tumbled down long, metal chutes into a large container and was hauled away by train. "Coal is still king in China, the world's biggest polluter," Chin said. "As a result, its citizens are suffering with widespread respiratory diseases. But China has also become one of the world's largest producers of wind and solar power in response to an increasing demand for clean energy." The screen cut to footage of miles of spinning turbines on a large wind farm.

"Chin, any indication how the government there will react to the CAPE's demand for phasing out fossil fuels?" Kalyn said.

"China's leaders say they're already in a position to step up their clean-energy production," Chin said. "They're waiting to see what the other top polluters decide, especially the United States. This is Chin Min in Beijing."

"Our CAPE members from China recently reported that they sent their government a letter with several hundred names on it," Jamie said.

"Now here's a surprising player in the clean-energy movement," Kalyn said. "Our correspondent, Ammar Azeem, reports from the city of Dubai, one of the United Arab Emirates."

Behind Amma the desert was covered with solar panels for what looked like miles. "Dubai is building here what it says will be the world's largest solar-energy park, and it's planning to install rooftop solar on every home. Dubai and the rest of the United Arab Emirates are the world's sixth largest producers of oil, yet their federation has ambitious plans for switching over to renewable energy. They're already making large investments in the effort.

"The CAPE's plan fits well with this Arab federation's vision for a future clean-energy economy. This is Ammar Azeem in Dubai."

"Can you believe that?" Jamie said. "Even the big oil countries are into clean energy."

Kalyn introduced correspondent Maria Domingos in Salto Caxias, Brazil.

Maria reported from an overlook high above a huge dam. Water below the dam surged from openings in opposite sides of stone walls. "Hydropower plants like this one supply over eighty percent of Brazil's electricity," Maria said. "Brazil is Latin America's largest renewable-energy market, with investments in wind, hydropower, and solar. Since so much effort here is focused on clean energy, the people of Brazil are seriously considering the CAPE's pleas for a pollution-free world."

"Thank you, Maria," Kalyn said. "Up next is another country that has substantial investments in renewables and energy efficiency. We have a report from Omar Karim outside of Ouarzazate, Morocco in northern Africa."

Omar spoke loudly over the din of helicopter blades as he flew over hundreds of rows of curved mirrors in a desert. "These half a million mirrors follow the sun in a solar plant that covers ten square miles. When this project is completed it will provide power for over a million homes in Morocco with enough left over to export to Europe.

"The plant is a new innovation in solar energy because it stores that energy in the form of heated molten salt. This allows for the production of energy even at night and on cloudy days."

A huge storage tower that glowed near the top arose in the center of the field of mirrors. "Molten-salt-heat-storage technology is an important breakthrough in solar energy. This technology can go a long way toward supporting the youth movement's goal to replace fossil fuels with clean energy. Omar Karim in Morocco."

"We'll be back after this break with the latest on striking CAPE factory workers in India," Kalyn said.

"Wow," Jamie said. "Look at all those countries on different continents that are really into clean energy." He scooped up the last few kernels of popcorn. "I didn't know about that new solar invention that makes energy at night, did you, guys?"

"My father does, he just started research on it," Raj said.

Keisha collected the empty bowls. "Anybody want more popcorn?"

"Bring it on," Tony said. "Oh, wait, the news anchor's back."

Keisha turned up the volume. "… children are striking at Indian factories. Here's our foreign correspondent Deepak Agarwal in Allahabad, India."

Deepak stood outside a large factory where dozens of striking children in CAPE t-shirts marched in a picket line and carried signs that, translated on the TV screen, said *We Want Clean Air*. Nearby a group of angry-looking adults yelled at them and waved their fists.

Jamie got a bad vibe about the striking kids. Especially when he looked at the faces on the grown-ups who shouted at them.

"India has half of the world's twenty most polluted cities and the largest number of child laborers on the planet," Deepak said. The children seemed to ignore the angry onlookers and continued to wave their signs. "These children are striking as part of a global kid's movement to replace dirty energy."

The scene shifted to CAPE-attired American kids collecting pennies at the CAPE's Halloween parade. Deepak reported, "Children in richer nations are financially supporting these factory-worker kids with a massive fundraising drive launched by their international organization, the CAPE—Children Against Polluting Earth."

Back in India smog filled a highway and cars crawled bumper to bumper. Thick, gray air swirled around young children trudging along a dirty sidewalk. "Their message is resonating in this country where many of its residents are suffering with severe lung disorders from air pollution."

Deepak continued, "But although India wants more clean energy, the CAPE's efforts here are creating conflict. The factory owners are suing the Planet Defense Council, an international nonprofit organization that's funneling the CAPE collections to the factory-worker children. In response, the council is suing the factory owners for their exploitation of these children."

"The striking children are not only fighting for cleaner air but are getting a temporary break from working in deplorable conditions," Deepak said.

Footage showed children sitting at spinning wheels and hand looms, packing garments, and stacking boxes. "At some of these textile and garment factories, children are forced to work almost every day up to twelve hours a day for very little pay," Deepak said. "They've been found laboring in cramped, filthy, hot and humid buildings contaminated with mold and littered with stray electrical wires. Some of them are beaten if they stop working, and many of them suffer from health problems due to the poor working conditions."

Deepak ended his report, "Allahabad, India."

Keisha turned off the TV but kept staring at the blank screen.

"That's awful," Jamie said. "How can anybody let that happen?"

"*Let* it happen?" Tony said. "Didn't you see the adults yelling at the CAPE kids who were striking? They looked pretty angry that those kids weren't inside working."

"You'd think people there would be glad the kids didn't have to be treated like that in those awful factories," Keisha said.

"You do not understand my country," Raj said. "It *is* awful, and there are laws against child labor, but they are hard to enforce."

"Why don't the parents protect them?" Keisha said.

"Both the children and parents work because the parents cannot make enough money to support the family," Raj said. "There is a lot of poverty in my country and making poor children work has been happening for generations."

"You didn't have to do any of that, did you, Raj?" Keisha said.

"No," Raj said. "My parents were from a higher class. But child labor causes many of us shame for our country."

"What's going to happen to our striking CAPE kids, Raj?" Jamie said.

"As long as the families have money coming in from our collections, I think most of the parents will wait to see what happens. But once that stops the children will have to go back to work."

"Are we putting them in danger, Raj?" Jamie said.

"Well, there is much attention on them now in the news media so—"

"What about those lawsuits against the factory owners?" Keisha said. "Maybe they won't want to do anything to make their cases worse."

"Yes, that and the media attention will probably help protect the strikers for now," Raj said.

"How do you think the kids feel about all this?" Jamie said.

"Do you remember the CAPE member from India in our Facebook group who replied to questions about striking?" Raj said. "She reached me through Facebook messenger. Her name is Anaya, and she is the one who has been working with the other kids to organize the strikes. She told me they want to support the CAPE with their strikes because so many of their family and friends are sick from all the pollution."

"They're brave kids," Tony said. "We just need to make sure we don't let 'em down."

"I wish we could help all of them so they never, ever have to work in those factories again," Jamie said.

"Hey, Captain America, let's save one thing at a time, okay?" Tony said.

Jamie flicked a chocolate raisin at Tony. Then he turned to Raj. "But I'm still nervous about the way those grown-ups were acting. Raj, maybe you could stay in touch with Anaya so we know what's going on."

Raj nodded.

Jamie realized this was way more complicated than he'd expected. It all seemed like such a good idea at the time. And Raj seemed to think so too. Maybe Raj still did, but he was sensing something that made him nervous about those kids.

CHAPTER 34

On his way home from Keisha's house Jamie kept thinking about the kids in India and worrying if the CAPE would cause even more problems for them.

Why does life always have to be like a rain cloud bursting all over you in the middle of a sunny day? Those kids in India probably feel like life is one endless cloud burst, pounding them into the ground. It's so unfair.

When he reached his yard, he went out back and crumpled on the lawn under the big oak. The grass was soft and cushiony and welcoming. He curled his arms around his knees and listened to the night. It was full of tree sounds, branches stirring in the dark, leaves whispering in the breeze, an acorn falling to the earth where crickets chirped out their songs to their mates.

The moon shimmered on his garden, illuminating his beets, bell peppers, squash, carrots, and collards, all ripe for the final harvest. He took in the brisk night air and all the good smells, the smell of fall, the smell of nectar from his flowers.

Then there it was: the whooshing noise, followed by a blast of sparkles. Mr. James stood before him. "Hello, Jamie."

Jamie almost fell over. "Mr. James! I didn't think I'd see you again!"

"I've been thinking about you."

Jamie uncurled his arms from around his knees and propped himself up on his heels. "I'm glad to see you."

"Are you doing okay?"

"Not really."

Mr. James slowly lowered himself onto the lawn. "Do you want to tell me about it?"

"I'm afraid if I start talking I'm just going to sound like a whiner."

"Why don't you try anyway?"

Jamie straightened up a little and stared at the old man. "Did you know they treat a lot of children in India almost like slaves? Some of these kids are trying to help us save the planet and they can hardly feed themselves. Why doesn't anybody care about them? And how can people in the future decide it's okay to protect only the strong kids? And how come Mr. King Fuel doesn't care about children with weak lungs? And why are so many people treating our planet like a big sewer and leaving their mess to us kids? And why doesn't our country care enough about us to do more about it? Why does it seem like grown-ups only care about themselves?"

Jamie folded his arms across his narrow chest, then he took a deep breath and huffed it out like a steam engine running out of steam.

"I understand why you feel like that, Jamie. It can be pretty discouraging. But if you give it a little more thought, maybe you can see the other side of things."

"What other side?"

"Well, you know your dad cared about you very much, and your mom does too. And Raj's father shows he cares by trying to make a product that can reduce pollution. Senator Pattern is doing everything she can because she cares so much. Ms. Tollhouse has shown you that she cares too with all the help she's given you. Think about all the other adults who have been supporting your efforts with the CAPE. And, Jamie, I care. That's why I came back here."

"How do you know about all those people?"

"For now, let's just say I have the benefit of knowing certain things because I live in the future."

"Well, you're right about all of them." Jamie rubbed his forehead. "I guess I wonder if this job is too big for us. We're just kids."

"It doesn't matter what age you are. Remember what I told you last time about how the mind is the most potent force in the physical universe? Your power is just as strong as anybody else's."

"It doesn't feel that way."

"Did you have a chance to think about what we discussed last time, Jamie?"

"You mean the garden hose and our Creator?"

"Yes."

"Well, I haven't thought about it much, my mind's been so full of other things."

"Do you remember what I said about powerful energy always flowing through you?"

"I remember, and I liked the story."

"Do you believe it's true?"

"I don't know. I want to believe it."

"Our power comes from our Creator, and we have been given free will to use that power. So hidden away in each of us is endless potential to create much good in the world and for ourselves."

"But if I've got all this power in me, how do I get to it?"

"Well, first it helps to get rid of false beliefs about yourself. Think you might have a few of those?"

"I wish they were false."

"You will become what you believe about yourself. If you don't like what you think about yourself, believe something better."

"I'd like to believe I'm confident and brave like Captain America."

"What's stopping you?"

"My false beliefs?"

"What do you think, Jamie?"

"Well, I guess I'm the one who decided I was a wimp."

"So maybe you could stop yourself from thinking that, along with any other negative thoughts that get in the way of you using your power."

"Like the dirt in the garden hose clogging up the flow of the water."

"Yes, just like that."

Jamie raised his eyebrows. "Is that all of it?"

"Well, it would also help if you replaced all your fears with gratitude. Sincere gratitude creates a feeling of openness and joy that not only makes you feel good but prepares your mind for doing good things in your life."

"I do have a lot I'm grateful for."

"I know you do, so focus on that. When you prepare your garden to plant seeds you use rich, fertile soil and nutrients, right? And then you see beautiful plants rise up.

You would never allow anything toxic in your garden and expect to grow something worthwhile, would you?"

"I get it." Jamie paused and clasped and unclasped his hands a few times. "Well, I *am* grateful for the way the CAPE's taken off, so not *everything* is worse like I first said. We've got a ton of really dedicated kids all over the planet doing an awesome job and lots of people supporting us."

"That's excellent, and it is a lot to be grateful for, Jamie."

Jamie still wasn't certain how to handle everything he was worrying about, but his shoulders felt a little lighter.

"Thanks, Mr. James. I'll think about what you said. And thanks for coming back to see me."

"You're going to do fine, Jamie. Look at how much you've already done." Mr. James smiled, then stood up and set his energy vibrator.

Jamie watched him until he was gone.

He leaned over his garden and thought about what Mr. James had told him. He plucked a ripe raspberry from its vine and popped it into his mouth. It brought back a memory from that day his dad helped him dig up this little wild raspberry bush to transplant into his garden.

"We'll have this as a reminder of our trip," his dad had said to him. "It'll come back every year."

"I have the perfect spot for it," Jamie had said.

"I think you're a natural at gardening, Jamie. So nurturing to all your plants. You'll be a good father someday."

"Thanks, Dad. I just want to take good care of them. I can't explain it, but being with them makes me happy."

His dad smiled. "That's the way I feel about you."

A single tear arose at the corner of Jamie's eye. He dabbed at it with his fingertip. Then he dug his hand into the soft, rich earth as if to draw strength from its life-giving source.

PART THREE

CHAPTER 35

Colton knew before he got to Thomas's office this wasn't going to go well. He'd watched all the news reports on the CAPE, and he was sure Thomas had too. Colton felt the familiar pressure on his chest, so he pulled out his bronchial meds and swallowed them in hopes of heading off any spasms.

The minute he arrived the assistant hustled him through the door. Thomas was standing at his wall bar, drink in hand, instead of his usual spot. He didn't offer Colton a drink.

"Do you remember when I told you I had a bad feeling about those kids?" Thomas said.

"Yeah … right after that first interview with that scaredy-cat kid Jamie."

"I warned you, and you just laughed at me."

"You don't have to rub my nose in it."

"You're not laughing now, are you?"

Colton's mouth tightened.

"And did you do anything to stop them?"

"I kept an eye on 'em."

"I repeat, did you do anything to stop them?"

"I'm going to stop them now."

"Kind of like closing the barn door after the cows get out, isn't it?"

"It's not too late. I'll take care of it."

Thomas turned back to his bar and refilled his drink. Colton waited. Thomas flicked his hand over his shoulder, his sign of dismissal.

Colton left and thought back to that day. Of course he'd laughed. The kid and his crazy crusade were a joke. But now the little pansy and his pansy followers had actually done a lot of what they said. Colton realized he'd been so preoccupied with Thomas's assignments he hadn't stayed on top of how fast their movement had mush-roomed.

But the thing that bugged him most was: Where did that Jamie kid get the gall to think he could take on the whole world? When Colton was a kid, he'd never have dared to stand up to adults like that. Hah, like what he said would actually have mattered even if he'd had the guts to speak up. He'd always kept his mouth shut about the miserable conditions in the mine and the long hours he'd worked under the legal age limit.

The first time he'd ridden into the mine he thought he'd pass out from claustrophobia. With his back flat against the top of that mantrip vehicle, his nose only missed the ceiling by eight inches the whole two-mile trip down.

Then there was that day he'd been alone when a mine rat raced between his legs and he fell, knocking off and breaking the headlamp attached to his hard hat. The total darkness made him feel the most helpless he'd ever felt in his life. He couldn't remember much after that except for the other light coming at him, then blood dripping from a gash in his forehead.

That mealy-mouthed Jamie would never last two seconds in a mine. But here the kid was teaming up with Ms. High and Mighty Pattern to replace the time-honored trade of Colton's family.

Thomas didn't have to say much this time for Colton to agree something had to be done about the CAPE. He headed over to Richard's office.

~

Richard had thought about having his assistant tell Colton he wasn't in. He wished he never had to deal with him again. But that's all it was—wishful thinking—and he knew Colton would keep scurrying back like a tenacious cockroach.

No sooner had Colton come in the door than he'd started pacing in front of Richard's desk, wired as a cheetah, shoulders drawn up so high they buckled the seams on his finely tailored suit. He'd brought with him some bushy-red-haired guy he called Sharkey, a big fireplug of a man who looked like he'd slept in his clothes. Sharkey stared idly out the window from a corner of the room.

"How in blazes did these kids ever get this far?" Colton said. "And yours one of 'em!"

"I learned about my son when you did, and I stopped his involvement immediately," Richard said.

"Better do more than that. Some Congressional idiots are actually considering the kids' insane demands. Right when my clients are pushing Congress to pass four important bills."

"Calm down, Colton. They're just kids, a novelty. Nobody's really going to take them seriously."

"The hell you say. The news media's jumping all over this damn thing."

"In a couple of weeks they'll move on to the next oddball story."

"What about those striking factory-worker kids? If that goes on long enough, a lot of those countries will scramble to save their economic butts—and so will the countries that buy from them."

"Well, companies in our country aren't supposed to buy from child-labor factories, so what do we care?"

"You're so naïve and short-sighted, Richard." Colton started to sit down and shot back up again. "And what about their boycott right here in the good ol' USA? I'm already getting calls from some heavy-hitter business clients."

"How long do you think a bunch of kids can keep that up?"

"This bunch of kids has a pending bill supporting them! Has Ms. High and Mighty lost her mind?"

"Pattern is an environmental extremist. Come on, Colton, how do you think her bill can ever pass when our party has so much control?"

"Not everybody is toeing the party line these days, and you know it. Too many are starting to think like Pattern."

"So what. We've still got the numbers. It'll never even make it out of her committee."

"Maybe not yet. But I'm telling ya … people are being taken in by these kids and their whining about saving the planet. Before you know it we'll be facing a global train wreck."

"Colton, Colton. Listen to yourself. You're blowing this all out of proportion."

"Don't patronize me, Richard."

"Well, what do you expect me to do about it?"

"Stop it now. Or you'll never get another dime from our clients. You decide."

Colton stormed out, Sharkey trailing him.

~

Richard decided he was sick and tired of that obnoxious Colton. Who did he think he was with his arrogant lectures and threats? And what audacity, treating Richard as if he worked for him. Wasn't there any respect for the office anymore? *That's the problem with these lobbyists. They throw a lot of money around and they think they're in charge. As if the voters don't matter one bit. As if none of us here have any principles.*

He leaned against the window frame and peered out at the darkening sky and the shadows filling the trees. *How did I ever get to this point?* When he'd started out, he was confident he could make a difference. He wanted to be the kind of man who stood for something. Something good and honorable. He was going to help the people back home live better lives. He was going to help make this a stronger, more prosperous country.

And now this is what I've come to? Errand boy for slimy lobbyists who would as soon steal your soul as buy your vote?

Richard observed his reflection in the window. His face looked slack and his eyes hollow. He was in too deep. It was too late. He'd gone too far down this path to retrace his steps.

He stared out at the wind shifting in the trees. The familiar numbness enveloped him. Then he buzzed his assistant and told her to get Arni Sanseria on the phone. He waited.

"Putting him through now, sir."

"Arnie?"

"Hello, Richard, how are you?"

"Could be better." His voice was flat. "I don't like having to make this call, Arni." Richard paused. "My committee may not approve renewed funding for your biofuel grant."

Silence. Then, "But it was supposed to be renewed for five more years."

The strain in Arni's voice wasn't easy to ignore. Richard liked Arni. He was a hard-working, decent man. Their sons hung around together. When Arni had first described his research, Richard agreed it could lead to a lot of new jobs, so back then he didn't hesitate to get his committee's support for the grant. But now he needed to put all that aside. He sought refuge in his numbness.

"Well, that's true, but it's competing with other projects. Some things have to be cut," Richard said.

"We are making some very important breakthroughs in our research, and if we have to stop, many of my people will lose their jobs," Arni said.

Yes, Richard already knew that. Of course he knew that. This whole thing was such a crock. But he had no choice. Richard steeled himself. "Look, I'll be straight with you, Arni. Your son's and his friends' involvement with this CAPE group is really complicating things around here."

"Why are you dragging the CAPE into this?"

"These kids are putting a lot of us in a very difficult position."

"Are you giving me an ultimatum?"

"Let's just say I'm giving you a heads up. I'm sorry, Arni." Richard ended the call. He told his assistant he wasn't taking any more visitors for the rest of the day.

Richard got up and opened a cabinet. He pulled out a glass and a bottle of vodka. He knew it would keep the numbness going. At least for a little while.

~

Jamie was in Raj's kitchen getting ready to leave after helping his friend work on the model rocket he'd bought at the planetarium. When Jamie heard Mr. Sanseria's phone conversation, he wrinkled his forehead and stared at Raj.

Mr. Sanseria sunk down at the kitchen table and put his head in his hands. Raj's mom came to his side. "What is wrong?"

He looked up at her. "My grant may not be renewed. I may have to eliminate our biofuel research and lay off many of my employees."

"That does not make sense," Raj said. "Making clean energy is more important than ever. Why would the government not want to keep funding your research?"

"It is not your problem, son."

"Sir, we heard you mention the CAPE?" Jamie said.

"There's nothing more I can tell you."

"We need to know, Father," Raj said. "Who is trying to stop you? Is it because of the CAPE?"

Raj's dad rubbed his forehead. "I will deal with this, boys. Just please be careful."

Jamie and Raj retreated to his bedroom.

"Raj, this is awful."

"I know."

"I have to go home now to babysit my sister, but why don't you come over after supper and we'll try to figure this out?"

"But what can we do?"

"I don't know—but we need to try."

Jamie was sure their luck was starting to run out, just as he'd expected.

See, that's just the way life is, no matter what Mr. James says.

CHAPTER 36

Jamie was almost done preparing Katie's breathing treatment with the tabletop nebulizer on her nightstand. Katie rested against her propped-up pillows and looked up at him with a weak smile. This was his first time operating the machine alone since his mother had taught him how to use it, and he wanted to be careful to do it right. The doctor had increased Katie's medication dose, so Jamie needed to check for signs that she was easily inhaling the medicated mist pumped through the plastic tubing.

He attached the pediatric face mask over Katie's nose and mouth. "There, munchkin, feel okay?" She nodded with trusting eyes.

He swept up wisps of her hair so they wouldn't get caught as he pulled the straps on the mask over her curly-topped head. All set now, he turned on the nebulizer and gazed at his sister, her small, oval face half-covered and hooked up to an electrical machine. Tiny face. Tiny lungs. He didn't want to think about how hard those sick lungs had to work just to keep her alive.

He turned his head away so she couldn't see his face. Katie pointed up at the ceiling to the glow-in-the-dark stars he'd affixed there and motioned for him to turn off the light. He darkened the room, settled in beside her, and listened quietly to her labored breathing. They stared at the glowing stars together on their make-believe sky.

Having her close to him like this helped him relax. The doctor had told his mother today that there still was very little improvement in Katie's condition. She had some good days and some bad days, but the bad days seemed to be more frequent. He was giving her this treatment now because this was one of the bad days.

The steady sound waves of the machine made him sleepy. After a while he dozed off and awoke with a jerk of his head. Katie's time on the nebulizer was just about up. She was playing an imaginary flute with her fingers to the rhythm of her breathing.

Jamie had just finished removing her face mask and unhooking her from the equipment when he heard the doorbell ring. "Wanna watch some TV, munchkin? I think that's Raj." He reached for the remote for her TV. Katie nodded and rubbed the little respirator creases from around her nose and mouth.

Jamie ran downstairs and pulled open the door for Raj.

"I'm sorry about what's happening to your dad, Raj."

"Me too, just when I was starting to think America was a great country."

"Are you trying to be funny?"

"No, I mean it. Look at what Senator Pattern is doing and all the other people who are helping us."

"Yeah, and then there's all the people who want us to fail," Jamie said. "But why would anybody want to stop your dad's research? How could anyone be afraid of algae?"

Raj hesitated. "I think there is something my father is not telling us."

"Like what?"

"Like why the government would not want to keep funding his research. And when my father would not tell us why the person on the phone was bringing up the CAPE."

"It must be somebody in the government who thinks what we're doing is wrong or will cause them problems," Jamie said.

Raj rubbed his forehead. "What if it is someone who is trying to get back at Senator Pattern by shutting us down?"

"That seems like a roundabout way to do that, though, Raj. Wouldn't it be easier to just get everybody to gang up on Senator Pattern against her bill?"

"Maybe it is someone in the government who thinks replacing fossil fuels will hurt the country."

"But I don't know anyone who thinks we shouldn't have any clean energy at all, so why stop your dad?"

Raj nodded. "You are right. Maybe the real reason is not my father's research. He is still far from a product he can sell. It makes more sense that somebody wants to get rid of us by threatening my father."

"Okay, so let's think about the people we know who are angry about us."

"Government people who also know the connection between my father and me and the CAPE."

"The first government person I think of when I think about angry people who know us is ... Tony's father," Jamie said. He paused. "Hey, I just remembered hearing your father call the person on the phone 'Richard' like he knew him." He was silent for another moment. "I bet it *is* Tony's father."

"I remember that name too, and I also remember my father saying another time that Senator Newsome's committee approved his grant. So why would he want to end it now?"

"I don't think Tony's father would try to stop us just because he doesn't agree with us."

"But he might have a reason that has to do with his job." Raj said.

"What if somebody is using Tony's father to get at us?"

"It is logical."

"It is, isn't it?"

"So who can we get to help us?"

Jamie thought a moment. "We need to come up with somebody who knows Tony's father."

"Somebody who has ... how do you say it in America? ... the balls to take him on?"

Jamie tapped his head, then grinned. "I think I know... I'm gonna call Keisha."

CHAPTER 37

Jamie had never been to the Capitol Building. Inside, every clatter of shoes on the stone floors echoed back from the high ceilings. Sunlight poured through the ring of windows in the huge dome.

Once they got through security Keisha's mom led Jamie, Keisha, and Raj to Senator Lydia Pattern's office where the senator leaned against the edge of her desk talking on the phone. She grinned at them and waved for them to come on in.

"Yeah, the pope's visit couldn't have come at a better time," the senator said to the person on the phone.

Then as she listened her grin disappeared. "I know it's a tough fight, but we need to keep the pressure on ..."

Her free hand rubbed the back of her neck. "No deal. The kids are right. We have to wean ourselves off fossil fuels. Period."

Jamie did a little cheer inside.

The senator slammed her hand on her desk. "Don't give me that bull. We already have the way. What we need is the will ..."

Yep, Keisha's dad was right, thought Jamie. A tough cookie.

"Yes, yes, I know very well how many on the committee are from fossil-fuel states ...

"No, you don't need to remind me how hard it's going to be to get the bill to the full Senate. I don't care. We show them how their dirty industries are sickening and killing their constituents ..."

Red blotches appeared on her neck and crept up her cheeks. "Well, I wasn't surprised when he pulled us out of the global climate pledge and started his fossil-fuel binge. Do you know how crazy it makes me that he's ripping up our environmental protections and trying to increase drilling in our national parks and oceans? But Congress is his equal and we need to step up to the plate ..."

The red blotches darkened. "Well, of course, he'll want to veto my bill, but we have public opinion on our side and an international kids' movement. We'll just have to get a veto-proof majority."

Jamie wished Tony could meet her. He'd really like her. *She sounds like such a fighter. Our fighter!*

The senator smiled at Jamie and his friends. "Hey, the public's getting behind this because of those kids," she said into the phone. "Let's use that to keep up the pressure to get it to the senate floor. In the meantime, I've also lined up some pretty persuasive speakers for our public hearing. You may be surprised at what you hear. I have to go."

Senator Pattern hung up the phone, strode over to them, and shook their hands. She started with Keisha. "It's good to see you and your friends, Keisha."

"Thank you, ma'am. You remember Jamie Sawyer? And this is Raj Sanseria."

"I've been following all of you in the news reports," the senator said. "I'm glad you kids are doing so much for our planet."

"You too, Senator," Jamie said. "We're all excited about your bill."

"Now I just need to keep my fellow senators from wimping out on me." Senator Pattern glanced at her phone then back to them. "Well, I understand you kids have a problem."

"I'll leave you kids with Senator Pattern," Keisha's mom said.

The senator closed her door. "Please come sit down."

~

An hour later Jamie scampered out of her office and down the hall with his friends. He was sure they looked like a trio of Cheshire cats.

As they headed from the Capitol for the Metrorail, Jamie noticed the bald guy he'd seen at the parade. The man ducked half-hidden in the doorway of a building across the street. Jamie nudged Keisha to look in the man's direction, and when she did he scurried away.

"Did you see him?" Jamie said.

Keisha nodded, eyes wide. "That's the same guy! Remember him from the parade, Raj? Why do you think he's spying on us?"

"No clue," Jamie said.

"We should tell our parents," Raj said. "Just so they know."

Jamie would tell his mom, but he was determined not to let this guy creep him out. At least he'd try.

CHAPTER 38

A few days later Richard hesitated when his assistant told him Senator Pattern was there to see him. He had cosponsored some national parks legislation with her in the past and admired how effective she was at working the system. But he didn't like her extreme position on fossil fuels and couldn't imagine what she might want with him today.

"Hello, Richard," Lydia said, with a big smile and a strong grip when she shook his hand. Richard liked a firm handshake.

"I'm sorry I don't have a lot of time for you today, Lydia." He offered her a chair and retreated behind his desk. She leaned back, her long arms spread across the top of the chair like she was settling in for a nice, friendly chat. That confident air about her impressed him, but sometimes it annoyed him too.

"I guess you know you're creating havoc with that bill of yours," Richard said and chuckled. He was convinced it wasn't going anywhere.

"Seems that way."

"Surely you're not here to ask for my support."

"Well now, Richard, I wouldn't be foolish enough to ask for your support on anything that would disappoint your fossil-fuel buddies."

"That's good to hear." Richard cleared his throat. "So what can I do for you?"

"I want Sanseria to continue his research on algae biofuel."

Richard was caught off guard. How did she find out so fast he'd threatened to cancel Arni's grant?

"I don't think that's any of your concern, Lydia."

"Well, it concerns me a great deal."

"There are many worthy projects, but my committee can't recommend funding for all of them. After careful review based on extensive impartial criteria and thorough analysis, my committee decided the algae project was one of the ones that had to be dropped."

"Actually, I think you wrangled enough support on your committee to cut Sanseria's funding, and I'm asking you to un-wrangle it."

"That's crazy. I'm the one who recommended funding for the project in the first place."

"I know. And I also know when you go to bat for a project, you support it all the way. So something's not adding up here."

"I already told you, we can't support them all."

"I'm sure you'll reconsider."

"Why would I do that?" The hairs on Richard's neck started to bristle.

"Well, I've recently found out some interesting things about you, Richard, and I think some of those interesting things might help change your mind."

"What interesting things?"

"Certain large, illegal financial gifts."

Richard felt his blood pressure shoot up, but he forced a tight smile. "I didn't think you were one to listen to false rumors, Lydia, and you certainly can't prove it."

Lydia grinned. "Can't I? Good day, Richard."

Richard clenched his teeth while he watched her stroll out the door. How dare she try to intimidate him. He wondered if she was bluffing ... but he couldn't take the chance if she wasn't. He never saw it coming: she'd just bustled in, ambushed him, and bustled out.

He played back in his head his conversation with Arni, the sound of Arni's voice when Richard told him about cutting the funding. Arni must have felt ambushed too. Richard was almost relieved that doing Lydia's bidding meant he wouldn't have to live with that guilt anymore.

He rested his elbows on his desk with his arms straight up and dropped his head into his hands. First Colton and now Lydia. An image of a puppet flashed though his mind. And the thing that really bugged him ... he was the one who'd given them the strings.

CHAPTER 39

The US Senate Kennedy Caucus Room was filled to capacity with three hundred people. Another one hundred people were escorted to a nearby overflow room to watch the proceedings live on C-SPAN.

Keisha's mom made sure Keisha, Jamie, and Raj got there early enough so they could get seats next to the aisle with a good view of the speakers and Senator Pattern's committee members. Jamie couldn't stop gaping at the magnificent room. The ceiling was so high he had to tilt his head all the way back to scope out its beautiful gold-and-white carvings and gigantic chandeliers. This seemed like an important room for very important business, and there he was right in the middle of it.

Keisha's mom had told them there was so much interest in the senator's public hearing she had to schedule this big meeting space for it. He hoped that was a good sign.

Raj leaned over to Jamie and Keisha. "My father got a call from Senator Pattern that he still has his grant."

"I knew we could count on her!" Jamie said.

Keisha bobbed her head. "She's totally major league."

Senator Pattern and her committee members arrived. After introducing the committee, she thanked the audience for coming and told them this was the first of several public hearings of the US Senate Committee on Energy and Natural Resources to receive input on the impact of fossil fuels on human health and the environment. Then she introduced the first speaker, Ms. Francis Powell, a researcher on children's environmental health at a major university.

Ms. Powell hauled a large cloth bag to the speaker's desk and piled two high stacks of booklets on either side of her. "I'm here to speak today for those who can't vote and who have no paid representation. I'm here on behalf of our country's children. These studies are just a sampling of the vast amount of research by dozens of health organizations and medical practitioners documenting the impacts of fossil-fuel pollution on our youngest and most vulnerable citizens.

"Let's start with what's in the air we breathe. The combined wastes from coal combustion, oil refineries, and extraction of natural gas produce carbon dioxide, nitrogen dioxide, sulfur dioxide, hydrocarbons, benzene, mercury, toxic microscopic particles, black carbon, and methane. Methane leaks out from natural-gas drilling sites, pipelines, and fracking sites and is thirty-four times more toxic than carbon dioxide. Any one of these substances is detrimental to human health.

"This pollution soup also often includes ground ozone, which damages the cells that line the respiratory tract. When sunlight heats some of the gases released from burning fossil fuels, smog is formed. Smog is harmful to both the lungs and the heart and, in fact, reduces lung function even in healthy people.

"Human-made smog is derived from burning coal, driving gas-burning vehicles, industrial waste, forest and agricultural fires, and photochemical reactions to all these emissions."

Raj nudged Jamie. "New Delhi is the world's most polluted capital city because of its smog."

"Another toxic air pollutant is carbon monoxide, most often from automobile exhaust," Ms. Powell said. "It passes through the lungs into circulating red blood cells, binding tightly to hemoglobin and blocking the blood's ability to carry oxygen throughout the body."

Jamie's breath caught in his chest.

"We can see smog. But do you think that because we can't see most of these other toxins in the air that they aren't doing any damage? Actually, visible or not, they're taking a huge toll on human health in our country in the form of premature deaths from heart and lung disease, pneumonia, asthma, cardiovascular ills, chronic bronchitis, and upper and lower respiratory diseases.

"So if dirty energy is a major health concern for adults, just imagine what it does to young children who are much more vulnerable due to narrower airways and lungs that are not yet fully developed. Children also inhale more pollutants per pound of body weight because they breathe a proportionately greater volume of air. But their lungs are far less equipped to protect them.

"Irritation caused by air pollutants that would produce only a slight response in an adult can raise havoc in the airways of a small child with immature defense systems. The toxins from burning fossil fuels can stunt the growth of children's lungs, permanently reducing their ability to breathe."

Jamie whispered to Keisha, his voice shaky, "Oh, Keisha, what's going to happen to Katie?"

"Maybe that hasn't happened to her yet, Jamie, you don't know for sure," Keisha said. "But boy, what a lot of junk in the air."

"I bet most people think it is not there unless they can see it," Raj said.

Ms. Powell continued. "… Several studies confirm that even fetuses have incurred damage when fossil-fuel pollution inhaled by their mothers passes through the placenta. Exposure to babies in the womb can exert multiple toxic effects including reduction in lung function, increased risk of chronic respiratory function, genetic damage, and cancer."

Jamie elbowed Keisha again. "She's talking about bad stuff happening to babies that aren't even born yet!"

"These debilitating conditions are growing each decade. For example, air pollution is an established trigger of childhood asthma—the major cause of chronic illness in our young citizens. In cities with poor air quality, even previously healthy children are developing asthma and other lung disorders. There are now seventy-five percent more asthma cases in the United States than in 1980. That's a shocking increase by any standard. We're concerned about the escalating number of Americans who are being deprived of the most basic of human functions—the ability to breathe freely."

Keisha grasped Jamie's hand. "With that many people they'll have to do something."

"Yeah, but I bet this is why Katie isn't getting better," Jamie said.

She gave his hand a little squeeze. "But she will, Jamie, you must believe that she will."

A wave of murmurs rolled through the public hearing room while Ms. Powell packed up her stacks of studies. Senator Pattern asked for questions from her committee.

Senator Wade Ringling spoke first. "Thank you, Ms. Powell. Aren't there a lot of factors that can cause or aggravate asthma? Like product chemicals in the home and other allergens?"

"That's true, Senator," Ms. Powell said. "But we also know that one third of asthma is due to environmental exposure, and the more fossil fuels we've burned over the last three decades, the faster the rate of increase for asthma and other pulmonary diseases. Conversely, cities with anti-pollution policies have seen a drop in the percentage of their children with respiratory ailments. For example, children in Southern California now have higher lung function and lower rates of asthma and bronchitis, thanks to years of clean-air laws in that state."

"Ms. Powell," Senator Jonathan Vine jumped in, "why does government regulation always have to be the answer to problems in our country instead of allowing businesses that are important to our prosperity determine how best to serve their customers?"

"I hope you all will read some of the reports from the American Lung Association, the National Health Association, and the American Public Health Association," Ms. Powell responded, "and try to put a little more credence into what you learn from them than what you hear from those who are making huge profits from fossil fuels."

"Good one!" Jamie whispered.

CHAPTER 40

When there were no more questions of Ms. Powell, Senator Pattern introduced the next speaker, Thomas Mandel, president and CEO of King Fuel.

Jamie nudged Keisha. "That's him! The guy we saw on the news who flipped off kids with weak lungs."

Keisha nodded. "Oh, yeah, and he said mean things about the CAPE. Maybe you could trip him on his way out."

"Keisha!" Raj said.

Keisha giggled. "Only kidding."

While Mr. Mandel approached the speaker's desk, a studious-looking man handed a booklet to each of the committee members. Mr. Mandel removed a folded paper from inside his suit pocket and glanced at it. "The study I'm having distributed to each of you is based on solid research regarding fossil fuels and the environment. It confirms that some of the so-called scientific studies linking fossil fuels with climate change and pollution are based upon flawed data."

Some of the committee members flicked through the pages of their booklets.

"In fact," Mr. Mandel said, "this study indicates there is evidence that increased atmospheric carbon dioxide is environmentally helpful."

Mr. Mandel glimpsed at his paper again. "The research here demonstrates not only that the effect of atmospheric carbon dioxide on the environment is likely to be benign, but that greenhouse gases cause plant life, and the animal life that depends on it, to thrive. There's a very simple reason for this. As most biologists know, plant life takes in carbon dioxide and expels oxygen for us to breathe. So the more carbon dioxide in the air, the healthier our plant life is, and the healthier we all are."

"Did some scientist really say that?" Jamie whispered to Raj.

Raj rolled his eyes.

"Your premise is misleading," Senator Ralph Walton said. "You're ignoring the greenhouse effect of carbon dioxide, and you're not addressing all the other toxins released by burning fossil fuels."

Mr. Mandel leaned forward. "This whole charade was started by advocates of government control and alternative-energy production. They're predicting a ridiculous array of exaggerated conditions and trying to blame them on fossil fuels. It's pure imagination disguised as science to prevent us from using our natural resources. There are no good reasons to keep us from more drilling on public lands and in the Arctic and Atlantic Oceans."

"What about the impact on our oceans, marine life, and shorelines when there's an oil spill?" Senator Frederick Tander said.

"The risk is extremely low, and the benefits far outweigh any potential risk. We have millions of acres of ocean floor ripe for drilling, and we ought to stop being afraid to take advantage of this storehouse of riches."

"Mr. Mandel, it appears one of the concerns about ocean drilling is that we'll experience more catastrophic oil spills like the Exxon Valdez supertanker that hit a reef off the Alaskan coast," Senator Tander said. "You may recall that it dumped millions of gallons of crude oil into the pristine Prince William Sound and was considered one of the most devastating human-caused environmental disasters in our country's history."

"An isolated incident," Mr. Mandel said.

"What about the BP oil well that blew out in the Gulf of Mexico?" Senator Tander said. "Many of us watched in horror at the scenes on our TVs as that oil well spewed five times more crude oil than the Valdez and polluted six hundred square miles off the Gulf Coast. As you must know, Mr. Mandel, that was the largest marine oil spill in the history of the world."

"Things have changed since then," Mr. Mandel said. "There are safeguards in place that didn't exist before."

"Those industry safeguards are dangerously lax," Senator Tander said. "And this administration's plan to roll back safety measures and oversight will greatly increase the risk."

"I have a question, Mr. Mandel," Senator John Pariser said. "What kind of measures can protect your ocean rigs from being blown apart by large-scale earthquakes on the West Coast or super hurricanes on the East Coast?"

"Well, if we worried about every remote possibility for what could go wrong, we'd never make any progress," Mr. Mandel said. "Everywhere you turn, the government is using a heavy hand to control the energy output in our country, and it needs to stop."

Jamie whispered to Keisha, "I wish we could go up there and show our video of Virginia Beach seventy years from now."

"Yeah, but I bet he'd say it's just another 'isolated incident.'"

CHAPTER 41

A fter Mr. Mandel finished, Senator Pattern introduced Ms. Norma Ratherson, an heir to Etone, a major oil and gas company. An elderly woman with white hair slowly made her way to the speaker's desk.

"I want to talk about carbon and climate studies by Etone, which was founded by my great-grandfather." She lowered herself to her seat. "In the 1970s Etone scientists were leaders in exposing the harmful impact of carbon emissions on the planet, and they warned about the future outcome. However, over the next decade the company financed think tanks and researchers who publicly denied the very science the company pioneered."

Ms. Ratherson sipped from a water glass on the desk. "In the midst of the company's denial campaign, its scientists warned management about what they called 'future global catastrophic weather conditions' that could only be averted by major reductions in fossil-fuel combustion. These findings were not released to the company's shareholders or to securities regulators. Internally, though, Etone not only accepted the correlation between burning fossil fuels and climate change but even projected business opportunities such as drilling for oil once enough polar sea ice melted in the Arctic."

Ms. Ratherson eyed each of the committee members. "Allow me to crystallize the point here. This is an oil-and-gas company whose own scientists sounded dire warnings against the continued burning of these fuels, but the company publicly denied what it knew to be true. I'm here today to insist that none of us can afford to live in denial."

She took another sip of water. "I inherited substantial shares of Etone stock. I recently donated all those shares to my family's nonprofit, which is investing the proceeds in clean energy. Other stockholder members of my family and I have repeatedly warned Etone representatives that they must transition to a clean-energy company."

"Thank you for your comments, Ms. Ratherson," Senator Sam Bernard said. "Are you saying we should all run out and sell any stock we have in fossil fuels? Do you think that's an economically responsible solution?"

Ms. Ratherson fixed a steely stare on the senator. "What I'm saying, sir, is that none of us can keep investing in dirty energy if we don't want to foist planetary devastation on our children and grandchildren."

There were no more questions. The old woman, her back straight as a ramrod, rose and walked out of the committee room.

"Boy, that took guts to tell on her own family's company!" Jamie said.

"My father would like her," Raj said. "She took all that money out of dirty energy and put it into clean energy."

~

Lionel Collings, a climatologist, took his seat as the hearing's next speaker. He stared intently at each of the committee members.

"I think there's been a lot of misinformation about our changing climate," he said. "First of all, the Earth's climate has gone through cycles of cooling and heating all on its own for billions of years. Second, warming over the past century has resulted primarily from natural processes such as fluctuations in the sun's heat and ocean currents. And third, glaciers have been growing and receding for thousands of years due to natural causes, not human activity."

"Mr. Collings, but if we're talking about scientific evidence, don't your conclusions have to be based on something measurable rather than on general assumptions?" Senator Lucas Browning said. "When you have climate scientists in many different parts of our planet measuring and recording sea-level rise and ice volumes, recording temperatures, collecting air and water samples, running computer-model simulations and historical climate reconstructions from ice cores, ocean sediments, tree rings, and other measurable indicators—and they all reach the same conclusion that climate change is the result of human activity—does that not provide valid scientific evidence?"

"Anybody can use numbers to their advantage," Mr. Collings said.

"Let's set aside the question of climate change and just look specifically at air pollution from burning fossil fuels," Senator Pattern said. "Will you acknowledge that burning fossil fuels produces several kinds of greenhouse gases that cause air pollution?

"With seven billion humans on Earth, there is likely some impact on nature." Mr. Collings glared at Senator Pattern. "However, I don't think anyone can prove to what degree human activity actually affects the air we breathe. I think this whole controversy about fossil fuels was started by radical environmentalists who have their own agenda and scientists who want to milk the government for high-dollar research contracts."

"Are we 'radical environmentalists'?" Jamie whispered to Keisha and chuckled. "Or non-radical environmentalists?"

CHAPTER 42

As soon as Mr. Collings left the speaker's table, Senator Pattern called on Mr. William Brown, chairman and CEO of Hunter Inc., an American multinational investment firm.

"I'm here today to talk about return on investment and job growth," Mr. Brown said. "There are three times as many jobs in wind and solar as in coal. My company has invested thirty billion dollars in clean energy because, based on our economic forecasting and international trends, we know that the largest future growth in energy profits is going to come from renewables. In fact, shifting from fossil fuels to clean energy represents a *multitrillion-dollar* investment opportunity.

"Now, why do I say this? Countries all over the world are investing heavily in clean energy and new clean-energy technologies."

"Raj, did you hear that?" Jamie said. "Trillions in clean energy. Great for your dad, huh?"

Raj grinned.

"For example, would it surprise you to know that China, the world's largest polluter, is making colossal investments in green energy? Do you think this is happening because

China's leaders suddenly became environmentalists? No. Not directly."

"We've got a ton of kids from China as CAPE members," Jamie whispered to Keisha.

"China's proliferation of coal plants has made its air toxic, and the country's Communist Party elites have no choice but to breathe it just like everybody else. But by developing more green energy to help clean up their polluted air, they're also building a national clean-energy economy as well as exporting their clean-energy products.

"Let's think about this a minute," Mr. Brown said. "China, a Communist country, is capitalizing on what it views as an international growth market. And China is garnering the largest share of that market."

"Is he saying they're doing more clean-energy business than everyone else?" Jamie said.

Raj nodded.

"Thank you for sharing your expertise with us, Mr. Brown," Senator Walter Rider said. "I believe we're all for sound investments. But you seem to be telling us that clean energy has to replace investment in fossil-fuel energy. Why can't we have both?"

"We have both *right now*," Mr. Brown said. "Our federal government is subsidizing fossil fuels by over three hundred and thirty billion dollars a year. That means we're fighting against an emerging international trend that's moving away from these dirty energies."

Senator Frederick Jones spoke up. "I represent a state with high unemployment, and many of my employed constituents are afraid of losing their jobs to this so-called clean-energy economy. What they're doing is all they know."

"I'm glad you raised that concern, Senator," Mr. Brown said. "Energy derived from fossil fuels is basically a holdover from the industrial revolution which ended in the early nineteenth century. We're in the process of building a twenty-first-century economy. There are even more opportunities today for job growth in a clean-energy economy than there were when we transitioned from an agricultural community to the Industrial Revolution."

Senator Jones said, "That all sounds good, but how do we ensure that the workers in the older industries still have jobs?"

"We offer them job training, like the coal miners who lost their jobs in Carbon County, Wyoming. They're being trained by a wind-turbine manufacturer to become wind-farm technicians in its Wyoming factory. And by the way, it's a Chinese manufacturer that's training them."

"That's cool, huh?" Jamie said to Raj.

"As our country moved from a farming community to the Industrial Revolution to a technological society, people acquired new skills that they used to enter new fields of employment," Mr. Brown said. "Equally important is the fact that by leaving their old jobs behind and using their new skills, they raised their standard of living."

"Just how is that supposed to happen now?" Senator Jones said.

"We can replace nineteenth-century jobs with better ones by leveraging what America excels at: creativity and innovation. By transitioning to an economy powered by clean energy, we can unleash a wave of innovation to create new technologies, lower the cost of clean energy, and create millions of new jobs. Doesn't it make sense to capitalize on the favorable conditions for these types of jobs rather than try to turn back the clock?"

"I like that the workers in the old jobs might get better new jobs," Jamie said to Keisha.

"We can be the world's leader in manufacturing innovative clean-energy products—by growing this market both in our own country and exporting all over the globe to countries who are hungry for clean-energy products." Mr. Brown said. "That is, if we don't let China beat us to it."

Mr. Brown leaned forward in his chair. "We can lead or we can be left behind."

Senator Pattern asked if there were any more questions, and when there were none Mr. Brown concluded, "Cleaning up and preventing more fossil-fuel pollution is one of America's greatest business opportunities in the twenty-first century."

"Whew-hoo, I didn't understand everything he said, but he sounded like a pretty smart business guy and he's all about clean energy," Jamie said to his friends.

Senator Pattern called for a short recess.

Jamie stood up and caught a glimpse of Senator Newsome sitting in the back of the public-hearing room. The senator shoved back his chair and stormed out. "Oh boy, Tony's father didn't look too happy."

"When does he ever look happy?" Keisha said.

After the recess Senator Pattern introduced several more speakers, who addressed impacts of fossil-fuel pollution and climate change on national security, the military, human health, people living in poverty, plant and animal species, waterfront communities, and the economy. By the end of the public hearing Jamie felt like his brain was packed to the brim with what he'd heard.

"You guys, I'm so glad we came to this," Jamie said. "I learned so much today."

But he wondered if it would help Senator Pattern with her bill. What Keisha's mom had explained to them about Congress made it hard for him to even guess.

CHAPTER 43

The unusually high humidity cloaked the late-autumn afternoon and the scent of dying leaves saturated the air.

Jamie glanced out his bedroom window on the second floor of the house and saw that Katie had snuck outside and plopped herself down next to his garden. She'd picked a small bouquet of yellow marigolds and placed it in Earthadilly's floppy arms. He knew Katie wasn't supposed to be outside, but she looked so happy lifting her face to the sun and the breeze that played with her curls.

She must be tired of being cooped up in the house all the time, and this was probably one of her rare good days. He watched her roll around on the soft grass with her doll, giggling as the grass seemed to tickle her bare legs. He decided to keep an eye on her and let her have her fun. He went back to writing his report for school.

After a while he noticed the sun's rays getting stronger, and he could feel the heat through his open window where his curtains started billowing. The wind seemed to be shifting from another direction. He focused on Katie. She appeared content playing with her doll, and the air looked clear. So he returned his attention to his report.

But the next time Jamie looked out to check on Katie, he spotted smog creeping along the ground in the backyard. And Katie wasn't in sight.

In a panic he headed downstairs and out the back door to the yard, but she wasn't around anywhere. He ran back into the house and heard Billy cry out in a loud voice, "Mommy, Mommy, come fast."

Jamie saw Katie and Billy at the end of the long hall in front of the entrance to her bedroom. She was gasping for air, her face turning blue. Billy had his crutch under one arm and the other around his sister's waist, barely holding her up, the two of them hobbling through the doorway.

Jamie dashed down the hall and helped Billy get their sister into bed. Their mom ran into the room, turned on the nebulizer next to Katie's bed, and poured liquid medication into the nebulizer flask. Jamie propped up Katie on her pillows and affixed the nebulizer mask over her nose and mouth. Sweat rolled down her blue face as she fought the familiar battle to keep from suffocating.

"Try to relax, sweetie," their mom whispered. "You're safe now." She wiped the beads of perspiration from Katie's brow with a washcloth from her nightstand and gently pulled a strand of hair back from her eyes.

Jamie held his sister's hand while she sucked in medicated air behind the mask. He inhaled and exhaled along with her. Breathe in. Breathe out. Breathe in. Breathe out. It must be hard for her to force her lungs to work when they hurt. Each time she inhaled, her eyes filled with pain. She must be scared too. Breathe in. Breathe out. She looked so tired.

After several moments Katie's face turned from blue to pale and she loosened her grip on his hand. The medicine seemed to be working. She could probably let her lungs breathe on their own soon instead of telling them to. Breathe in. Breathe out. Her eyelids closed and she slept.

"I'm calling the doctor," their mom said. "Jamie, when she wakes up please take her temperature." She left the room.

Jamie watched Katie sleep and dabbed the washcloth on her moist forehead with a trembling hand. Her long lashes fluttered and her breathing slowed. For a moment he took comfort in how peaceful she seemed. Peaceful but worn out and worn down.

But he'd made a horrible mistake. When the wind changed direction, he should've known it might blow in smog from the highway. But everything had seemed okay and she'd looked so happy. He just wanted to let her be happy.

Billy leaned his crutch against the wall, then pulled himself up on the bed and nestled beside his sister.

When their mom returned, her face was as pale as Katie's. "The doctor would like to see Katie right away."

"Billy and I will come with you," Jamie said.

"Honey, I don't know how long we'll be gone, so please stay home with Billy."

Jamie carried Katie out to the car. She awoke, looked up into his eyes, and gave him a weak smile. "I can walk," she said.

"I know, munchkin, but I like carrying you, okay?"

~

Hours later Jamie was in the middle of playing a board game with Billy but had a hard time concentrating. His phone rang. It was Raj.

"I have some bad news, Jamie. Anaya said some of the striking kids in India had to go into hiding because the factory owners were after them."

"Oh no, Raj!"

"I am surprised they are doing this with the world's attention on their factories now. But they are having to pay higher wages to replace the striking children and they are very angry."

"I had a bad feeling about this after we saw that news report. What should we do?"

"I need to think about it," Raj said. "I will see how much more I can find out from Anaya. How many kids are in hiding. If any other kids are in danger."

"Let's talk about it when we get together at Keisha's tomorrow night," Jamie said.

Jamie's attention was drawn out the window to his mom's car pulling up in the driveway. "Raj, I gotta go. See ya tomorrow."

Jamie waited for his mom to put Katie in bed. His mom's face looked strained. "Honey, Katie's infection isn't responding to the new antibiotic, and now she's in the early stages of pneumonia."

Jamie's breath shot out of him. "Oh, no, Mom, what are we gonna do?"

His mom started to say something, then seemed to change her mind. "Dr. Abrams has put Katie on a different antibiotic. She needs lots of rest and fluids, and she'll continue on her pain medication and cough medicine."

"Geez, now pneumonia!" Jamie's whole body trembled.

"I know it sounds bad, honey. But we'll give her the very best care."

Jamie could tell that was his mom's fake cheery voice.

CHAPTER 44

Jamie retreated to his garden after his mom told him about Katie's pneumonia. The wind had shifted again and the smog had moved on to its next victims.

He spotted the little bouquet of marigolds Katie had dropped. He knelt, gathered up the flowers, and started to wrap a raspberry vine around the stems when he heard a familiar sound. Sure enough, Mr. James appeared.

"Geez, I never get used to you showing up like that out of thin air!" Jamie said. "But I'm glad you came."

Mr. James searched Jamie's eyes. "I take it things aren't going well?"

"Worse than last time you came. My sister's got pneumonia and the antibiotics aren't working, and I didn't stop her from playing in the yard so she had a really bad asthma attack."

Mr. James frowned. "I'm very sorry to hear that." He settled near Jamie and said in a gentle voice, "It all sounds pretty discouraging."

"Yeah, very."

"Well, it's natural to feel helpless at times like these. Especially with your little sister. You can't give her healthy lungs, but you can give her your love, and sometimes that's one of the most healing things we can do."

"You think so?"

"Yes, I do."

Jamie finished wrapping the raspberry vine around the bouquet Katie picked. "I really love her," he said softly.

Mr. James lightly squeezed Jamie's arm. He was quiet for a few moments. Then he said, "How's your youth movement doing?"

"That's my other bad news. Some of the kids helping us in India had to go into hiding. I keep trying to practice what you've told me, but then things seem to get worse. You talked about overcoming obstacles, but I think our obstacles are too big, Mr. James. I'm afraid I'm going to fail."

"Please try not to let yourself slide into fear and doubt, Jamie."

"Easy for you to say."

"Yes, it is." Mr. James hesitated. "Yes, it is easy for me to say because I *am* you."

"What do you mean?"

The old man's face softened. "You always felt like you should've been able to save your dad. And you still cherish the raspberry plants in your garden that he helped you collect on your camping trip. And you'd like to be tough like your friend Tony. And you admire how talented your friend Keisha is. And you wish you were as smart as your friend Raj. But you don't have to try to be like any of your friends because you have everything you need inside you right now."

"How could you know all that?"

Mr. James turned up the palms of his hands.

"You really *are* me—like in the future?"

The old man nodded.

"This is so hard to believe. Me, you're me, seventy years from now."

"I wouldn't lie to you."

"And I'll be a scientist when I grow up? A scientist who grows plants to feed people?"

Mr. James smiled. "But if your generation is successful in saving the planet, you'll be a scientist who does so much more than what I'm doing in the timeline you saw."

"So even though I'll be you in the future, you're telling me I could be a *different* you in the future?"

"Just think of it this way, Jamie. The future I come from is based on what's happening today in your timeline. But there are many other alternatives to the future I showed you. When I was you in my past, I didn't do as much as I should have to protect our planet. But now you can. You're getting a second chance to set things right for the Earth. You and the people in the present timeline can drastically change who you'll be in the future and what kind of a life you'll have."

Those words whirled around in Jamie's brain like a pinwheel. He gaped at Mr. James, his future self. *Is this for real?* What he'd seen in the future seemed real enough. And how else could this mysterious old guy know all that stuff about him?

It was so weird to see himself as an old man. But this old Jamie did seem kind of familiar. Not so much how he looked, but how he sounded talking about the Earth. And how this future Jamie had helped him look at things in a way he never did before. Like thinking he could save Katie by saving the planet. Like having confidence in his idea for the CAPE. It felt good to know that his future self had come back to help him. It seemed like something his dad would do.

His dad! Why didn't he think about his dad before?

"Okay, I believe what you said about who you are," Jamie said. "And I think I believe we can change the future." He sat back on his heels. "So if you can come back here to get us to save the planet, you can go back two more years and save our dad!"

Sadness crept into the lines of the old man's face. "I wish I could."

"Oh, please, try!" Jamie said. "Set your energy vibrator to before Dad died and warn him."

"I did that already, Jamie. But when he got tested, nothing showed up. Sometimes there's no evidence for when a blood vessel in the brain is going to bulge and rupture."

"Couldn't you try harder to find a way to help him?" Jamie said.

The old man sighed and his whole body seemed to sag. "Don't you think if there was anything I could do to save our father, I would have done it?"

"So even my future grown-up self couldn't save him?"

"There's nothing either the young you or the old you could have done. It's important that you accept that, Jamie. It was his time to go. I'm sorry."

Jamie glanced back at his house. That awful memory arose of him with his father's motionless body on the kitchen floor. The shock of it was still just as strong. But this time there was something different about that scene, as if something peaceful settled all around him and his dad.

He closed his eyes and absorbed it into his heart. "Goodbye, Dad," he whispered.

Mr. James wrapped his arm around Jamie's shoulders and joined his silence. They stayed there together like that for several moments. Then Jamie opened his eyes and looked up at Mr. James. "Thank you."

A warm breeze brushed up against them and carried a few falling leaves from the old oak off into the night.

"Our dad was a very caring man and you have that quality in you, Jamie. That's going to serve you well in ways you can't even imagine yet."

Jamie let those words enter his mind like a welcome friend.

"Are you going to be all right?" Mr. James said.

"Yeah, I think I *am*."

"I think so too."

Mr. James got to his feet. "I've got to get back to the future, Jamie. I'll be waiting—hopefully—for what will be a whole new Earth."

Jamie nodded. "Thanks for coming back to help me. And for telling me who you are."

Mr. James set his energy vibrator and disappeared.

Jamie surveyed his garden and watched the hummingbirds flit around, poking their beaks in and out of the flowers bordering his fertile little plot.

Suddenly a hummingbird shot past Jamie's ear like a miniature guided missile and hovered over his red impatiens. He knew his speedy little companion, one of the world's smallest birds, soon would migrate thousands of miles south for the winter, as far as the Caribbean islands.

This little guy doesn't realize how tiny he is. When he starts off on his southern journey he doesn't worry if he'll get where he wants to go. He doesn't wonder if he has the power to fly or find food or return at winter's end. He just beats his wings as fast as he can, and off he goes to his destination.

Jamie focused on the hum of the little bird's beating wings and breathed easily.

CHAPTER 45

J amie was eager to get to Keisha's house to talk about the striking kids and watch another CAPE story on the news. He could relax a little this time because he knew this news story wouldn't have an interview with him like too many of the others did. He still didn't like doing interviews, and he especially didn't like watching himself when they aired.

When he joined Raj, Tony, and Keisha in her dad's huge entertainment room he found she'd gone all out this time. Cookies, potato chips, pretzels, peanuts, three different kinds of soda, and of course—their favorite— chocolate-covered raisins. Tony and Raj had already finished off half a bowl of popcorn.

"Keish, I think we should hang out here every week," Jamie said.

"Well, my dad might not think so," Keisha said with a chuckle. "He's out with his buddies right now, but when he's home he practically lives in this room. This is one of *our* special nights, though, so we deserve to hang here." She was all beaming and fidgety and Jamie thought she seemed especially wired tonight.

"These treats are the best, Keish," he said. "Thanks for doing all this." He paused, his voice turning serious. "Could we all talk first and maybe Keisha could record the news for us?"

"I've already done that," Keisha said. She bounced up from her seat. "Listen, I need to tell you guys something, something totally fantastic. It's why I got my mom to buy us all this stuff, kind of as a little celebration."

"So tell us already," Tony said.

"Well, you know how the pope is coming to DC?" she said.

"Your mom got us better seats to see him in his pope-mobile?" Jamie said.

"Oh, much better," Keisha said. She looked like she might leap out of her skin. "He's been following the news on the CAPE and … catch this … he said he wants to meet the kids who started it!"

"Holy cow!" Jamie said.

"Yeah, but that's not all," Keisha said. "He wants us to speak to Congress right after him so we can tell Congress and the American people why we started the CAPE!"

"No way! Are you sure?" Jamie said.

"Totally. My mom said the Vatican contacted Senator Pattern's office about us. Remember, Senator Pattern was the one who got him invited to speak at a joint meeting of Congress."

"This is big, *really* big," Jamie said.

"He's the ultimate, cool, environmental dude," Tony said.

"We're calling the pope a dude now?" Keisha said. "Real nice, Tony."

Tony laughed.

"This is an honor even for a Hindu," Raj said.

Jamie felt like his brain was splitting in half. The first half was cheering about meeting the pope and getting a chance to make their case before Congress. The second half was jeering about him speaking in front of all those elected officials. He told the second half to just shut up.

"You all know what this means for us?" Jamie said. "To speak directly to the politicians who will be voting on Senator Pattern's bill?"

"Yeah, I think that's why he invited us," Keisha said. "My mom said if our big, polluting country is willing to vote for that kind of huge commitment, we'll have a better chance of getting the rest of the world to speed up its efforts."

"Keish, that's just what we need!" Jamie said.

"You know what?" Keisha said. "I think I'm beginning to love being with the CAPE as much as I love b-ball."

She picked up a popcorn kernel and tossed it into a cup on the far side of the coffee table. Then she turned to Jamie. "So, Jamie what did you want to talk about?"

"Geez, now I feel like I'd be busting everyone's balloon," Jamie said.

"Just spill it, dude," Tony said.

Keisha tilted her head to the side. "Is something wrong?"

"Well, yeah," Jamie said. "You wanna tell 'em what you found out, Raj?"

"Anaya told me that ten striking kids had to go into hiding because the factory owners have threatened them with beatings and are trying to force them back to work any way they can."

Keisha grimaced. "Oh, no!"

"What monsters," Tony said.

"What about all the other strikers?" Keisha said.

"Anaya got as many reports as she could on all the striking CAPE members and she found that so far, only these ten kids who worked at one small factory are in danger," Raj said. "But other factory owners could get the same idea."

"What about that group that was suing the owners?" Tony said. "You know that group that's been getting the money to the kids for us?"

"The Planet Defense Council," Jamie said.

"They have offices in India and they are still suing them," Raj said. "But it takes a long time to get into court."

"Oh, Jamie, I think we should tell all the striking kids to stop," Keisha said. "What if more kids have to go into hiding?"

Raj tapped the side of his head. "I just got an idea. What about asking the Planet Defense Council to drop its lawsuit against the factory owners if the owners agree to conditions that protect the kids and maybe even make things better for them?"

"You think that would work?" Jamie said.

"It might," Raj said. "The owners probably do not want to spend a lot of money defending themselves in court. Maybe this will also bring more attention to what they are doing and finally start getting the laws enforced that are supposed to protect kids."

"Well, at least it's a start," Keisha said. "I especially like the idea that we try to make things better for the kids."

"Yeah, and if the owners of this factory back down it might keep other ones from threatening other kids," Tony said.

"Okay, then, we all agree we'll try this?" Jamie said.

His three friends nodded.

"Ms. Tollhouse got the Planet Defense Council to help us, so I'll ask her to talk to them," Jamie said.

"Sounds good, Jamie," Keisha said. "So ... wanna watch the news on the CAPE now?" She turned on the recording and fast-forwarded to the network news anchor, Kalyn Roberts, introducing the story.

"... and here's Steve Headley, our network affiliate reporter in Washington, DC, with the latest on a controversial environmental protection bill in Congress."

Steve was on the sidewalk in front of the Capitol. "The fossil-fuel industries are lobbying heavily against Senator Lydia Pattern's bill to phase out fossil fuels in ten years, and our sources say there still isn't enough support to get it to the senate floor for a vote. Our sources also tell us the lobbyists have no problem getting the legislators' attention. Their fossil-fuel clients have contributed over sixty-four million dollars to members of Congress." Steve appeared on camera. "Back to you, Kalyn."

Keisha hit pause on the remote. "Gee, how can we beat that kind of money?"

"We have leverage, remember?" Tony said.

"Oh, and guess who signed up to be CAPE members?" Jamie said. "Keisha tell 'em what you told me about a lot of kids and grandkids of people in Congress."

"Yeah, my mom heard about it at the Capitol," Keisha said. "It was the big buzz all over the building this week."

"Ha!" Tony said. "I hope those kids are leaning on their folks big time. Gee, maybe I should try leaning on my dad, the big senator." Tony did his hyena laugh but it sounded a little weak.

Keisha hit play and the camera zoomed in to the anchor desk. "But Congress is also hearing from frantic business owners whose sales are plummeting due to the boycotting efforts of an international kids' group known as the CAPE who are working to rid the planet of fossil-fuel pollution and stop climate change."

The newscast ran footage of children in CAPE t-shirts picketing with signs that read *Adopt Our Plan – Save Our Planet* at a large children's pizza restaurant, a toy store, and a skateboard park. "We reported on the boycott when it was launched, and since then it's had a devastating impact on thousands of businesses from coast to coast," Kalyn said. "They're a stark contrast to the businesses that have publicly committed support for the CAPE. Some of the major motion-picture studios and online retailing giants were among the first to express their support, and their bottom lines are steadily increasing."

"You were right, Tony!" Jamie said.

Aerial footage showed container ships in the ocean. "World markets are also being impacted by CAPE child laborers striking at factories overseas," the anchor said. "The strikes are having a severe financial impact on countries that export and import goods from these factories. The factories can't sell enough goods, and the businesses who buy from them can't restock their inventory."

"Good job, huh, Raj?" Keisha said.

At the anchor desk Kalyn said, "We switch now to our business reporter in New York City, Alan Stone, for a look at how the CAPE is affecting Wall Street."

The reporter stood above the pit of the New York Stock Exchange. A ticker tape crawled across the screen above him showing losses for a number of businesses. "Stock prices continue to fall in many of the retail, restaurant, electronics, and entertainment sectors targeted to young people. Wall Street is getting jittery about the high volatility of the market right now and what it means for the global economy."

Brokers talked loudly on their phones behind Alan, who held his mic in front of one broker. "What's your reaction to the downward spiral in kid-oriented segments of the stock market lately?"

"I'm shocked that this kids' network is having such a negative international impact on the market," the broker said. "The youth sector was such a steady, lucrative niche we didn't see this coming."

The reporter faced the camera. "This is Alan Stone, New York."

"Thank you, Alan," the anchor said. "These young people are flexing quite a lot of muscle to get their countries to phase out fossil fuels. That concludes our special edition."

Keisha turned off the TV.

"Here's to leverage!" Jamie said. He and his friends toasted with their soda cans.

CHAPTER 46

After they left Keisha's house, Jamie and Tony headed to Tony's to catch up on their homework, though all Jamie wanted to think about was the TV news show they'd just seen about the CAPE. He did several wheelies on his bike down the sidewalk to celebrate.

But the minute Jamie saw Tony's dad, he wanted to kick himself for not realizing how stupid it was to come over here right after that big broadcast. They found him next to Tony's mom on the sofa, hollering at the TV.

"Hello, sweetie," his mother said to Tony. "Nice to see you, Jamie."

"What's goin' on?" Tony said.

"I'll tell you what's going on," his dad said loudly. "Worldwide panic over these kids and their wild schemes. Ridiculous."

"Your father and I watched a news report tonight on Jamie's group, dear," his mom said, a note of cheeriness in her voice.

"Jamie, you already know how I feel about all this." Tony's dad had lowered his voice. "You're not my son, but I'm telling you anyway that you and your group have gone way too far."

"I'm sorry you're upset, sir." Jamie said.

Mr. Newsome gestured at the TV and raised his voice again. "And all these so-called 'news' people falling all over themselves to make y'all look good. What in hell is wrong with them?"

Tony switched on his android face but couldn't hide the smirk that tugged at the corners of his mouth. His father turned and glared at him.

"Don't you dare mock me or I'll wipe that smug look right off your face."

Tony tightened his lips. "I'm not mocking you. I worked my butt off raking your yard this morning, so why can't you just get off my case?"

"You will not back-talk me, boy."

Jamie noticed the bulging veins in Mr. Newsome's forehead.

"I haven't done anything wrong," Tony said. "You're just making up stuff to get mad about. Why? Why are you always so angry with me?"

His father leaned forward on the sofa and hesitated. "I'm not angry. I'm just tired of being treated with disrespect."

"If anybody's treating you with disrespect, go get mad at them instead of me."

To Jamie's surprise, Tony's dad sunk back on the sofa and appeared to crumple like used wrapping paper. Tony didn't say anything. Neither did his father. Jamie wondered what had just happened.

Mrs. Newsome rubbed the back of her husband's neck. "Sweetheart, please don't get yourself all worked up. And please let Tony be." She stood up. "Come with me out to the kitchen, darling, and I'll make you a nice cool gin and tonic."

She took his hand and he quietly followed her. Jamie enjoyed watching Tony's mom work her magic. She was so good at it sometimes he wondered if she had secret powers.

The minute his parents left, Tony jabbed his fist in his dad's direction and led Jamie to his room. "See, he gets mad at me and I haven't even done anything!"

Jamie paused for a few seconds. "I need to ask you something."

"Shoot."

"What do you think about speaking to Congress?" Jamie had been trying to figure out what to say to Tony ever since Keisha told them the good news.

"I really want to, but I'm still thinking about it," Tony said.

"We don't expect you to do it. We want you with us, but we don't want to cause you any more trouble with your dad. And that would be very big trouble."

"You know I get crap from him no matter what, so don't sweat it. I'll let you know what I decide."

Jamie avoided Tony's eyes.

"Now what?" Tony said.

"I wonder if maybe one day you and your dad won't have to be like this with each other."

"Fat chance. We can't stand each other."

"We both know it used to be different."

"Well, now he's always riding me. Treats me like dirt."

"But remember when we were in first grade and your dad took us down to Virginia Beach and helped you build a sand fort? And he put you on his shoulders in the ocean when you saw a jellyfish … and he caught you in his arms at the bottom of the big slide at the water park and—"

"Stop it, Jamie." Tony shook his head. "Those days are over. That guy is long gone."

"Tony—"

"Look, Jamie, you gotta stop worrying about me and my dad. Maybe he was different when I was a little kid. But he changed when I got older and he turned into a jerk. He's been a jerk ever since. And the more power he gets in his job, the more he gets on me."

"But maybe things could change back."

"It's a waste of time thinking my dad and I could feel different about each other." A slight crack wedged in Tony's voice. "It could never happen."

"Okay, I'm sorry—"

"Don't be sorry for me, dude. I'm fine, and in a few more years I'll be outta here. So are we going to do homework or what?"

"Yeah, let's do homework."

Jamie was as eager to change the subject as it seemed Tony was. But he still wished there was something he could do to help Tony with his dad.

~

Jamie didn't do any more wheelies on his way home from Tony's. This was turning out to be one of those good-news-bad-news days.

Then just as he was about to ride his bike up his driveway, he caught a glimpse of someone in the shadow of a tree across the street. He made believe he didn't see them and once he got inside his house, he peeked out the window with the lights turned off in the den. The bald guy came out from behind the tree, then hurried down the sidewalk to a car parked next to the curb and drove off. Jamie shuddered.

"Mom, that guy I told you about was spying on me again," he yelled to his mom in the kitchen.

His mom rushed into the room. "Where?"

"Right across the street, but he's gone now and I couldn't see his license plate."

"I think it's time we told the police."

"What can they do? I've never even been able to get a good look at his face."

"Doesn't matter. I'm calling them anyway."

Jamie tried to stop the tremor in his body. It seemed like his life was one big roller coaster ride. First he was up, then down … up, then down. This guy was definitely a downer. He just wished he could figure out what was going on.

Chapter 47

Richard took one look at Colton storming through his senate office door with his creepy sidekick in tow and secretly groaned. For weeks it had been one blasted thing after another. First his kid turned on him. Then everybody and his grandmother showed up at the public hearing to bash fossil fuels. Then he got threatened by Pattern who— *God help us all*—had just coerced her crazy bill out of her committee. Then the news media went wacko supporting that idiotic kids' crusade.

And now here comes another diatribe from that lowlife lobbyist. If he has to deal with one more crappy thing, he just might hang himself from the senate balcony.

Colton did his usual pacing in front of Richard's desk. Sharkey slouched down in a chair against the wall and dug dirt out from under his fingernails.

"You're not the man I thought you were, Richard," Colton said. "How did Pattern ever get her bill to the full Senate? It shouldn't have even gotten out of her committee."

"Pattern's like a battering ram and knows too much," Richard said.

"She's going to put my clients in a very big bind."

"Don't be such an alarmist. There'll be two or three days of political posturing on the senate floor, picked up by the mainstream media, and then it'll die a quick death by the next news cycle."

"A quick death doesn't seem to be such a sure thing anymore, Richard."

"Surely you don't think that ridiculous bill can sustain public support in our fickle country. We'll just do a counterattack in the media that support us."

"Without those conniving kids, she wouldn't have a prayer," Colton said. "Their blasted boycott's working."

"It just needs time to peter out. They can't keep it up much longer. Kids have short attention spans."

Colton slammed his hand on Richard's desk. "And what about the pope having them join him when he addresses Congress?"

"So what," Richard said. "Nobody but the pope cares what some twelve-year-olds have to say."

"Stop trying to ignore the fact that these particular kids have gotten a lot of attention and public support," Colton said.

"It's the news media's fault. They're making them into heroes."

"Exactly. And you know damn well Pattern's using all that press to get more votes."

"Look, Colton, it doesn't matter what she does. How many times do I have to tell you? She's never going to have enough votes. You should know that better than anyone, thanks to all the money you and your cronies have tossed around here. You've covered all the bases."

"You're a fool, Richard. Sitting up here in your isolated tower you're not in touch with what's going on the real world. This insane kids' crusade has been gaining momentum all fall. By the time they finish their sob stories about saving the planet in front of Congress and the whole country, the situation is going to be totally out of our control. We have to stop them before that happens or there'll be hell to pay from my clients."

Richard decided he was not going to listen to another word from this guy. Partly because he was afraid Colton was right. Partly because he was tired of being pushed around by some sleazy lobbyist.

"We're done here today, Colton. I've tried, but there's nothing anybody can do to stop them."

"Don't be so sure about that!"

PART FOUR

CHAPTER 48

The final days of autumn arrived quickly as if Nature had waved an invisible baton, signaling the leaves to pick up the tempo. After weeks of an exuberant performance, she seemed spent and calling for the finale. Traces of her recent splendor descended in swirling clusters, floating about like lost notes in a dying tune.

Outside Jamie's house a small eddy of fallen leaves spun across the den window on the updraft of a light breeze. Jamie cringed at the sight but pushed his thoughts away. He wanted to believe that his sister was going to live through the fall and the winter and the spring and the summer and grow up to be healthy and strong.

Jamie helped Katie get settled on the sofa with Earthadilly after her return from another visit to the doctor with their mother. Then he joined their mom in the kitchen where she was writing on a tablet.

"I need to get this all down before I forget," his mom said.

Jamie waited until she was done. "What did the doctor say?"

"No improvement in Katie's pneumonia. Antibiotic can take longer in highly resistant cases like hers. Need to prevent lung infection from spreading to her bloodstream." She grimaced, then continued reviewing her notes. "Her asthmatic lungs making recovery difficult. Keep up the nebulizer treatments. Give her plenty of fluids. Increase the home nurse visits. Call immediately if her symptoms get worse ... but then what?" His mom turned away from Jamie and faced the wall.

"You okay, mom?"

She nodded but didn't turn around. Jamie went up to her and hugged her.

He joined his sister on the sofa and gently ran his fingers through her blond ringlets. He tried to smile. She studied him, then rattled off a stream of chatter like jellybeans bouncing from an overturned jar.

"Jamie, I really like Dr. Abrams," Katie said in a croaky little voice. "She told me I'm going to be a great astronaut. I said I know I am! I'm going to bring Earthadilly with me too so she can see how she looks from way up in the sky."

Katie coughed several times and sucked on her inhaler. "Billy says climbing our tree is good practice for being an astronaut because we get to feel what it's like to be up high. Oh, but we know we have to wait to climb our tree until we're older like Mommy said, right? But while we're waiting to get older maybe you and Mommy could take us on a plane ride somewhere so we could be up high without falling down. Maybe we could fly to Disneyworld, huh? That would be fun don't you think, Jamie?" She inhaled and coughed several times, followed by a grin.

"That would be fun, munchkin," Jamie said. He stayed close to her until she leaned her head back against the sofa and closed her eyes.

His mom entered the den. "Weren't you going to meet up with your friends at the park, sweetie?"

"I don't have to go. I can call them and ask about meeting another time."

"No, go ahead, it will be good for you to get out and take your mind off Katie."

Jamie knew nothing could take his mind off Katie, but he headed for the park anyway.

~

Unseasonably high temperatures had quickened Nature's fading palette, and the once lush, green grass had turned a sickly shade of dying wheat. An occasional light breeze brought little relief.

When Jamie arrived at the park it was deserted except for his friends. He straddled a bench across from Keisha and Raj at their usual picnic table under a partially denuded tree.

"I got some good news from Ms. Tollhouse about the factory-worker kids," Jamie said. "Our idea worked. The Planet Defense Council got the factory owners to meet its conditions for the kids by agreeing to drop its lawsuits."

"Does that mean the kids in hiding will be able to come out and be safe?" Keisha said.

"If the owners have agreed to the conditions, that should apply to all the kids," Raj said.

"Yeah, I hope we'll be able to ask them to stop striking soon," Jamie said. "Those kids have already helped us a lot."

A beep on Jamie's phone signaled a text. "Tony says he can't come today because he got in another fight with his dad."

"Because of the CAPE?" Keisha said.

"He didn't say why, but he's still deciding whether he's going to join us with the pope," Jamie said. "I hope Tony doesn't think he can keep it a secret from his dad and just show up."

"That's the worst thing Tony could do!" Keisha said.

"I know." He scrunched up his face like a rotted pumpkin.

Jamie had been thinking a lot about his own secret from his last talk with Mr. James. He was trying to get used to the idea that the old man was actually himself, Jamie, seventy years in the future. But he didn't feel right that he was still keeping that from his friends. "I have something really strange to tell you guys."

Jamie swerved his legs around under the bench and leaned his elbows on the picnic table.

"Mr. James came to see me a few days before our last time at Keisha's house," Jamie said. "I didn't tell you sooner because ... well, because he told me something I needed time to think about. It was just so bizarre ..."

"So tell us already," Keisha said.

Jamie lowered his hands on the table palms up. "Mr. James is me seventy years in the future."

Keisha giggled. "Right, and I'm gonna be captain of a starship."

"No, Keish, it's true," Jamie said. "He knew so many things about me that nobody could know unless they lived inside my head."

"You serious?" Keisha said.

"Yes."

Keisha twisted her mouth to the side. "That's just plain crazy. It was hard enough believing all that other stuff about the future, but now you're telling us we met *you* instead of some old scientist? Come on, Jamie."

"Well, you did meet an old scientist from the future … but he says that will be… ahh is … me in his 'timeline' or whatever he calls it."

"Why do you believe him?" Raj said.

"Like I told you, he described feelings and thoughts I've had that nobody else but me could know about. And everything he said was true."

"What if he was reading your mind?" Keisha said.

"I don't think so. It made more sense that he … or me as a grown-up—I'm just gonna keep calling him Mr. James because that's the way I still think of him—would want to come back and try to change things."

"It seems logical, does it not?" Raj said. "Why pick us out of all the kids in the world unless he … you … your future self … knew us very well, especially you, Jamie."

"Yeah, and I had a strange feeling about him almost from the beginning, but I couldn't figure out why. It's still hard to think of myself as ever getting that old."

"How did you feel when the old man said he was you?" Raj said.

"Totally weirded out at first. But the more we talked, the more I believed him."

CHAPTER 49

After Jamie told his friends about his last visit from Mr. James, they continued to chat around the picnic table. When a large cloud drifted away from the sun, its rays slipped between the sparse leaves on the tree above them and prickled Jamie's skin.

He wiped sweat off his brow with the back of his wrist and scanned the empty park. "No wonder it's like a ghost town."

Then he noticed a brown Hummer slowly pull close to the park sidewalk a few hundred feet from their picnic table. Two men got out and ambled down the sidewalk, each wearing blue gloves and carrying small plastic bags—like doggy-poop bags. Both men wore grimy-looking t-shirts on stocky frames. One had bushy red hair and the other wore a baseball cap.

Keisha and Raj had their backs to the men as they approached the picnic table.

Jamie thought it was strange that they wore gloves like his dentist and carried doggy-poop bags but didn't have dogs. Maybe their dogs got away from them and—

"Hey, you kids seen two pit bulls around here?" the bushy-haired guy said when he and the other guy got within a few feet of the picnic table. Before Jamie could answer, bushy-haired guy pulled two rags out of his plastic bag, bolted behind Raj and Keisha and shoved the rags over their noses and mouths with his huge hands while pulling each of them back against his barrel chest.

At the same time Jamie leapt up and charged toward bushy-haired guy, but the other guy grabbed him and covered his nose and mouth with a powdery rag. Jamie kicked and twisted as hard as he could, but something in the rag started making him weak and sleepy. He flailed his arms against the man like a pinned butterfly. The last thing he heard before he passed out was his friends' muffled screams.

Sundown brought no escape from the sweltering autumn evening. Even the crickets sounded weary in their attempts to fill the night with their usual chirpy song. A new moon hung high in a barren sky, its face frowning down at the weary inhabitants below.

Light from a street lamp slid between the slits in the plantation shutters of an old, weathered house. Inside, Jamie was in a deep sleep, slumped in a wooden chair against the wall of a dark, laminate-paneled den, his head hanging down on his chest. A pungent odor permeated the air like swamp moss in an ancient lagoon.

The room was dimly lit with one wobbly, freestanding lamp next to a stained, sagging couch. A cheap coffee table, pocked with cigarette burn holes, separated the couch on one side and two battered, stuffed chairs on the other.

A fly buzzed around Jamie's head and landed on the tip of his nose. He wiggled his nostrils, squinted, then drowsily looked around for Keisha and Raj, who were asleep in wooden chairs on either side of him.

All he could remember was his friends struggling in some big guy's arms and somebody else dragging him away as he passed out. His head hurt and his brain felt fuzzy. He tried to use his hands, but they were tied behind the chair. They must be prisoners, kidnapped. Wait … *kidnapped?*

He heard two men's voices on the other side of the wall. This was bad—really bad. What were these guys going to do to them? He forced back a scream. Oh, his poor mom. She'd be so worried. They had to figure a way out of here fast.

"Raj," Jamie whispered. "Wake up, Raj."

Raj rotated his head a few times, as if trying to loosen the muscles in his neck, then looked over at Jamie.

"You okay, Raj?" he whispered.

"I think so," Raj said.

Jamie gently kicked Keisha's chair with his foot.

Keisha awoke slowly and stared at her two friends. She raised her shoulders and tried to pull her hands out of the tied rope, then lowered her shoulders when she had no success. "I feel kind of woozy."

"The drug," Raj said.

Jamie motioned with his head toward the wall. "We need to be quiet because they're in the next room."

Keisha gasped. "Kidnappers?" She barely squeaked out the word. "What are we going to do?"

"Drag your chair behind me, Jamie, and I will try to untie you," Raj said.

Jamie scooted his feet on the floor and quietly slid his chair around so it backed up to Raj's tied hands. Raj fumbled with the knot in Jamie's rope until Jamie pulled out his hands. Then Jamie freed Raj and Keisha, who rubbed her wrists where the rope had made grooves in her skin.

The two voices in the other room got louder. Jamie listened for their names.

"Damn it, Sharkey, it's bloody hot in here," the first man said.

"Yeah, the AC's broke," Sharkey said. "No wonder Colton's tenants run out on him."

"He's not paying us enough to hole up in this dump," the first man said. "I even seen a rat."

"Look, Baldy, you know how cheap he is. Pays us peanuts to do his dirty work while he lives like an Arab prince."

"Maybe we oughta try to get a cut of the ransom money," Baldy said.

"We're not actually gonna collect ransom money. We're gonna botch it up."

"So what's the point?"

"It's all a cover for keeping these kids out of commission."

"Well, at least Colton don't have me running all over the place keeping an eye on 'em anymore," Baldy said. "What a boring job that was."

Jamie flashed back to the bald guy who'd been spying on them. So that's who he was!

"But it made it easy to find 'em when we needed to," Sharkey said.

Jamie heard a chair in the other room scrape against the floor, then footsteps.

"Got any more beer in that fridge?" Baldy said.

"There's only a couple left in here. We finished off the last two six-packs," Sharkey said. "You can buy more down the street. I gotta get that Sawyer kid's mother on the phone to demand the ransom. Then I gotta feed 'em."

Jamie pleaded in his head. *Oh please, don't call her. Please don't do this to my mom.*

"I'm going out for beer and a fan," Baldy said. A door slammed.

"Is this Sarah Sawyer?" Sharkey said. "… I'm calling about your kid. If you want him and his friends back in one piece, we'll need a million bucks. I'm giving you and the other parents twenty-four hours to get it together. Then I'll call you back with instructions."

Jamie squashed another scream. *Noooooooooo. This can't be happening. It all has to be a bad dream. If I shut my eyes really tight, I can go back to sleep and wake up in my own bed. It's just a dream, it's just a dream, it's just a dream.* He opened his eyes.

It's not just a dream.

Jamie got up and started toward the window when he heard footsteps again. He leapt back into his chair as fast as a tick on a dog. He loosely wrapped the rope around his wrists behind his back, and Keisha and Raj did the same.

Sweat rolling down his face, the guy with the bushy red hair stomped into the room with a McDonald's take-out bag. "I'm gonna untie your hands so you can eat, and I don't wanna hear a peep outta ya."

At the sight of the man, Jamie started to quake so badly he thought he might keel over. Mr. James's words whizzed through his brain. *We attract more of what we focus on.* He tried not to think about his quaking body.

Negative thoughts clog up our mind. Geez, he had nothing but negative thoughts right now! *Come on, Jamie, find one positive one ... our Creator is always moving powerful energy through us.*

Oh God, please help me be brave.

"We're not hungry, sir," Jamie said, staring down at his lap. He thought the man sounded like the one the other guy called Sharkey.

"Suit yourself." Sharkey returned to the next room.

Jamie heard the lid of a beer can pop open and remembered that the other guy said he was leaving. *There's only one of them now. Maybe we'll have a better chance. I can't just sit here freaking out.*

Jamie pattered over to the shuttered windows, pulled back one of the shutters, and slowly opened the window. Raj stood as lookout and motioned for Keisha to escape first. She lifted one knee onto the sill when suddenly a bald guy appeared outside the window right in front of her. Jamie recognized him from the park.

"Ahhhhhhhh," Keisha screamed and leapt back, slicing a long cut on her knee on a rusty nail that protruded from the edge of the window frame. Baldy shoved the window down from the outside and disappeared. Jamie dashed to the den door and slammed it shut. Raj and Keisha joined him, and he and his friends pressed their backs against it as hard as they could.

The door started to open, and Jamie and his friends pushed back. He dug his heels into the floor for leverage. But the door kept opening more and more. Jamie tried to kick the door shut, slammed his fists against it, and howled like a caged animal. Finally the two men barged into the room, flinging Jamie and his friends off the door.

"Good thing I came back for my wallet and caught 'em sneaking out!" Baldy said.

"If you're looking for trouble, you're gonna get it!" Sharkey said. He grabbed Jamie with his massive hands and slammed him hard onto the couch. Baldy threw Keisha next to Jamie, then the two men went after Raj and knocked him onto the couch.

Sharkey backhanded all three of them across their faces. "That's just a taste of what you're in for if you try that again!"

Keisha rubbed her hand over her cheek and whimpered softly, then tore off a piece of her t-shirt and wrapped it around her bloody, wounded knee.

Sharkey glared at her. "You better knock off that sniveling or I'll glue your mouth shut."

Keisha quieted down and Jamie patted her arm. His mouth was still stinging from being backhanded, but he couldn't stand to see Keisha like this. "Our friend has a bad cut from a rusty nail," Jamie said, fighting a tremor in his voice. "She needs something to keep it from getting infected."

Sharkey glanced at the blood-soaked strip of cloth wrapped around Keisha's knee. "Tough. I don't wanna hear another word outta you little brats, and you better stay put!"

Baldy wiped sweat from his brow and sneered. "I'll fix 'em so they don't get up for a week."

"I took care of 'em for now. We'll drink in here and watch 'em good."

All the energy in Jamie's body drained out of him. How dumb he was to think he could help them escape. *I've just made things worse. It's all because of me that my friends are in this whole mess, my mom will be hurting like crazy with worry, and I'll never get to save my sister.*

If God was always streaming powerful energy through him, how come he'd failed?

CHAPTER 50

Richard gaped in shock at the TV in his study as Steve Headley reported on the kidnapping of Jamie and his friends. Other news reporters and camera crews swarmed behind him across Jamie's front lawn and sidewalk.

Richard couldn't believe Colton would stoop this low. But he had to be behind this, especially after the threat he'd made the other day.

"We're outside the home of Jamie Sawyer," Steve said. "He's been kidnapped along with his friends Raj Sanseria and Keisha Taylor, daughter of star Washington Wizards basketball player Sam Taylor. The kidnappers are demanding one million dollars in ransom for the three middle-school children. The ransom call came in on a stolen cell phone."

On the TV the front door of Jamie's house opened a little and Billy's head peeked out. Jamie's mother appeared behind him and pulled him back inside, slamming the door shut.

Richard was sure Sarah and the other parents must be frantic. And those poor kids. They were causing a lot of trouble, but they certainly didn't deserve this. How could this whole thing have gotten so out of hand? And they demanded ransom? What the hell got into Colton?

Steve continued with his report, "Over the last several weeks, we've been covering the fascinating story of these children who started a group they call the CAPE, an acronym for a worldwide kids' effort to stop fossil-fuel pollution and climate change. The group's leader, Jamie Sawyer, and his two friends were last seen at their neighborhood park where the FBI found evidence of their kidnapping. The agents are trying to track down the supplier for a knockout drug, traces of which were found at the scene of the crime. No suspects have been identified in the case so far."

Good Lord, they drugged the kids too. Tony's going to go crazy over what they've done to his friends.

Behind Steve, Billy and Katie popped up in a picture window and waved to the reporters. Their mother closed a drapery over the window, hiding them from sight.

"It appears that the kids' high visibility made them marks for soliciting ransom," Steve said. "People from all over the country and the world are expressing concern for the children. We hope to have an update from the FBI on our eleven o'clock news report. This is Steve Headley in Alexandria, Virginia."

Richard worried about whether he'd be implicated because of his connection with Colton. He should have cut ties with that parasite years ago. He was tired of selling his soul piece by piece. So now on top of everything else, he was also dealing with criminals?

Tony yelled from his bedroom down the hall. "Dad, my friends have been kidnapped!"

Just before Tony raced into Richard's study with fiery eyes, Richard turned off the TV and jumped to his feet. He tried not to look guilty. "What are you talking about?"

"The news guy just said it."

"They wouldn't go that far. I mean, how could anybody go that far?" Richard wanted to bite his tongue.

"Like who?"

"Nobody."

Tony narrowed his eyes and Richard avoided them. "Wait a minute ... I heard the news on in here at the same time I was watching in my room," Tony said. "Why are you acting like you don't know about this?"

"My TV wasn't even on."

"Yes, it was."

"Don't contradict me, boy." Richard was having a tough time getting his normal voice back. It sounded weak to his ears.

"Do you know who did this?" Tony said.

Richard felt shorter and Tony suddenly seemed taller. "Of course not."

"Who do you think did this to my friends?"

"The FBI will take care of it."

"If you know something, you've got to help them," Tony said.

"I don't know a damn thing, boy."

"I don't believe you. You're always making me feel like I need to be a better kid. Ha! What a hypocrite!"

Richard shivered. "Go to your room!" He still couldn't seem to control his voice.

"I should have snuck out to be with my friends that day. If I was with them maybe I could've stopped the kidnappers. Or at least if we all got kidnapped together,

I could help them escape. I hate the way you've made me stay away while they did all the work and took all the chances. And now they're in danger and they have to face this without me. All because of you, my dictator father."

"That's it! Get out!" Richard flung his hand toward the hall and Tony slammed the door shut on his way out.

Richard picked up his phone and made a call. He lowered his voice and hissed into the receiver. "You've crossed the line, Colton!"

He drummed his fingers on his desk as Colton tried to give him a line of bull.

"Don't give me that crap," Richard said. "I know you're responsible. Let them go. *Now!*" Richard slammed his hand against the wall, then ended the call.

Of all the words Tony had thrown at him, a few bothered him the most.

What a hypocrite.

CHAPTER 51

Jamie drifted in dazed semiconsciousness with eyelids half open, weak from the heat and humidity. Raj and Keisha slumped against the couch on either side of him. Beads of perspiration ran in thin streams down his flushed cheeks. A few yards across from him in worn, cushioned chairs slept their kidnappers, snoring loudly in sleeveless dirty undershirts soiled with sweat. All that separated Jamie and his friends from their captors was a rickety old coffee table, littered with dozens of empty beer cans and a cell phone.

Jamie started to fall asleep, but his head dropped down and woke him with a start. He eyed the kidnappers. How could he give up and escape into sleep? After he'd worked so hard to be brave, he was just going to roll over like a beaten dog?

Mr. James had told him *you will become what you believe about yourself.* He didn't want to believe he was a wimp any more. *Replace your fears with gratitude.* Gratitude for what? How about gratitude for Raj teaching them Adithada? He elbowed Raj and Keisha out of their drowsy state and got them to untie each other's hands. Then he gestured toward the door.

Jamie rose quietly from the couch in a stooped position, followed by his friends. They tiptoed toward the door. Suddenly, the cell phone on the table rang. Sharkey awoke, saw the kids and clumsily charged at them like a drunken bull. They scattered in three directions, but Keisha's injured knee slowed her down, and Sharkey grabbed her by the arm. When Sharkey raised his fist to punch Keisha, a sudden energy burst through Jamie's body and propelled him into action.

"Get away from her," Jamie yelled. He chopped the edge of his hand down on Sharkey's wrist and freed Keisha's arm from the big man's grasp. "Go for it, Keish. You know how."

Keisha twirled around, lifted her good leg, and kneed Sharkey in his ribs. Raj leapt through the air and jabbed his heel into the middle of Sharkey's back. Sharkey fell forward moaning. Before he could straighten up, Jamie wound up a strong kick to the side of the tipsy man's head. It was as if Jamie's body was filled with the force of a fierce ocean wave—building, crashing, and pounding its target. The bull thumped face down on the floor, motionless.

Baldy rose to his feet in an alcoholic daze and stumbled toward Raj, who swung his foot into the man's abdomen. Baldy doubled over and Jamie slammed his elbow into the back of the man's neck. Baldy toppled onto the couch. He started to raise his head, then dropped it.

Jamie gaped at the defeated men. It didn't seem real. He didn't remember planning what he was going to do, he just did it. It must have been all those Adithada lessons, repeating over and over until the moves became part of him. Or maybe it was more than that.

Jamie raised his hand in a high-five and his friends each returned it. "Can you believe what we did?" Jamie said.

Then he focused on Raj. "All thanks to you, Raj."

"I just taught you how to use what you already had," Raj said.

Jamie didn't know where the kidnappers had hidden the kids' phones, so he picked up the cell phone from the coffee table and tapped in three numbers. "I want to report a kidnapping."

Within five minutes a white Chevrolet Malibu police car pulled up the driveway to the house and its two uniformed officers went inside. Shortly after, a gray Ford Crown Victoria parked in the street. Four men in cargo pants and navy-blue, short-sleeve polo shirts emerged, their shirts emblazoned on the back with *FBI* in yellow letters. The FBI agents and police officers found three kids standing guard over two burly, unconscious men.

One of the agents interviewed Jamie and his friends and said he would contact them soon for more information. Another agent discovered with a phone app that Colton Slone was the house's owner, then began forensics work on the property. As soon as Sharkey and Baldy regained consciousness, the other FBI agents handcuffed them, read them their rights, and asked them some pointed questions, but they wouldn't answer anything without an attorney. The agents hauled away the two kidnappers as easily as taking out the garbage, and the two police officers filed initial reports with their phones.

With Colton's thugs arrested and reports filed, the officers just stared at the children. Then the older officer broke into a grin. "Twenty-five years on the force, and I've never seen anything like this."

His partner, a younger officer, cocked her head. "How'd you kids do it?"

"We have our ways," Keisha said with a laugh.

Jamie looked at Raj and Keisha. "I just wish Tony could've been here. He would've loved it."

CHAPTER 52

When Jamie and his friends were settled in the back seat of the police car for their ride home, he silently reflected on their latest adventure. He was proud of himself for not letting his fear turn him into a wimp. *But how did I do that?* Just because he'd learned some martial arts didn't make him the kind of kid who could actually use them to knock out grown men. He'd never been a fighter. Ever. That was Tony's thing.

Why didn't he think about how they could have been hurt really bad ... or killed? But that was just it. He didn't think. He didn't have time to think. He felt something rise up in him and he followed it. And for the first time in his life, for a few minutes, he'd glimpsed what it was like to feel brave in the face of something really scary. Way more scary than public speaking!

Raj and Mr. James said their minds were powerful. Jamie didn't know if he'd totally believed them before. But now he knew there'd been something that came from deep inside him, a sense of his own power ... and a power much greater than that.

The first thing Jamie saw as the police car pulled up to his house were the reporters and camera crews stationed across his front yard. The photographers recorded his homecoming, with his mom dashing out of the house carrying Katie while Billy ran ahead to greet him. She set Katie down, and for a few seconds his mom's teary eyes lingered on his, then she engulfed him in her arms.

The twins hugged him like bear cubs clinging to a tree. Katie coughed and wheezed, but her emerald eyes kept smiling.

At first Jamie buried his face in his mom's shoulder because he was determined not to choke up in front of the cameras. But the twins wrapped themselves around him so tightly they almost toppled him, so he bent down to their level and they smothered him with kisses. Despite being kidnapped, if Jamie had ever had a better day than this, he couldn't remember it.

CHAPTER 53

Colton's lawyers dropped him off at his high-rise luxury condominium in Washington, DC, after they got him out on bail. He had to reassure them that he didn't need anything to help him calm down. He trudged out onto his open balcony and glared down at the city below. A city he was starting to hate.

It looked different to him now. This damn town had turned into a snake pit and he was fed up with it. Everything he'd worked for was going to be taken away from him, including his freedom. If he had to go to prison, somebody was going to pay. First Thomas, then that annoying kid. If the kid and his friends hadn't started this mess, he would never have had to stick his neck out.

He went back in and poured himself a stiff, cold drink, flopped down on his sofa, set the drink on his end table, and turned on the TV to the six o'clock news. Then turned it off. Why torture himself? But he wanted to know what they were saying about him. He turned it back on.

Steve Headley, the Capitol reporter, was outside the Alexandria Adult Detention Center with his TV cameraman, along with dozens of other news reporters and photographers.

"We're waiting for Washington, DC, lobbyist Colton Slone, who was arrested today on kidnapping charges," Steve said. "His attorneys appeared before the magistrate here today and just got him out on bail with the posting of a five-hundred-thousand-dollar secured bond. Slone has denied the charges and his trial date hasn't been set yet."

The newscast cut to a shot of Colton and his two attorneys exiting the main entrance of the jail earlier in the day. Steve and a mob of other reporters had surrounded him trying to get him to speak to them, but he turned away.

Colton cringed at the news report, the sight of himself associated with a jail. And he looked awful, like one of those back-alley crazies.

The camera zoomed in on Steve. "Slone, a well-connected lobbyist for fossil-fuel clients, allegedly hired two ex-convicts to kidnap the child leaders of the CAPE, a global kids' group that's fighting fossil-fuel pollution and climate change."

The report cut to video of Thomas Mandel at a public hearing. Off camera, Steve reported, "Slone's largest client, King Fuel CEO Thomas Mandel, denied any involvement and has fired Slone, expressing outrage at his actions."

Colton had an urge to throw his glass at Thomas's onscreen face. Then he started coughing and couldn't stop. He pulled out his bronchial meds and downed them with his drink.

Steve was back onscreen. "Even with Slone out of the picture, other industry lobbyists are still pressuring Congress to vote against a controversial anti-fossil-fuel bill supported by the CAPE."

Colton stiffened like an overstarched shirt. He turned off the TV. Yeah, *out of the picture*, what quaint news lingo. He picked up his phone and tapped on a number in his contacts.

"Why are you calling me on my home phone, Colton?" Thomas said. "I gave you this for emergencies only."

"This *is* an emergency," Colton said. "Did you really think you could avoid me, you stinking coward? Your assistant wouldn't put my calls through when I got out of jail. But you'd better listen to me now or I'll tell everything I know."

"Don't you dare threaten me or you'll be in an even worse predicament than you are already."

"Oh, you think so?" Colton slid his lips back from his teeth. "How dare you fire me—and I haven't even been to trial yet! Why didn't you take any of my calls? You owe me, Thomas. Year after year I've done your dirty work while you hid in the background. Now it's your turn to take care of me."

"I'm not doing anything of the kind," Thomas said.

"Yes, you are." Colton had to stop himself from biting right through his lip. "This is the most outrageous thing that's ever happened to me. Arrested! Fired! Facing prison! All my years of hard work on the Hill down the drain. The cost to fight this thing in the courts will wipe me out, and I'll probably still end up in prison. You've got to hire the kind of attorneys who can get me off, and you've got to be my character witness, tell them I'm not capable of having anybody kidnapped."

"You broke the law all on your own, and I don't owe you a thing."

"So what if you didn't ask me to do it? How did you think I was going to stop them? That's why you hired me. To figure out how to get the job done, no questions asked. It's your fault. And now I'm not going to let you sit there and hang me out to dry."

"Listen to me, Colton, I'm not the reason you're in hot water," Thomas said. "It's those kids. The news media made 'em so popular that now everybody's out to get you. It's because of those kids that your whole career got wrecked."

"That's the one thing we agree on." Colton took a sip of his drink. "The kids, yeah, it's really their fault. If it weren't for them and their little ringleader, I'd still be sitting pretty."

Colton rubbed his cold drink back and forth across his hot, sweaty forehead. "How I despise seeing that little idiot on TV. All righteous in his stupid cause … trying to wipe out my people … *our* people, Thomas. They're trying to wipe out *our* people and nobody cares. My dad didn't die in the mine so they could take down everything he stood for. We can't let them get away with it, Thomas." Colton felt his eyes water.

"I know, Colton, it's not right. Look, I have to go. I'm sorry things have gone so badly for you, but you've hired some good attorneys and I can't do any more for you than they can. I'll keep fighting to protect our people. Goodbye."

Colton heard the line go dead.

But who's going to protect me?

He knew a kiss-off when he heard one. He was all alone again. No one to look out for him. His brain raced back to his days in the mine as a fourteen-year-old kid.

He'd taken pride in his work like his dad, but every day he went down that shaft the foreman rode him as if he was trying to break him.

Old images kept working their way up to the surface of his memory. He was alone in the total darkness … groping around for his headlamp, which had broken when it detached from his hard hat and hit the ground. Another light came toward him and shined in his eyes, blinding him. An angry voice: "What the hell are you doing here without your headlamp?" He turned away, just as from the corner of his eye he saw a pickax swing at him. A searing pain on the side of his forehead. Something warm oozing down his cold face. The foreman dragging him out of the shaft. Then darkness again.

Colton hunched over on his sofa with his arms wrapped around his chest. He shook so hard his teeth rattled. Then his hand crept up to the scar on his forehead and he checked it for blood. Nothing. An adult hand. He was all grown up now. He forced himself to stop shaking.

He got up and went out on his balcony. Stared out at the lights of the city. Made a promise to himself. He wasn't going to let anybody grind him down again or try to wipe him out.

CHAPTER 54

J amie was in his bedroom finishing his homework before going to sleep for the night when his phone rang. The ID said *private caller* but he answered it anyway out of curiosity.

"Hello?"

"Jamie?"

It was a man's voice he didn't recognize. "Yes," Jamie said. "Who's this?"

"I'm a fan of yours," the man said in a friendly tone, but Jamie felt there was something odd about it.

"A fan? What's your name?"

"That's not important."

"How do you know me? Who are you?"

"I have something important to tell you."

Jamie was torn. He wanted to hang up the phone. Was this another person who wanted to hurt him? Jamie was still jumpy from the kidnapping. But what if this person really was calling about something he needed to know?

I understand you plan to join the pope when he speaks to Congress," the man said.

"Me and my friends."

"Well, you know, that's a very large group of important people." The man's voice got stronger. "The most important group of people in the world, some would say."

"Yes, sir," Jamie said. He started gnawing on his fingernail.

"Millions more all over the world will be watching on TV because of the pope."

Jamie surveyed his room as if searching for someplace to hide. "Yes, sir."

"Even grown men have frozen up before Congress."

Jamie had a hard time breathing.

"You could be so scared you might not be able to speak at all. Humiliate yourself in front of the whole world. *Humiliate* yourself in front of all those people who think you're sticking your nose where it doesn't belong. You know what I'm talking about, don't you?"

"Yes, I mean no ... No!"

"I'm just trying to warn you that some people are so angry they'd like to squash you like a cockroach." The words slithered through the phone and snaked their way into Jamie's brain.

He shut off his phone and flung it across his bed as if it had caught on fire. *Who was that?* His hands trembled so badly he cupped them around his skinny thighs. His mind conjured an image of a big shoe squishing a Jamie-faced cockroach.

The nasty voice thundered in his ears over and over. He knew there were angry people out there because of him. But it was a good thing he was doing. For Katie. For the planet. He couldn't let their anger shut him down.

Still, now he'd have to get up in front of all those important people with that horrible man lurking out there somewhere. Even if he managed to get through the Congress thing, was this man going to try to hurt him after he did? Or even before?

He should tell his mom. The police. His friends. But hadn't his mom already been through so much with the kidnapping—and had enough to worry about with Katie? Wouldn't he sound like a big whiner if he complained to the police? It wasn't a crime to say mean things to somebody. And what good would it do to tell his friends? So some nasty guy was angry about their cause. They knew there were still people fighting against the CAPE.

If he was ever going to be a real leader, he needed to have courage during tough times—like he did when they were kidnapped. He tried to get back the feeling he'd had when he knocked out his captors. Yeah, the new and improved Jamie proved he had courage, didn't he? He was determined never to let the wimpy Jamie come back and humiliate him again.

That was the most awful part of what the scary man said. That Jamie might humiliate himself if he spoke before Congress—and it would be in front of the whole world, too. On the other hand, getting squashed like a cockroach was pretty scary, but at least he'd be the only one who knew about it. Yeah, humiliation in front of millions of people was probably the worst. This was like that silly game Billy tried to play with him: *Would you rather get a hot stick in your eye or walk naked through a swarm of bees? A bucket of worms down your throat or a bunch of snakes in your bed? Come on, Jamie, pick one!* Jamie wanted to scream: *None of them! No squishing like a cockroach and no humiliating!*

But Jamie couldn't get the man's words out of his head. They triggered those familiar old thought creatures that crawled out of some dark cavern in his mind and scratched at the edge of his brain like ravenous beasts, feasting on every fear he'd ever had. Gnawing on every bad memory of when he didn't measure up. Jamie's mind offered up a banquet for beasts like these.

Truth was, he'd stored up a warehouse full of embarrassing memories. Moments of running away when he should've run forward. Sitting down when he should've stood up. Closing down when he should've blasted out of his anxious little prison and done something.

The sound of his mom's footsteps interrupted Jamie's thoughts. She appeared in his bedroom doorway looking frantic. "Katie's in respiratory arrest. They're coming to take her to the hospital."

"Oh, Mom," Jamie cried, as the beasts circled closer.

CHAPTER 55

A streetlamp's sharp glow cut through the early morning darkness outside the hospital waiting-room windows. Jamie's mom leaned against the back of a couch. Shadows hung under her eyes and worry lines curved around her mouth. Next to her, Billy cradled his child's doctor kit.

Jamie slumped in a chair across from them, gazing at the hospital's aquarium. This silent, ever-changing, reality show of underwater sea life calmed and distracted him. Bright green seaweed, anchored on the sandy bottom, swirled gently back and forth like graceful, slender, aquatic trees. Bubbles gurgled in rhythmic patterns as they streamed to the surface. The constant, subtle wave action almost mesmerized him. Tiny purple fish darted back and forth while several other species swam lazily around the tank.

Jamie's tensed muscles started to relax. But then he noticed that some of the fish had transparent bodies, their beating hearts on full display. He peered closer at them. It didn't seem right to Jamie that their hearts were exposed. It made them seem so fragile and unprotected.

Dr. Abrams entered the room. When their mom jumped to her feet, Jamie and Billy did too and stood on either side of her.

"Mrs. Sawyer, I just received the X-ray results. Katie's pneumonia is causing fluid to build up in her lungs."

Their mom wavered and Jamie wrapped his arm around her waist.

"We need to suction out the fluid so she doesn't suffocate."

Jamie's heart started pounding. *Suffocate?* He pictured Katie gasping for air like a fish out of its tank. She was getting worse and there was nothing he could do. Just like with his dad. His heart pounded louder.

"Can I see her before you take her in, then wait in the recovery room?" their mom said.

Jamie wished he could go too.

Dr. Abrams motioned for their mom to follow her. "You boys will need to stay here," the doctor said.

Jamie led Billy by the hand to chairs by the aquarium. "What are they going to do to Katie?" Billy said, eyes widening. "Is Dr. Abrams gonna use a plunger on Katie's lungs?"

"No, not a plunger," Jamie said. "A special lung tool."

Jamie fought the urge to run after the doctor and beg her to make his sister well. It took every bit of strength he could muster to keep from letting his little brother see how shaken he was.

"But I should be with her when they use the lung tool." Billy pulled hard on Jamie's arm. "She wants me to be with her when she's scared, and I know she's scared now." His voice cracked and faded to a whisper.

"We can't be with Katie right now, but we can see her later, okay Billyboo?" Jamie grazed his hand over a cowlick on top of Billy's head. He knew what he'd heard about twins was true for his brother and sister. Like two little peas in their own private pod, Katie and Billy often seemed to know what the other was feeling.

His mom said the pictures of them before they were born showed their arms wrapped around each other, and when the doctor had to open her stomach to deliver them, that's how they came out. Since then, you'd hardly ever see one without the other. Katie the cheerleader. Billy the protector. If anything happened to Katie, would Billy ever recover? Would any of them?

Jamie had always had the same need to protect his sister as Billy did. The same need to protect his whole small family. But now his sister was lying in some operating room while they tried to keep her lungs from drowning. And all he could do was wait.

Jamie shut his eyelids as tightly as he could to dam up his emotions. He needed to think about something else or he'd surely lose control in front of Billy.

It seemed as though Billy's usual high energy had been sucked right out of him. He was crouched down in his chair with grown-up weariness covering his child's face. Jamie gestured toward the aquarium. "Look, Billyboo, aren't these fish cool?"

Billy slowly turned his head to the tank and stared blankly. Jamie pointed to a fish—its front half hot-pink and back half bright yellow—swimming across the front of the glass. "How do you think he gets his bright colors?" Jamie said.

Billy leaned closer to the tank. "I think that must be a *girl* fish 'cause she has girly colors. If Katie was that girl fish she wouldn't need a lung tool 'cause she could breathe in water." He paused. "Jamie, why did God make me with good lungs and not Katie?"

Jamie couldn't believe he'd never wondered how Billy must feel about this difference between his twin sister and him. But at least he could try to keep his little brother from feeling guilty or disappointed in God.

"God made you and Katie both perfect," Jamie said. "It could be that because Katie is smaller than you, her smaller lungs weren't able to fight the bad things in the air that made her lungs weaker."

"Katie's going to get better though, right, Jamie?" Billy's voice was tight.

Jamie forced a smile to hide his true feelings. "Of course, she is, Billy."

~

After what seemed like a very long time, Jamie's mom returned from the recovery room and said Katie was unconscious but Dr. Abrams would be here soon to tell them how she was doing.

A few minutes later, Dr. Abrams joined them. "We got out most of the fluid," she said. "The rest will be draining through a tube we inserted between the ribs of her chest cavity. Right now she's breathing on her own, and hopefully that will continue."

"Thank you for all you're doing for her," Jamie's mom said.

"Unfortunately, all we've been able to do at this point is remove the fluid. The bacteria that's causing her pneumonia is still active."

Jamie knew that didn't sound good. How much longer could Katie's little body keep fighting this awful bacteria?

"In her weakened state this particular strain of bacteria has become even more resistant to antibiotics," Dr. Abrams said. "The culture and sensitivity tests have helped us identify the organism, but we're running out of options."

The doctor took a step toward their mom. "With your permission, Mrs. Sawyer, there's one last antibiotic we can try that's experimental and not without high risks. But it's our last resort."

"High risks?" Jamie said. "Last resort?" He turned to his mom.

"Let's hear the rest, honey." Her voice was flat.

"We want to combine this experimental antibiotic with a new alternative form of treatment that entails an intravenous intake of a potent antioxidant," Dr. Abrams said. "It should help boost her body's immune-system response to the foreign organism threatening her lungs."

"Could you please tell me what the high risks are for the experimental drug?" his mom said.

"Every patient is different, but it could affect her liver," Dr. Abrams said. "But we'll be monitoring her the whole time, and the immune-system booster should help protect her. Unfortunately, we seem to be running out of options."

His mom sighed. "All right. Please, doctor, do whatever you think is best."

Dr. Abrams nodded. "We'll do everything we can to ensure we're giving her body what it needs."

Jamie wondered if Dr. Abram's unspoken words at the end of that sentence were *to survive*. He bit his lower lip.

"I think you boys should go home and get some rest while we're waiting for the outcome of Katie's latest treatment," their mom said. "You haven't had much sleep."

"No, Mom, we want to stay here with you and Katie," Jamie said.

"I know, honey, but we don't know how long it's going to take and I need you to be rested to help me with whatever comes next."

Jamie didn't like the sound of that, but he didn't want to go against his mom's wishes. So he let her call a cab for them. He was afraid to think about what they might be facing when they returned.

CHAPTER 56

After Jamie got Billy into bed for a nap, he sought refuge in his garden. His place of solace in all seasons. He inhaled the familiar, musky scent of dying leaves and observed the few remaining subtle signs of life that had once sprung from the soil in great abundance. Tidy, empty troughs aligned like naked soldiers in formation. A tiny squash that had lost track of time. A stubborn, stray tomato holding fast to its wilting vine. And an autumn crocus: her showy, yellow head lifted skyward with confidence, ushering in the final curtain to the seasonal concert first announced by her spring sister.

His beloved garden. It always held a promise of new life to come. Like the leaves that released themselves to the earth, returning home to become part of another life another day. To Jamie's mind there was no death in nature. Only renewal. So he chose for his little sister the destiny of the autumn crocus, which rose in full bloom in the midst of a season of endings.

Jamie felt the sun warm the back of his neck. It was still hot for autumn, so he poked his finger into the soil next to the crocus to make sure she had enough water.

Suddenly, the sun was gone, and the long shadow of a person fell over him.

Colton had been watching Jamie from the side of the house for several minutes. His obsession with the kid had accelerated since his arrest. He knew he must be losing it when he found himself parking just down the street from where the kid lived. But it looked like nobody was home. No car in the driveway and no lights on inside. He had gone around to the back to peek in the windows when he spotted Jamie in the backyard.

There he was: with his perfect little life in his perfect little yard and a big, expensive house. How friggin' lovely for him. A nice, safe, protected life full of butterflies and oak trees and flowers. And not a speck of coal dust.

One part of Colton's brain told him he should leave right away before anyone saw him. He knew he was asking for trouble lurking around in the house's shadow. But he felt like he was in a car and somebody else was driving. All he knew was that his heritage was at stake—and he wanted to break this kid to keep him from destroying it. Break him the way he'd been broken.

Colton quietly sauntered across the lawn as if he were just a friendly neighbor come to visit. Jamie was bent over his garden. When Colton got within a few yards his shadow enveloped Jamie.

"Aaaaaarrh!" Jamie screamed after he turned around. "Who are you?"

"Did I scare you?" Colton said. He adjusted his silver-coated sunglasses.

"What do you want?"

"To talk to you."

"I'm not supposed to talk to strangers."

Jamie drew back. The look on the kid's face reminded Colton of a small, trapped animal.

"This won't take long," Colton said.

"I don't have time. I need to go inside now." Jamie inched his way around the garden in the direction of his house.

Colton blocked his path. He recognized the fear in the boy's eyes. The same kind of fear had tormented him when he was a boy. "I think you'll be sorry if you don't hear what I have to say."

Jamie swerved around him and started toward the house.

"If you need to run in the house and hide because somebody just wants to talk to you, you'll never be able to get up in front of a huge room full of important people," Colton said. "But that's your choice. Go ahead, go hide in your house."

Jamie stopped in his tracks, turned, and stared straight at Colton. "I know your voice. You're the one who called me and tried to bully me." Jamie's eyes flickered.

"I wasn't trying to bully you. I was just trying to warn you."

"You're trying to scare me into not speaking before Congress. But the kids are depending on me and so is my little sister."

"What's up with your sister?"

"She has sick lungs," Jamie said softly.

Colton scanned the boy's face. *He looks so … vulnerable.* Colton winced. *So what.* It was because of this boy that he could go to prison and his people could be wiped out.

"Then you shouldn't be out raising havoc and screwing up peoples' lives," Colton said. The hot sun created drops of sweat along Colton's brow. He removed his sunglasses to mop up the sweat, revealing his eyes. Then he wiped the lenses with the bottom of his shirt.

Jamie recoiled. "I saw you on TV. You're the guy who had us kidnapped!"

Suddenly a much smaller boy slammed open the back door and shot out of the house. "Jamie, I'm done with my nap." Then, "Hey, who's that guy?"

"Billy, call 911," Jamie yelled.

Colton sprinted out of the yard, around the house, and down the street to his car, then took off with his tires spinning. He wanted to kick himself. He should have grabbed the kid as soon as he had the chance. What had gotten into him? He wouldn't make the same mistake next time.

~

Seconds after the man bolted out of their yard, Jamie and Billy heard tires squealing. Jamie hugged his brother a long time. "Come on, let's call the police," Jamie said.

After a police officer arrived and interviewed Jamie, the officer told him, "I'll put out an APB."

"A what?" Jamie said.

"An all-points bulletin to be on the lookout for Colton Slone." The officer entered some notes in his phone.

"Don't worry. Once we catch him he won't get out on bail again."

Jamie hoped they'd catch him soon. He didn't know how he'd ever feel safe until they did.

"You've started quite a movement," the officer said.

"Yes, sir," Jamie said.

Billy tugged on the officer's sleeve. "My brother's famous!"

The officer smiled at Billy. "You did a good job scaring the bad man away from your brother."

"So could I get a ride in your police car?" Billy said.

"I think that can be arranged," the officer said.

Billy beamed. "Now? A ride to the hospital to see our sister? And with the siren too, okay?"

The officer chuckled. "We might have to save the siren for another time, but I'd be happy to drop you both off at the hospital."

The officer told Jamie that when they got to the hospital he'd come in with them to speak with their mom about what happened. But Jamie begged him to talk with her later instead because she was already so upset about their sick little sister. The officer agreed. Jamie also convinced his brother to wait to tell their story until Katie could hear it too.

Before they headed for the hospital Jamie picked a bouquet of flowers from his garden for Katie. He tried to imagine her coming home and playing in their yard. But the image kept disappearing.

CHAPTER 57

J amie and Billy approached the hospital in the patrol car as the sun slid down toward the horizon and some of the last shards of sunlight broke on the flickering windows. A huge swarm of chattering blackbirds shot up in unison from a nearby maple tree as if to signal the end of another day. Shadows hemmed in the yellow sphere that glowed from a light pole in front of the hospital entrance.

The boys found their mother alone in the waiting room on the couch, her head bowed and eyes closed. When they settled on either side of her, she opened her eyes with a start and rubbed her temples. She gave them a weary smile and wrapped an arm around each of them, as if forming a cocoon with their bodies.

"Any word on Katie yet, Mom?" Jamie said.

"Not yet, sweetie. The nurses are removing the drain from her lungs right now, so I came out here for a few minutes to rest my eyes."

"Is she awake?"

"No, she's still unconscious, and her fever from the bacterial infection hasn't broken yet."

Jamie dug his nails into the palm of his hand until the pain came. "Not after all this time, Mom?"

"They hope the new medicines will knock out the infection soon."

Jamie didn't think his mom sounded so sure of that.

Before Jamie could ask any more questions, Dr. Abrams entered the waiting room. "Mrs. Sawyer, we've encountered another complication. The pneumonia has damaged Katie's lungs to the point where she's having a hard time breathing on her own."

Jamie stiffened.

"I need your permission to put Katie on a ventilator."

"Artificial life support?" their mom said, her voice quivering.

"Yes, it will push air in and out of her lungs and provide the oxygen and pressure she needs to hold her lungs open so the air sacs don't collapse."

Jamie grabbed hold of his mother's hand, both for her and for himself.

"Of course you have my permission," their mom said in a feeble whisper. "But how long will she have to depend on the ventilator?"

"We need to buy her some time, Mrs. Sawyer. By taking the strain off her lungs we hope they'll heal enough for her to eventually breathe on her own. We'll wean her off the ventilator just as soon as possible."

"But what if she can't be weaned off it?" Jamie said.

Dr. Abrams touched Jamie's arm. "We'll do everything we can to get her lungs functioning on their own."

The color drained from Jamie's face. After Dr. Abrams left the room, he noticed his mom's hands trembling. Jamie squeezed her hand tighter.

Jamie didn't know much about ventilators, but what little he did know wasn't good. He'd heard about people who went on them and could never come off. Or got infections from being on them too long. Or worse. The thought of his little sister hooked up to a breathing machine made his own chest tighten.

He could sense panic building in his mother too. When she finally spoke, she sounded like she had rubber bands pulled around her throat. "Honey, I know you're afraid for Katie, but she has very good doctors, and they're working very hard to get her well."

His mom pulled her purse into her lap and took out some tissues. She rested her elbow on her purse and shielded her eyes with her hand. "When the doctor's done hooking up Katie, we'll visit her," she said.

Jamie swallowed hard, stood up, and touched his mom's shoulder.

"A machine has to breathe for Katie?" Billy said, his voice cracking. "She needs me to be with her, Mommy!"

Their mom looked up. "I know she does, sweetie. As soon as the doctor finishes with Katie I'll check with her healthcare team to see when you can visit her."

"But she needs me now!" Billy said. "Please, Mommy, please let me be with Katie right now!" Billy tugged on his mom's elbow. "She needs me, she needs me," he sobbed loudly.

She pulled Billy into her lap, wrapped her arms around him, buried her face in his hair, and rocked him. Jamie thought all this was way too much for their mom.

After a few moments the rhythmic back-and-forth motion seemed to help soothe them both a little. She ran her fingers through Billy's hair. "Okay, honey, you'll see Katie soon. It's all right. I'll make sure you can see her as soon as possible."

Billy's sobs slowly stopped, followed by a few hiccups. But he continued to cling to their mom, and she continued to rock him.

For the first time, Jamie admitted to himself that it might be too late to save Katie. His love wasn't enough to save her. Being brave was not enough. Believing he could make a difference was not enough. Standing up for what was right was not enough. There was nowhere else for him to turn. He was being pulled toward a dark tunnel with no light at the end.

The final rays of the falling sun filtered through the hospital window. One golden beam fell across Billy's face. He rubbed his fists in his eyes, then peered up at a sky streaked with gigantic swirls of purple, red, and pink. Bolts of white light streamed through billowy, luminescent clouds. "When Katie and me are up in our tree, we see God finger painting in the sky. To let us know he's there for us. And look, Mommy, he's doing it right now."

Their mom blinked away little pools in her eyes and followed Billy's gaze.

Jamie approached the window. He observed the celestial canvas above him and felt touched, even in his grief, by its majesty. Was God really there for them? Jamie wanted very badly to believe it. He inhaled deeply for a few moments. The heaviness in his chest started to lift. Then he began inching his way out of the tunnel like a blind man feeling his way home.

Jamie was surprised to suddenly feel his chest vibrating until he realized it was his phone in his shirt pocket. He pulled it out and recognized the number.

"Raj?"

"Jamie, where are you? You were going to tell us where to meet tonight."

"I'm sorry, Raj, I forgot."

"But you know we only have a few more days before we speak to Congress, and we all still need to practice the speech you wrote."

"I'll email you the speech, but I don't think I'll be able to go with you and Keisha to speak to Congress. My little sister's going on life support tonight."

"I am so sorry, my friend. Do you need anything?"

"Just a miracle."

Silence on Raj's end.

"Raj, are you still there?"

"Yes, Jamie." Raj paused. "I know this is a very bad time, but this is our last, big chance. What do you think we should do without you? Keisha got a bad infection from that nail when we tried to escape the kidnappers."

"Poor Keisha! Is she all right?"

"Yes, but she is still recovering and cannot come."

"Oh no."

"I cannot do it by myself," Raj said. "We need an American citizen ... the only one left is Tony."

"I can't ask him. You know why."

"He said he wanted to help, so you should give him that choice."

"I can't do that to Tony. I know he'd do it for us ... and just to spite his dad. But then there'd never be any hope—"

"Jamie, you cannot save everybody. You should ask Tony and let him decide."

"I'll think about it, Raj. And let you know. I gotta go."

Jamie didn't see how things could ever get better between Tony and his dad if Tony spoke out against what his dad believed in front of Congress. Especially with his dad and his dad's friends right there in the room.

He leaned his forehead against the hospital window and thought about what Raj said. But Raj hadn't seen how hard it was for Tony.

Jamie decided he was seeking an answer he'd already given himself. He wouldn't call Tony. He'd save Tony from having to decide.

But as soon as that thought entered Jamie's mind, he felt like a thief. *Why do I feel this way?* He wasn't taking anything from Tony. He was doing what was best for Tony. His best friend. He was protecting Tony the way Tony once protected him from bullies. It was kind of the same, wasn't it? Tony would understand, wouldn't he?

Jamie had always admired how fearless Tony was. The way he never backed down. He always seemed to know what he wanted, then went after it. Good ol' Tony, who did things his own way. Would he really be okay with Jamie making this decision for him?

Jamie watched a bead of pink clouds pearl on the horizon just before the tip of the sun sunk out of sight. In the twilight, he faced the truth.

CHAPTER 58

Richard quietly paused in the half-open doorway of his son's bedroom with a clear view of the TV. Tony was watching old DVDs from when he was a small child. Richard saw himself running around the yard, bobbing up and down like a horse, with his son's little body on his shoulders. After a few more gallops he watched himself lower Tony, nuzzle his neck, toss him in the air, and smile up at his giggling face. The scenes touched a place inside him he thought had disappeared.

Elizabeth crept up and looked over his shoulder. She gave Richard a knowing expression and signaled for him to follow her to his study.

"What are you doing sneaking up on me like that?" Richard said after closing his study door, his cheeks burning.

"I wasn't sneaking, darling, just observing," Elizabeth said.

"Well, it felt like sneaking to me," he said.

"Those were good times, honey, weren't they?" she asked, voice silky as fur on a fox.

"Yeah, they were okay."

"He was such a happy, loving child, wasn't he?"

"I know what you're trying to do, Elizabeth."

"What's that, sweetheart?"

"You're trying to make me all mushy about when our son was a sweet, fun boy and forget about the disrespectful little tyrant he's become," he said.

"Now I wonder why you'd use the word *tyrant*."

"Well, that's what he is. Dictating to me how he's going to behave. Insisting on his own way."

"You know, honey, my father considered those things part of the growing process. He said a child discovers his own identity by pushing against adult boundaries and expressing himself. It doesn't mean the adults have to agree. But maybe the adults can set those boundaries without making the child feel suppressed. Maybe our son thinks you're the one acting like a dictator with him."

"Me, a dictator? You think that's what I am?" Richard said. He raised his voice, but he cringed inside.

"No, darling. But I do wonder sometimes if you press down a little too hard on our son and hardly ever acknowledge when he does something good."

"Well, I'm not going to be disrespected."

"How has he disrespected you, sweetheart? He may disagree with you or resent what you tell him, but he doesn't get into trouble. He's a good student, he works hard, he earns his own spending money from his part-time job, he helps around the house, he's home by his curfew. He tries to learn how to do the things you enjoy, like hunting. The worst thing he's done is not agree with some of your political views. Wouldn't you rather Tony learn *how* to think rather than be forced into *what* to think? You don't want a robot for a son do you, honey?"

Richard ran his hand through his hair and resisted the urge to pull on it. He scanned his wife's beautiful smiling face, her eyes filled with love and something else familiar. Determination.

Richard knew when she looked at him like that he was a goner. And here they were again, her logic making it hard for him to disagree with her. "I wish you wouldn't do that," he said.

"What?"

"Make me feel like the bad guy. You're trying to save me from myself."

"No, darling, I'm trying to save you from losing our son."

"Okay, okay. You made your point," he said. "I know you'll never give me any peace if I don't lighten up on the boy. Fine. But I'm not going to accept him being involved in that crazy CAPE thing. That's where I draw the line."

"I think you've made the right decision to go easier on him," she said. "I know you love him as much as I do. But, sweetheart, I hope you'll think about his reasons for trying to protect the environment and not see it as an affront to you. You know he has strength of character. Just like you."

"Please don't push me, Elizabeth," he said in a quiet voice." I'm done talking about this right now."

Richard didn't want to think about how Elizabeth looked at him when she said he had strength of character. She seemed to actually believe it.

CHAPTER 59

J amie's fingers were sore from gripping the arms of the chair in the hospital waiting room. He didn't want to think about anything else except Katie. But he had to do something about making sure the CAPE was represented before Congress. He finally went out in the hall and called Tony.

"Hey, dude. What's up?" Tony said.

"I'm at the hospital. My sister's on a ventilator."

"Geez, that's really rough, Jamie. How long are they keeping her on it?"

"We don't know."

"Want me to come over there?" Tony said. "I should … I can come right now."

"Thanks, Tony, maybe later. But … there's something else."

"Anything you want."

"I know I told you before that we didn't expect you to go before Congress, but things have changed." Jamie explained their predicament.

"What a mess," Tony said. "So now you're asking me to do it?"

"It's okay if you can't do it. Really, Tony. I just wanted to let you be the one to decide."

"I'm not worried about my father, if that's what you're thinking. I'd love to do it. It just seemed like I'm the worst choice because of him. Like I'm tainted or something by being his son. You know, the son of a jerk that thinks the whole thing's a hoax."

"He doesn't want to believe what we know is true, but that doesn't make him a jerk."

"Whose side are you on?"

"You *know* whose side I'm on," Jamie said.

"Look, I'll do it."

"Really? Don't you want to think about it?"

"Okay … I thought about it. So what's the plan?" Tony said.

"Well, before I decided I couldn't go, Keisha's mom had scheduled a senate driver to go to my house. So you and Raj can still get picked up there. I wrote a speech with parts for all four of us and I'll email it to you. Raj already has the speech, the two of you can just double up."

"Okay, I like to do speeches."

"But there's one other thing," Jamie said. "You need to get your dad's permission."

"Ha, good luck with that."

"Please, Tony."

"Why are you always acting like my dad is normal? And trying to get us to be like a normal father and son?"

"It could happen if you give it another chance. Just stop being angry at him for a little while."

"He's the angry one."

"Tony, just try."

"I wanna do this, with or without my dad's permission. He's gonna say no. But I'll ask him. For you. I'll call you back."

Jamie tightened his grip again on the arms of his chair. What were the chances that Tony's dad would give his permission? Tony was right. Probably zilch. But they had to try.

~

Richard sometimes wished his wife didn't know his husband side as well as she did. She could get to him too easily. But then there was that other side he never let her know. And would *not ever* let her know if he could help it: the side that did what he did to remain in office. He was starting to think he didn't want to keep that Richard around anymore.

He glanced up from his large, mahogany desk when Tony appeared in the doorway of his study.

"I need to talk with you, Dad."

Richard removed his glasses. After Elizabeth's not-so-subtle lecture, he'd made a commitment to himself to try to have a better relationship with Tony, and he figured this was a good time to start. He motioned for his son to pull up a chair next to the side of his desk.

"Jamie's little sister is on life support," Tony said. "He's at the hospital."

"I'm very sorry to hear that. Jamie must be having a terrible time with this."

"Yeah, you know he is. First his dad and now his sister."

"Is there anything your mother or I can do for Jamie? For Sarah?" Richard wished he'd done more for the family when Jamie's father died. Maybe that's why he couldn't bring himself to come down hard on Jamie about the CAPE.

"I don't think so, Dad."

Tony ran his hand along the edge of his father's desk. "You remember when I was little, and I used to crawl under here and sleep next to your feet on that thick rug you used to have?"

Richard was caught off guard. Where in the world was Tony going with this?

"What about it?"

"And did you know that back in kindergarten Jamie and I used to hide out under here when you weren't around and pretend it was our own secret fort?"

Richard shook his head and allowed himself a slight smile. He'd never heard Tony talk like this before.

"You know Jamie's been my best friend practically forever, Dad. And I'd do anything for him."

Richard dropped his smile. "Loyalty is a good thing, son, but not to the extreme."

"Well, Jamie's always been very loyal to me, and now there's something I need to do for him." Tony paused. "Jamie can't represent the CAPE before Congress, and he asked me if I could go in his place."

"You've got to be insane!" Then Richard caught himself and lowered his voice. "You already know my answer."

"Please, Dad. It's bigger than a lot of stupid politics."

"I can't have you going against me, Tony."

"But we've got so little time left to save the planet."

"You know I don't buy any of that."

"Dad, it's real. You saw that video we have of the future. It wasn't computer animation. Jamie filmed that with his phone seventy years from now."

"Don't insult my intelligence, boy!"

"We saw it for ourselves."

"I will not have you lying to me!"

"Some old scientist used what he called an energy vibrator to transport us to the future."

"You will not ..." As Tony's words sunk in, Richard stopped abruptly and stared at Tony, the shock jolting him.

"You know about that?" Richard recalled that the military had been conducting secret experiments with energy vibrators and time travel, but he didn't think they'd made much progress yet.

"Like I said, we learned about it from this scientist guy who was *from* the future, and he used his energy vibrator to travel here to warn us so we could do something before it was too late. Look at the video again, Dad. What we're doing to the planet right now is putting us on the path to that kind of future."

Richard's brain kept trying to anchor itself in a storm of incomprehensible, opposing waves of reality. He grasped his eyeglasses and alternated unfolding and folding the arms against the lenses. Then he stopped and looked at his son.

"Look at me," Richard said flatly.

Tony stared up at his father and held his gaze. "It's all true. It's horrible."

Richard rubbed his forehead. This was way too much to absorb even for Richard's quick mind. Scientists from the future? Energy vibrators? Nobody in Defense knew if those experiments would pan out. And now his son had been transported to the future by one? A future so awful it was unfathomable how anyone could live like that. Seventy years meant in his son's lifetime. Impossible! It had to be a hoax, just like the rest of the climate-change craziness.

Richard gaped at Tony. "This can't be real. I don't believe it."

"I swear on the Bible it's real, Dad!" Tony said.

"Well, there must be some other explanation. It goes against what I believe."

"It's not about what you believe," Tony said. "You don't have to accept that it's real. *I* accept that it's real and I want to do something about it. You taught me to stand up for what I thought was right, remember?"

"And if I say it's not right?"

"Then you're telling me I shouldn't think for myself."

"You're just a boy."

"I'm old enough to know the truth when I see it."

"Your version of the truth."

"Dad, you live your life based on what you believe in. Wouldn't you want me to follow what I believe in?"

Richard peered into Tony's pleading eyes and saw naked sincerity staring back at him.

Tony spoke with a halting, passionate voice. "If you don't let me go, all my life I'm going to regret that I had a chance to do something good, something important, something I really care about, but you stopped me from even trying."

Tony leaned toward his father. "Please, Dad. Let … me … do this."

Richard looked away from his son and didn't speak for several minutes.

Then he said, "I won't stop you."

CHAPTER 60

The first time Jamie entered Katie's hospital room, he was shaken by the sight of her on a ventilator. Even though he was used to how she looked when he attached the nebulizer mask on her at home, he wasn't prepared to see her hooked up to a machine that did her breathing for her.

A large, clear, plastic cup was strapped over her nose and mouth. Two tubes, one blue and one white, forked out from the mask and extended to a boxy machine with a monitor next to her bed. Three zigzag lines waved across the monitor, ending in a column of colored, flashing numbers. Intravenous tubes were taped to one of her arms, and another IV was taped to her finger. The only normal sight was Earthadilly, lying by Katie's side.

It had now been five days since Katie was hooked up to the ventilator in the intensive care unit. Five days of Jamie and their mom taking turns watching over Katie in an unconscious state and listening to the monotonous sound of the ventilator forcing air in and out of her lungs. Each time they visited her, they donned hospital caps, masks, gloves, booties, and gowns to protect her from contracting more infection.

Fortunately for Billy, the hospital had a lenient policy for young family member visitors. Whenever Jamie or their mom brought Billy to visit, he stood by Katie's head in his own little hospital gear and whispered comforting words in her ear.

Yesterday they'd finally had some good news. Dr. Abrams said the tenacious bacterial infection was at last under control! The first major hurdle overcome!

But their relief was short-lived because another big hurdle remained. Dr. Abrams had started reducing the ventilator's oxygen level and pressure for longer periods of time to try to wean Katie's lungs off the machine. Jamie knew today was the day her doctor would try to remove the ventilator and see if her lungs could function on their own. He didn't want to think about what it would mean if Katie had to stay on life support.

Jamie was near the end of his turn keeping vigil. He leaned over from his chair next to her bed and gazed at Katie. "I love you, Katie," he whispered.

He lowered his head onto the bed next to her little hand. His head felt so heavy. He still couldn't bear the thought that the only thing keeping her alive now was a machine. He rested there for several moments. Then something brushed gently against his cheek. It was Katie's finger. He lifted his head and saw her pale-green eyes flutter open. She looked dazed. Then cross-eyed at the plastic cup on her face.

"Katie, can you hear me?"

She glanced around the room then back at Jamie.

"Munchkin, lift your finger again if you can hear me."

She raised her finger an inch off the bed.

Jamie buzzed for the nurse. As soon as the nurse arrived, she alerted Dr. Abrams that her patient was conscious, and notified Jamie's mother in the relatives' room.

Katie peered down at the mask again, then looked up at Jamie with fear in her eyes. She tugged on one of the hoses as if trying to pull herself free.

"Dr. Abrams will be here soon, Katie. Just hang on, okay?"

She tapped his hand with her finger.

"Munchkin, we really love you. We've all missed you so much. You're the best little sister anyone could ever have. You're going to be fine. As soon as you're well we'll go to the planetarium. We'll pick flowers from my garden. I'll take you and Billy to Super Saturday. We'll put more stars on your ceiling and planets too … you can choose any ones you want …"

Her eyes started to close.

"Katie." He waited. "Katie." She raised her eyelids halfway and blinked up at him.

Their mom arrived with Billy. When they saw Katie was conscious they rushed to her bed. "Katie, my love." Their mom caressed Katie's cheek. Billy held Katie's free hand in his own and stood there misty-eyed.

The nurse left briefly and returned with Dr. Abrams. "Well, Katie, how do you like your welcoming committee?" the doctor said.

Katie's eyes smiled.

"Okay, honey, let's see how you're doing." Then Dr. Abrams asked Jamie and his family to go to the waiting room while she tested whether she could remove the ventilator. Jamie thought those steps away from Katie to the waiting room were some of the most difficult ones he'd ever taken. He knew there was a good chance that today would determine Katie's fate.

After what seemed like forever, Dr. Abrams appeared.

It was all over.

Katie was breathing on her own.

Jamie had no urge to hoot and holler. His relief was beyond words. A quiet celebration arose in his heart and gently floated to the surface like joy-inflated helium balloons. He hugged his mom and brother in silent gratitude.

Only when Jamie entered Katie's hospital room and saw her wide, dimpled smile did he allow his pent-up tears to flow. Once the floodgates opened, all the fear and stress and worry of the past days gushed out.

Dr. Abrams proclaimed Katie *our little miracle girl* and said Katie had beat the odds in overcoming the resistant bacterial infection and damaging pneumonia. "We'll monitor her here for the next few days, and she'll need to continue on the antibiotics and immune-system booster, but she seems to be on her way to recovery."

"Can Katie play outside with me when she comes home?" Billy said.

"That depends, Billy, on when the air is safe for her to breathe," Dr. Abrams said.

Turning to their mom, the doctor said, "Mrs. Sawyer, Katie still has to contend with her asthma, and we don't know yet to what extent her lungs will fully heal from the damage she suffered as a result of all the inflammation. You'll still need to monitor the Air Quality Index for pollution levels anytime Katie wants to go outside."

"I always do," their mom said.

"That reminds me," Dr. Abrams said and glanced over at Jamie. "Aren't you supposed to be somewhere tonight, young man? Something about the pope and Congress?" She gave Jamie a little wink.

"Yes, ma'am, seven o'clock, but I don't want to leave Katie."

"There's no need for you to stay, Jamie," Dr. Abrams said. "Katie is going to be all right. She and your mother and brother can watch you from the TV in her room, and you can come back to see her when you're done."

"Yeah, go, Jamie," Katie said in her raspy munchkin voice. "I wanna see you on TV!"

Jamie turned to his mother.

"Go ahead, honey," his mom said.

Jamie hesitated, then kissed Katie on the forehead. "Stay well, munchkin. I'll be back soon."

He headed down the hospital hall and turned on his phone. A text had come from Tony while it was off. Whoa! Jamie couldn't believe it. Tony's dad was letting him speak before Congress. Well, *kind of* letting him, Tony said. But that was good enough.

Then another text from Tony—*Keisha coming too. Knee still weak but tetanus shot working.* "Double whoa!"

He texted Tony the news about Katie's recovery and that he could go with them now. Within seconds Tony texted him back with a string of happy face emojis. Jamie told Tony to have the senate driver pick him up at the hospital's patient entrance after they left his house.

Then he went into the men's room and practiced his part of the speech out loud in front of the mirror. This was going to be the mother lode of all public speaking for him and he couldn't blow it. If someone came in, he practiced in a whisper staring at the sink. After a while he stopped and studied his reflection. He looked exactly the same as when they'd started this whole thing. But he knew he wasn't. He nodded at himself and grinned.

A text appeared from Keisha. She'd checked with her mom because the senate driver was late … her mom was furious when she found out the driver had been cancelled … all the parents except Jamie's mom were already at the Capitol … Keisha's mom would send another driver … they'd stop for Jamie at the hospital on the way.

Jamie's antenna shot up when he read that someone had cancelled their driver. But he knew they were in good hands with Keisha's mom.

CHAPTER 61

When Jamie bustled outside through the electronic doors of the hospital entrance he was greeted with a brief gust of cool, fall air. It was a welcome change from the record-breaking high temperatures they'd had this season. He decided to wait for his friends on a wrought-iron bench next to the hospital curb. He plunked himself down and played back his recent moments with Katie, cherishing them like precious mental photographs. Her finger brushing his cheek. The first time he saw her eyes open. When she smiled free of the breathing tube.

A few drivers had been picking up discharged patients in the circular driveway and loading small suitcases into car trunks. But all activity had stopped now and Jamie was the only one there.

His memories of Katie were interrupted when he noticed a black Lincoln Continental glide up the hospital-entrance driveway and stop just a couple of yards from him. A man in a navy-blue suit and tie stepped out from the driver's side with a navy chauffeur's cap pulled low on his face. A long, navy scarf wrapped loosely around his nose and mouth and trailed down his back. Jamie assumed the driver was there to pick up a patient, like all the others he'd seen.

Instead, the man approached Jamie.

"Jamie Sawyer?" the man said in a muffled voice. "I'm your driver—"

Jamie immediately recognized Colton's poorly disguised voice, jumped up and started toward the hospital door. But Colton grabbed him, put him in a headlock, and wrapped his scarf around Jamie's head, covering his face.

Jamie tried to scream but the scarf blocked his mouth and nose so tightly he could barely breathe. The lack of oxygen made him weak. He flailed his arms and kicked in the direction of his captor, who pulled him off the curb onto the driveway.

Then he heard the pop of a car trunk opening. He felt Colton's grip tighten as he tried to thrust him inside. Jamie swung his heel back, ramming it into what seemed like Colton's kneecap. Colton cursed and knocked the side of Jamie's head against the edge of the trunk, inflicting a sharp pain along the side of Jamie's forehead. He fought to keep from passing out, then thought to fake it instead, letting his body go limp. Colton groaned, struggling to lift Jamie's dead weight into the trunk. It gave Jamie the few seconds he needed.

He thought of the powerful energy always inside him. He shifted his attention away from his fear and tapped into that energy instead.

Jamie lifted his foot against the car bumper and used it for leverage to heave his body against Colton, who fell away and released the scarf. Jamie heard a thud on the driveway and yanked the scarf off his head in time to see Colton spring up and push him backward over the open trunk.

Colton grabbed a long, steel lug wrench from the trunk and swung it at Jamie. Jamie ducked out of the way, but Colton shoved him down on the ground.

Suddenly Colton leapt on top of Jamie, his knees pinning Jamie's arms, steel wrench raised above Jamie's head where blood was trickling into one of Jamie's eyes from the gash on his forehead. Jamie stared up into Colton's eyes. He saw rage there, then thought he saw a flicker of sadness as Colton stared back at him, eyes glazed over and wrench frozen in his hand.

Jamie wiggled one arm out from under Colton's knee and elbowed him hard in his abdomen. Colton snapped forward and dropped the wrench. Jamie pulled his other arm free and chopped the side of Colton's neck. Colton rolled off Jamie and onto the ground, motionless.

Jamie quickly tied Colton's hands and feet with the long scarf, then took a deep breath. He closed his eyes and filled his heart with gratitude. He knew his victory was no fluke.

What Jamie didn't know was that his friends had pulled up the hospital's long driveway in a senate limousine, in time to see the end of the fight.

"Jamie!" Keisha said and threw her arms around him.

Tony looked like he might hug Jamie too, but he just grinned instead. "Dude, you were awesome!"

Raj grasped Jamie's shoulder and nodded.

Jamie smiled at his friends, then scowled at Colton. "This is the guy who had us kidnapped."

"We called the police from the limo," Tony said. "I bet they'll put him away for a looooong time."

Jamie wiped blood from his eye with the back of his hand and turned his head back and forth to loosen his neck.

Alexandria police officers arrived in two separate cruisers. They had Colton's car impounded and arrested him for assault, a second attempted kidnapping, and violation of his bail.

After one of the officers interviewed Jamie, he checked Colton's phone and found a record of calls to and from the senate drivers' pool. The officer verified the senate driver's identification, then told him and the kids they could leave. He wished the kids good luck with their appearance before Congress, while the other officer read Colton his rights and drove away with him in his squad car.

Jamie and his friends scrambled into the senate limousine and took off for the Capitol.

CHAPTER 62

Resting in the back seat of the limo, Jamie pressed his hand against the gash on his forehead. An image of his Captain America poster flashed through his mind.

"How's your head?" Keisha said.

"It's okay. Just a little throbby. Probably looks worse than it is."

"Most of the blood's dried." Keisha asked the driver if he had anything they could use to clean Jamie's wound, and the driver handed back a package of Handi Wipes. Keisha pulled one out and cleaned the streaks off Jamie's face.

"How's your knee?" Jamie said.

"Still sore. But there was no way I'd miss this."

Tony slid his hand along the black leather seat of the limo and whistled. "Hey, at least we get to ride in style. Your mom did good, Keish."

"Do you think we should text our parents about what just happened to Jamie?" Keisha said.

"No!" Jamie said. "I don't want to worry my mom. Let's not tell them until after our speech, okay?" Jamie said.

Tony nodded. "Yeah, it'd just be a big downer."

After about twenty minutes the car hit heavy traffic and slowed to a crawl.

"This ain't rush hour. What's the holdup?" Tony said.

Jamie stretched his head out the window for a better view of the lines of cars ahead, barely moving.

Raj pulled up a news report on his phone. "Thousands of kids and adults are streaming into DC to watch the pope's speech live on a jumbotron on the Capitol West Front Lawn and to show their support for an environmental bill and the young leaders of the CAPE who are scheduled to appear with the pope before a joint meeting of Congress tonight. The CAPE is a global youth movement fighting fossil-fuel pollution and climate change. Traffic into the capital is backed up for miles. Even the Potomac ferry service has a long waiting line."

Jamie looked at the clock on his phone and moaned. "We'll never get there in time."

"Maybe if we run fast enough," Raj said.

Jamie looked at Keisha's injured knee. "Keish, can you run?"

"I've run with worse," she said.

Jamie told the driver, "We gotta get out or we'll be too late."

Before the driver could answer Jamie jumped out, followed by his three friends. They raced along the median strip of the George Washington Memorial Parkway and made good time all the way to the Arlington Memorial Bridge. Jamie led them, weaving through a steady stream of walkers funneling over the Potomac River crossing to the nation's capital.

From atop the bridge they had a clear view of the other side. A sea of people flooded the National Mall and surrounding area.

"Holy smokes," Jamie said. "It's packed!"

A news helicopter flew overhead, its camera crew shooting aerials of the scene.

"I'd better text my mom and let her know we're on our way," Keisha said.

Jamie steered them near the Lincoln Memorial at the beginning of the National Mall, where orderly grids of green grass, lined with gravel sidewalks, led to the Capitol. But there was nothing orderly about the throngs crammed into the mall area and overflowing onto Constitution and Independence avenues on either side.

"We need to find small openings so we can squeeze through single file," Jamie said. With Jamie in the lead they slithered in and out of the crowd like a garden snake through a thicket of weeds.

Suddenly a toddler shot out in front of Keisha. She swerved to avoid him and fell on her injured knee, smashing it into the gravel sidewalk. She rolled on her side groaning. Jamie was right behind her. "Let me see your knee, Keish." He knelt beside her, helped her sit up, and inspected the damage. The knee was already starting to turn red and swell with fluid.

Jamie tried to help Keisha stand. She grimaced in pain and asked him to lower her back to the ground.

"You guys go ahead without me," Keisha said. "Hurry, we're running out of time."

"We're not leaving you here, Keish," Jamie said.

"But you have to. I can't walk on this stupid leg."

"No!" Tony said. "I'll carry you on my back. Let's go! Jamie and Raj, lift her onto my back."

"Forget it, Tony," Keisha said. "I'm heavier than I look and—"

Tony held up his hand like a stop sign.

"Let him carry you, Keish," Jamie said. "Please."

Keisha sighed and nodded. Jamie and Raj helped her get up on Tony's back, her arms wrapped around the top of his shoulders and her legs around his waist.

Jamie slowly trekked with his friends single file through the tightening throng. After a while Jamie noticed sweat dripping down Tony's face, even in the cool night air.

"Tony, can you even see with all that sweat dripping into your eyes? Why don't you let me or Raj take turns?"

"I can see well enough, dude," Tony said. "Thanks, but I got this."

"Tony, this isn't going to work," Keisha said. "You have to put me down!"

"You're coming with us, so just shut up, Keish," Tony said.

Jamie trudged on, looking back from time to time to check on his friends. He figured the weight of Keisha's muscular body must be zapping Tony's strength by now. Tony was bent over a lot more than when he'd first started carrying her.

When they got within sight of the Washington Monument, Jamie checked his phone clock and groaned. It was only about a mile to the Capitol, but at their snail's pace he didn't see how they could get there in time.

Jamie's heart sank. After all they'd been through, they weren't going to show up at the event that could finally propel the CAPE's movement over the top. Keisha's mom had said that public opinion was in their favor, but also that the fossil-fuel industry was increasing pressure on the nation's legislators to vote against Senator Pattern's bill. She'd said it could make a difference if the elected officials heard directly from the kids themselves. With the live TV coverage, this was also their biggest chance to make their case directly to the country and to the world. But although they had only a mile to go, it might as well be a million.

Jamie again started to offer to relieve Tony when he spotted a young girl pulling a Miniature Schnauzer in a red wagon with one hand and holding her mother's hand with the other.

Jamie approached the mother, who wore a red dot on her forehead. "Hi, I'm Jamie Sawyer. Our friend can't walk, and we need to get her to the Capitol right away."

The mother and her little girl looked at Keisha hanging on Tony's back, then at Tony's sweaty face.

"So I was wondering if we could borrow your little girl's wagon to carry our friend faster," Jamie said. "I promise we'll return the wagon by tomorrow. I'll give you my phone number."

The mother studied Jamie's face. "Are you the boy we keep seeing on TV who's trying to stop pollution and climate change?"

"Yes, ma'am, all four of us," Jamie said.

The mother turned to her daughter. "It's okay, sweetie, if you want to let them borrow it." The little girl whispered to her dog, and the dog yelped and jumped out of the wagon.

"You can take it, but please give it back, okay?" the little girl said.

"I promise," Jamie said. "We really appreciate it."

The mother pulled out her phone, and Jamie repeated his name and gave her his phone number.

"Thank you for what you're doing, all of you," the mother said.

Jamie and Raj lowered Keisha off Tony's back onto the wagon. Keisha smiled at the little girl. "What's your name?"

"Avani," the little girl said.

Raj's jaw dropped. "That means *Earth* in Hindi."

Jamie knelt next to the little girl, "Thank you, Avani. We won't ever forget you."

The little girl grinned and passed the wagon handle to Jamie.

Tony led their little procession through the throng, waving both arms high in the air and yelling at the top of his lungs, over and over, "Emergency! Injured girl! Make way!"

The crowd parted as Jamie pulled the wagon along the gravel pathway, greatly increasing their pace. The people around him became a blur, all his attention focused on getting them to their destination on time. Finally the Capitol loomed just ahead, and Jamie asked Keisha to text her mom.

CHAPTER 63

Members of the Senate and the House of Representatives were assembled in the Capitol's House Chamber amid its majestic vaulted ceiling, Ionic black marble columns, gigantic American flag, rich walnut paneling, and semicircular rows of connecting armchairs.

The historic room was filled to capacity for today's joint meeting of Congress. Joining the four hundred and thirty-five members of the US House of Representatives on their chamber floor were the one hundred US Senators, as well as members of the US Supreme Court and other dignitaries. Behind the speaker's rostrum at the center of the chamber was the vice president and the Speaker of the House.

Hundreds of visitors and the press corps packed the gallery that ringed the chamber's upper level. Many of those visitors were children wearing green capes and t-shirts with the CAPE's emblem. Everyone's attention was riveted on the speaker's rostrum where the pope was concluding his remarks. "… and I thank you for this opportunity to speak with you today. May God bless America."

The members of Congress and the gallery audience gave him a standing ovation.

The pope glanced off to the side for a sign of the youngsters and saw Capitol Security ushering them in. "I've asked four children to join me here tonight. They're the founders of the Children Against Polluting Earth ... Jamie Sawyer, Keisha Taylor, Raj Sanseria, and Tony Newsome."

Jamie helped Keisha hobble up the steps on her good leg to the rostrum, with Tony and Raj following close behind them.

Applause filled the chamber.

The pope, vice president, and Speaker of the House each shook hands with the youths. Then the pope took a seat in the front row of the rostrum area.

So here we are, thought Jamie. Finally. It was all so mind-boggling. When the pope shook his hand, Jamie's knees wobbled and he couldn't get out any words. He was drawn to the pope's eyes, struck by how much kindness he saw there. This was a special moment he knew he would always remember.

When Jamie stepped up on the platform to reach face level with the podium microphones, he wondered if his friends on either side of him were as stunned as he was.

He stared out at the packed chambers. Hundreds of men and women stared back at him from the grand, cavernous room. Somebody out there coughed, and the sound echoed against the high walls.

Jamie scanned the full width of the chamber and up to the gallery. It was hard to take it all in. This was more terrifying than he'd ever imagined. In the race to get here he hadn't thought about how he'd feel once he did.

He swallowed hard. So many eyes, and all on him. *Don't look at the eyes, look above the eyes*, somebody had told him. But it didn't help. It was still a gigantic room full of very important people … people who could decide whether the CAPE's mission succeeded or failed.

He refused to freeze up. It didn't matter how he used to be. He was a different boy now.

Jamie opened his mouth to speak, but nothing came out. The only sound was more coughing in different parts of the chamber.

He tried to speak again. Nothing.

Keisha slipped her hand into his and squeezed it gently.

Jamie squeezed back and began softly. "I … I … I have a small garden. Every year, fruits and vegetables sprout up from the soil. My garden has taught me that our planet is a living thing, just like us."

Keisha leaned against the podium to steady herself and said, "Our planet gives us oxygen, food, and water. Plants for curing illnesses and to create clothing and shelter. She offers us endless beauty all over the world, peaceful settings, places to climb and swim and hike and play and know pure joy. Places that help us feel our close connection with her."

"Planet Earth is the most wonderful home we'll ever know," Jamie said. "All she needs is for us to treat her with respect. But we're not. We're poisoning her with toxic gases from burning fossil fuels … trashing her air and water as if she were a giant garbage can … making our planet and her people sick."

"If you poison someone, there are symptoms," Raj said. "Earth's symptoms are the extreme changes in climate that are getting worse every year. We need to stop the way we are treating her, or she will turn into a place where nobody wants to live."

"That's why kids like us all over the planet are fighting against fossil fuels," Tony said. "We want to see these dangerous fuels phased out within ten years and replaced with clean, safe, renewable energy."

"We want strict conservation laws and protection for our forests," Keisha said. "We want clean air and clean water for ourselves and for our future children."

"Many countries are already working very hard to replace dirty energy with clean energy," Raj said. "But we cannot have a healthy planet if we only stop poisoning parts of her. We need to stop the poisoning everywhere and very soon. There are many clean-energy businesspeople like my father who are showing us that if we have the will, there is a much better way. A way for us to have a clean-energy economy where everyone benefits."

"Our planet is home to all of us," Tony said. "She doesn't belong to one group. She doesn't choose who can breathe her air or drink her water or fish in her oceans. She belongs to all of us, and she depends on all of us to protect her."

Jamie's voice became stronger. "My little sister, Katie, can't go outside to play some days because the air is too polluted. Katie has asthma, like six million other kids in America.

"Asthma makes her lungs burn and she feels like she's suffocating. It hurts her just to try to take a deep breath. Polluted air weakened Katie's lungs so badly that just this month, she got pneumonia and almost died. She had to depend on a machine to breathe for her. Today her doctor took her off life support and she was able to breathe on her own. But next time she might not be so lucky. Today we hope things will start changing so Katie and all the other kids won't have to suffer any more from dirty air."

Jamie scanned the room. "I love my little sister and I love our planet. I want them both to be well."

"We all know how to start the healing," Keisha said. "We can begin the cure if you support Senator Pattern's bill."

"As kids we don't get to vote," Tony said. "So we have to depend on you grown-ups. That's why we're here. To ask you to make good decisions for us and our planet."

"Other countries are watching what America decides," Raj said. "We are all in this together."

Jamie eyed the legislators and with a steady voice said, "We represent the children of the world who are asking you to lead the way in saving our global home from fossil-fuel pollution and climate change. Please don't let us down. Please put our future first. Thank you."

The great hall was completely silent as if time stood still. Jamie held his breath.

Suddenly the children in the gallery leapt to their feet and cheered loudly. Gradually, dozens of legislators stood and clapped. Then, as if a spark had ignited a bonfire, a thunderous roar of applause erupted in waves throughout the chamber, and all the legislators rose from their chairs. Jamie caught a glimpse of one of the last legislators to rise, his hands by his side. It was Tony's dad.

Jamie exhaled. Goose bumps all over his body. When he looked up at the CAPE children still cheering in the balcony, he thought his heart would burst right out of his chest and ricochet against the wall.

Jamie waved to his fellow CAPE members and mouthed, "Thank you."

CHAPTER 64

In the months that followed, Jamie compiled a scrapbook on their CAPE website of headlines around the world: *US Congress Passes Veto-Proof Bill to End Burning Fossil Fuels; China and India Follow America's Lead to Save Planet; Other Nations Sign on to Ten-Year Plan to Save Planet;* and *Children Against Polluting Earth Celebrate Victory!*

After he'd finished his last entry for the day, he went out to his backyard. His friends were going to meet him there soon for their celebration. He'd just knelt to pluck a raspberry from his garden when he heard the familiar sound. Mr. James appeared holding a gift from the future: a bouquet of red impatiens with a hummingbird hovering above.

The sun started its nightly descent. Katie and Billy, nestled together high up in their oak tree, exchanged a knowing glance as they watched majestic strokes of orange splash across the horizon.

Nearby Jamie, Keisha, Raj, and Tony formed a circle around Raj's model rocket in the middle of Jamie's backyard, eager for their own private celebration.

Raj flipped a switch on a small, white box. His rocket shot into the air. About twenty feet up the rocket released hundreds of tiny, silver stars that sparkled in the setting sun.

Jamie gazed up, his face glowing, as the silver stars floated toward Earth.

Inspiration for the Title

The title for this novel was inspired by the song, "I'm Tying the Leaves So They Won't Come Down," which the author's grandfather sang to her when she was a little girl. The song was written by Erasmus Huntington in 1907.

Please consider posting a review of this novel at www.goodreads.com, www.bookbub.com, or one of your favorite online retailers.

Twitter.com/AuthorJuneToher

Facebook.com/AuthorJuneToher

ACKNOWLEDGMENTS

Thank you to my father, Al Toher, who taught me to love books and the magic of words, and my mother, Sophie Toher, who instilled in me the importance of perseverance.

I am grateful for my sisters, Jeannie Toher and Kathy Toher Reed, and my brother, Steve Toher, who all offered me helpful ideas and ongoing encouragement for my novel. And for my other family members who, along with my siblings, regularly demonstrate the preciousness of sibling love: Zany Toher; Tanya Toher; John Reed; Christopher Reed, Kelly Reed Waters, and Jen Daughton; Hunter Graham, Alyssa Reed, Christina Reed, and Lexie Carpenter; and Kalyn and Colin Waters.

Immense appreciation for the folks at The Editorial Department: Julie Miller, my editor, who pushed me to bring forth my best, and Ross Browne, president, who guided me every step of the creative process. And for Jane Ryder at Ryder Author Resources for her marketing savvy.

Much thanks to Kitty Drury, Donna Campbell and Jane Cosner, who cheered me on from the first page. To my other supportive friends: Peggy Cadigan, Jeanne Bonar, Pamela Powell, Patty McQuade, Lin Smith, Connie Sage

Connor, Jan Matsoukas, Kathy Bernardi, Gayle Short, Vanessa Valdejuli, and Ann Mock. To my book club members for their valuable feedback: Sandy Bolcar, Shelley Christenson, Karen Detweiler, Debbie Drees, Carolyn Lammers, Carol Naumann, Bette Noe, Carol Pariser and Susan Rogge. And to Peter Slepsky, Dennis Bushnell, Kevin McPartland, Tom Conroy, and Charles Brewer for sharing their expertise.

My gratitude to former producer Chris Zarpas for critiquing the screenplay version of my novel and to Mike Zarpas for helping me make that connection. This story was first developed as a full-length feature film with the title *The Children's Alliance for Planet Earth,* and the final script was registered with the Writer's Guild of America, East in May 2008. Since that time many youth organizations have taken on the challenge of protecting the planet.

These organizations and agencies influenced my writing: American Lung Association; Asthma and Allergy Foundation of America; Centers for Disease Control and Prevention; Columbia University's Center for Children's Environmental Health; World Health Organization; World Federation of Public Health Associations; National Institutes of Health; National Academies of Science, Engineering and Medicine; Climate Leadership Network; Energy Information Administration; U.S. Geological Survey; National Oceanic and Atmospheric Administration; NASA Langley Research Center; U.S. Congressional Record; Environmental Protection Agency; Union of Concerned Scientists; Intergovernmental Panel on Climate Change; Climate Central; Natural Resources Defense Council; and Skeptical Science.